D0557347

"I HATE YOU, BEAU."

"I know you do, Rebecca. I'm the enemy. And yet, if I touched you—"

"Don't!" she gasped.

"Why not?" he asked. "Because you hate me? Or because of something else?"

"I don't know what you mean!"

"I think you do, Rebecca." He moved toward her. "I think it was more than mere duty to your country that brought you into my arms that day. I think there was desire, passion, and I think they're still there, however you might want to deny it."

"You're wrong."

"Am I?" he asked doubtfully. "Why don't we put it to the test?"

Rebecca whirled, intending to flee, but it was too late. Beau's arm snaked about her waist and he pulled her against him. His body was like a rock wall at her back and his embrace was a band of iron, imprisoning her in his embrace....

By Love Betrayed

Sandra DuBay

LEISURE BOOKS NEW YORK CITY

A LEISURE BOOK®

May 1993

Published by

Dorchester Publishing Co., Inc.
276 Fifth Avenue
New York, NY 10001

Printed in the United States of America.

Prologue

March 1812
Fort St. Joseph
St. Joseph Island

"A spy? Are you out of your mind, Sumner?"

The twin rows of brass buttons adorning Sumner Meade's scarlet coat flashed in the firelight as he turned toward Rebecca. He was tall, even without the feathered, cocked hat that was part of his uniform as an officer of the Tenth Royal Veterans Battalion. His dark brown hair nearly brushed the heavy beams of the low cottage ceiling.

"I only ask you to think about it," he said to the woman sitting in the chair before him.

Rebecca Carlyle shook her head. Her hands were clenched in the folds of her black velvet,

9

high-waisted gown. Her hair, caught up in an ebony comb, gleamed blue-black as it tumbled to her shoulders.

She rubbed her arms, shivering, for the spring here, on the small island in the upper Great Lakes, was late and the chill of the too-long winter seemed to hang in the air of her small, two-room cottage.

"I don't know why you're asking this of me," she told him. "I know nothing of spying. Surely you have contacts on Mackinac Island who can—"

"Rebecca," Sumner interrupted, dropping to one knee beside her chair and covering both her small hands with one of his. "It is true, we have friends on the island—people who are sympathetic to England, loyal to the king despite the revolution in the colonies. But we need someone on the inside, someone above suspicion who can gain their confidence. Don't you see? Men are always quick to suspect other men, but a woman . . ." He lifted a curl from her shoulders. "Particularly a beautiful woman . . ."

Rebecca's startling, amethyst eyes flashed. "I'm not sure I like the sound of that!" she hissed. "Are you suggesting I should—"

"I'm not 'suggesting' anything," he assured her quickly. "I'm only saying that a man is less likely to suspect a beautiful woman of duplicity. He is always willing if not eager to believe her above reproach."

Rebecca gazed into the dancing flames, troubled. "I don't know, Sumner . . ."

"Perhaps I should not have asked you," he said, rising. "I think I was mistaken about you. I thought you bore no love for these 'Americans' after what happened to William."

Rebecca's slender hand went to the locket at her throat, containing a lock of her dead husband's hair.

"I hate them!" she hissed. "I hate them all!"

Pushing herself out of her chair, she went past Sumner to the window. Outside the night wind howled, rattling in the still-bare branches of the trees. Tears scalded her eyes but she blinked them back. William Carlyle had been her first, her only, love. She, the daughter and granddaughter of military men, had fallen madly in love with the handsome young captain. They had married and she had followed him to the remote outpost in North America. Relations between Britain and her former colonies, always strained, now bordered on warfare. Six months earlier William Carlyle had ventured into American territory to gather information. Captured, he'd been imprisoned. But before he could be tried as a spy, he'd died of pneumonia in the cold, dank confines of an American guardhouse.

Rebecca, suddenly a widow after less than a year of marriage, had remained at Fort St. Joseph. She'd intended to return to England when the summer finally came. In the meanwhile, her late husband's best friend, Lieutenant Sumner Meade, looked after her. She suspected he intended to court her when her first mourning ended. And now here he was, on behalf of his commanding officer, asking her to become a spy for Britain—for the king she'd been taught to revere.

"I'm sorry, Rebecca," Sumner said, reaching toward her, longing but not quite daring to take her into his arms. "I'll tell Captain Roberts to find someone else."

"No, wait." Rebecca caught at his brass-buttoned, blue-cuffed sleeve as he started to pass her on the way to the door. "I'll go."

Sumner took her arm and pulled her close, gazing down into her eyes. "Are you certain?" he asked seriously. "Be very certain. You know it's not without risk. We are on the brink of war. It may be a matter of months, even weeks, before the shooting starts. If you were still there when the battle began, you could be caught in the midst of it."

"I said I'll go," she repeated firmly. "I'll try to get whatever information Captain Roberts needs."

Smiling, Sumner lifted her hand to his lips. "So brave," he murmured. "So beautiful. I'll be waiting for you when all this is over."

Rebecca said nothing. She could not tell him that part of her decision to go was a desire to be away from him. It was too soon after William's death to think of loving again. Sumner's obvious admiration aroused no answering emotion in her. But surely that was only because she still loved William. Sumner was a good man, a kind man.

Wearily, she pushed those thoughts out of her mind. Perhaps it would do her good to get away. Perhaps when she returned—when her sojourn among the enemy was over—she would be ready to love again.

Chapter One

April 1812
Mackinac Island

"Your first visit to the island?"

Rebecca pushed back the edge of the hood she'd drawn forward to protect her face from the biting wind that tore at her voluminous black cloak. She stood at the railing of the ship, an American schooner she'd boarded after traveling to Detroit so no one would suspect her true point of departure. A stout, uniformed man stood beside her. It was he who had spoken.

"It is," she confirmed. Her eyes went to the verdant island rising from the whitecapped waters of the straits of Mackinac. "It is a beautiful sight."

15

"Indeed. Nestled here between the northern and southern peninsulas. It was a sacred place, you know, to the Indians. Many of them still come here though mostly to trade furs for goods." He laughed. "Forgive me. My enthusiasm outstrips my manners. I am Dr. Sylvester Day, post surgeon at the fort."

Rebecca looked at the island. The small village lay near the water's edge. Behind it, the land rose sharply, gray stone promontories jutted from the undergrowth. The fort had been built on top of a bluff, its solid blockhouses and high walls providing lookouts from which no approaching ship could hide.

"A formidable place," she murmured, understanding the British dilemma of how best to mount an attack on so seemingly impregnable a fortress. Even if a ship could reach the island without being detected, no cannon could hit the whitewashed fort sitting so proudly atop the limestone cliffs.

"Do you have family on the island, Miss . . ."

"Carlyle," Rebecca told him. "Rebecca Carlyle. And, no. I know no one here."

"Forgive my saying so, but it seems a lonely place for a lovely lady, Miss Carlyle."

"Mrs. Carlyle," Rebecca corrected. "I am a widow, Dr. Day. And as to the loneliness, I was raised in such places. I should surely be lost in a great city."

"Your family is a military one?" The doctor's words were punctuated by the sound of the anchor as it splashed into the choppy blue

16

water surrounding them. The few passengers and their belongings would be ferried ashore in tenders.

"It was," she revealed. "Both my father and my late husband were military men. My grandfather, too, was in the army. He, like yourself, was a doctor."

"Ah. He fought in the battle for independency?"

Rebecca forced herself to hide the disdain she felt for these colonials and their pride in having gained their much-vaunted independence.

"He did," she agreed. She wondered what the doctor would think if he knew which side her grandfather had fought on.

The doctor was about to say something more but two voices shouting from below interrupted him. He looked down toward the water and grinned.

"There you are! Hawkins! McAllister! Anyone die while I've been gone?"

Rebecca looked down to see two men in the red-trimmed blue jacket and white breeches of the American First Artillery. One was dark, his hair the same ebony as Rebecca's own. The other was fair, his hair a burnished gold that caught the sunlight in its glistening waves. Each was, in his own way, a handsome man, and each regarded Rebecca with more than casual interest.

"No one's dead, sir," the fairer man replied. "Private Cary swears his leg is broken. Seems to work well enough when he's had too much rum, though."

The doctor laughed. "I'll have him back on guard duty soon enough," he called down. "I think I'll tell him the leg'll have to come off."

Noticing the two men's interest in Rebecca, he said, "McAllister, I've a job for you. Let me present Mrs. Carlyle. She has come to live on the island. Will you see her safely settled into her new home?"

The golden-haired man grinned, pulling off his hat. "Gladly, Doctor. Mrs. Carlyle? Beau McAllister, at your service."

"Lieutenant McAllister and his companion there, Lieutenant Anthony Hawkins, serve under the fort commander, Lieutenant Hanks."

"Gentlemen," Rebecca said, smiling.

"After I conduct the doctor to his home, ma'am," the black-haired lieutenant, Anthony Hawkins, volunteered, "I'll be happy to see your baggage is brought to you."

In spite of her mission, in spite of the fact that these men were the enemy—part of the same military machine that had committed treason against the king and killed her beloved husband—Rebecca could not help being flattered by their eagerness to play the gallant gentlemen for her.

"Thank you, Lieutenant," she called back. "I've taken a house owned by a man named Dunnigan."

"I know the one," he assured her. "I'll have your things there as soon as possible."

* * *

In short order Rebecca was walking along a narrow road that ran behind the row of houses and businesses that hugged the shoreline. Her escort, the brass buttons and gold braid of his blue jacket glinting in the sun, seemed to dwarf her, though at five feet six inches she was taller than most women she knew.

His nearness was oddly disquieting to her. It gave her a feeling of delicacy, of femininity, a feeling Sumner had never evoked in her—a feeling she had not known since . . . since William. Resolutely, she pushed that troubling thought to the back of her mind.

"Here is the house, ma'am," Lieutenant McAllister said, turning off the street and into an overgrown path.

The house was weathered, its log walls and shingled roof bleached gray by the sun and rain, the wind and snow. Like its neighbors it had a small backyard with a tall cedar fence. Chimneys rose above the steeply pitched roof at either end. It was not, Rebecca reflected, so very different from her own house on St. Joseph Island.

"I'll get the shutters off for you," the lieutenant offered.

Thanking him, Rebecca took out the key sent her by the house's owner, a secret British sympathizer, and opened the door.

The main room occupied half of the house. It had a huge, gaping fieldstone fireplace, a long, heavy trestle table, a pair of rough-hewn

19

benches flanking the table, a bulky, carved, scarred sideboard, and a pair of chairs. The stone-flagged floor was covered with a worn Turkish carpet whose once-bright colors had faded to dusty pastels. The other half of the house was divided into two rooms. One opened onto the main room. As the shutters came off its windows, Rebecca saw that it contained a desk and chair, an armchair whose worn damask upholstery matched the rose damask at the windows, and a set of shelves for books.

Returning to the main room, Rebecca opened the door to the third room. It was furnished with a carved double bed, a chest, a chair near the small fireplace, a table beside the bed, and in the corner a cradle, obviously handmade with loving care.

The room was flooded with light as the shutters came off the windows. In the backyard Rebecca could see the overgrown garden, the privy, and the well with its rough plank cover.

Rebecca went to the small cradle and rocked it, lost in thought.

"Dunnigan made it himself," Lieutenant McAllister told her from the doorway.

Rebecca started. She had not heard him come in.

"In our correspondence about the house, nothing was said of a family. I did not know Mr. Dunnigan had one," Rebecca told him.

"He hasn't," Beau replied. "Not anymore, at least. Mrs. Dunnigan died in childbed and the child with her."

"How very sad," Rebecca murmured.

"Perhaps you will fill the cradle," Beau suggested, "after Mr. Carlyle joins you."

"There is no Mr. Carlyle, Lieutenant," Rebecca informed him, squeezing past him in the doorway. "Not any longer. I am a widow."

Beau McAllister barely suppressed the relieved smile that sprang to his lips. "Is that so? In that case, if you need anything, please tell me."

"I could use a broom." Rebecca glanced around. "And a bucket of water. This house needs a good cleaning."

"There was one . . ." Beau went to the back door and reached outside. The broom he retrieved was worn and looked as if it had been outside all the previous winter but it would serve Rebecca's immediate purpose.

"I don't suppose you saw an apron out there," she joked, taking the broom from him.

"Sorry," Beau replied. "I'll get the water. There's a small pile of wood out there as well. Why don't I lay fires for you while you sweep?"

Rebecca studied the handle of the broom. They were certainly accommodating, these Americans. Perhaps Sumner had been right in suggesting that his commanding officer send a woman to gather the information they needed.

"I don't like to keep you from your duties, Lieutenant," she told him.

"If I were needed at the fort, ma'am, I'd be there," he assured her. "And call me Beau."

While Rebecca swept, Beau went into the yard and drew a bucket of water from the well. Leaving it on the stone hearth, he went back outside and returned with an armload of firewood apparently cut by Mr. Dunnigan before he'd left the island.

She watched as he knelt before the empty fireplace. Her eyes swept from the top of his golden head to the white gaiters that covered his white breeches from his knees to the leather boots on his feet. He was tall, more than six feet; he had towered over her when they'd stood side by side. His features were strong, chisled. His eyes, she remembered having noticed, were a deep sapphire-blue. He was handsome, a very handsome man.

She turned away as he rose and took up the rest of the firewood to lay a fire in the bedroom. Opening the front door, she swept the dirt out into the narrow path. Up the street she could see the other officer, Lieutenant Hawkins, coming with three other men carrying her trunks.

She smiled as the black-haired officer turned into the path. "This is very kind of you, Lieutenant," she said, stepping back to allow him and the other men to enter.

"It is not kindness, ma'am," he said, his dark eyes roving quickly and blatantly over her. "It is a pleasure. Where would you like these trunks?"

"Put them anywhere," she directed. "Once they're unpacked, they can be stored in the attic."

At Lieutenant Hawkins's signal his three helpers set down their burdens and left the cottage.

"Is there anything else you need?" he asked, a hopeful note in his voice.

His smile faded when he saw Beau McAllister emerging from the bedroom, dusting the dirt of the firewood from his hands.

A look passed between the two men. Women, especially young, pretty, unattached women, were a rare commodity in such far-flung outposts. Dr. Day had told Anthony that the lovely Mrs. Carlyle was a widow. He'd decided at that moment to pay court to her. It did not bode well for his chances to see McAllister already there, looking so pleased with himself.

"There's nothing else I need," Rebecca answered, speaking to both men. "I thank you both for your kindness."

"Well, then," Beau hedged. He, like his fellow lieutenant, wished he could think of some reason to stay. But there was none.

With a smile and a respectful bow, each man took his leave of the beautiful, raven-haired widow they had suddenly become rivals for.

Standing in the doorway, Rebecca watched them go. She would have to encourage one or both of them, for only in that way could she gain access to the fort and garner the information the British on St. Joseph Island needed.

23

Rebecca sighed as she closed the door. She opened the lid of the nearest of her trunks. Inside, carefully wrapped in a quilt, was the small painting of her late husband she took with her everywhere.

"Oh, William," she said softly, sinking into a chair, the painting held gently in her arms, "what a dirty business this is. If I am to help our cause, I must smile and try to captivate the very enemy I hold responsible for your death. The very thought makes me shudder, but I know that if I succeed I will have avenged, if only a little, their taking you from me. So I will—I must—succeed!"

Her heart was heavy as she settled herself into her new home. But Rebecca was filled with determination to see the Americans ousted from this island and her contrymen in possession. Once the British had captured the island, they could control shipping through the straits—the only water route from the east to the west for the trading schooners.

From her window Rebecca could see the fort high atop the bluff. The American flag with its stars and stripes flew from the flagpole. But one day—and soon—she would see the Union Jack there in its place and hear the cry, "God Save the King!" shouted from its battlements.

Chapter Two

Rebecca walked back toward her house, her basket over her arm. Ships anchored periodically, bringing supplies to the island as did the *voyageurs*, the traders who arrived in their forty-foot canoes capable of carrying tons of goods. In her basket, in addition to her supplies for the immediate future, Rebecca carried the seeds she would need to plant the garden that was every villager's main source of vegetables.

She did not, at first, hear the footsteps of the man walking behind her. She did not sense his presence until he collided with her, knocking her basket from her arm and sending her packages of seeds and her food cascading over the ground.

"*Pardonnez-moi, madame,*" the man said. He was a *voyageur*, Rebecca knew immediately, for their clothing was almost a uniform. This man wore a shirt of red-and-green plaid, brown corduroy trousers, and deerskin moccasins. A gray woolen toque was perched on his jet-black hair.

"My name," he told her in a heavy French accent as he helped her gather her belongings, "is Pierre LaRoux."

"Thank you, *Monsieur* LaRoux," Rebecca said coolly, wondering at his actions. He had deliberately run into her, she was sure. But why? Merely to introduce himself?

She took the basket from him and started to turn away. But then among her things, she saw a folded square of paper that was not hers.

"*Monsieur?*" she called, turning back to see him already moving off in the other direction. "This is not—"

Over his shoulder the Frenchman shot her a look filled with warning. Instinct made Rebecca tuck the paper back among her packets of seeds and go on her way.

"Mrs. Carlyle?" another voice said when she was halfway home.

Rebecca closed her eyes and sighed. The men on this island were friendly if nothing else, she reflected. Looking around, she found the black-haired lieutenant from the fort approaching.

"Lieutenant . . . Hawkins, isn't it?" she asked. "It occurs to me that you officers do not spend much time at the fort."

The lieutenant laughed, his dark eyes sparkling in his tanned face. "I live in the village, ma'am," he told her. "Quite a few of the officers do. Only Lieutenant Hanks, our commanding officer, and those immediately under him live in the stone quarters." He nodded toward the fort. The stone officers' quarters were at the forefront of the fort. It was actually a part of the battlements, for its lower balconied level had been dug right into the limestone of the bluff.

"What if the fort were attacked?" Rebecca asked, adopting a teasing tone to lessen the import of her question. "She'd be in a sorry state if all her officers were down here rather than up there."

Anthony Hawkins laughed. "Look out there." He pointed toward the straits where the crystalline water sparkled in the spring sunshine. "Can you really imagine we would not see our attackers in plenty of time to make ready our defense?"

"I suppose not," Rebecca admitted, wondering how her countrymen could capture so impregnable a fortress.

"Let me carry your basket for you," he offered, taking it from her. "It looks heavy."

Unable to think of a viable reason to refuse, Rebecca let the lieutenant take the basket from her arm. The folded paper the Frenchman had placed in it was tucked in among her packets of seeds. She could only hope the lieutenant would not be too inquisitive.

Together they walked to Rebecca's door. Smiling, she took the basket from him.

"Thank you, Lieutenant," she said. "I will not keep you from your duties."

"Oh, but you're not," he assured her, following her into the warm, cozy cottage which her cleaning and her personal touches had rendered inviting and homey.

"Lieutenant Hawkins," Rebecca began, taking the basket to the sideboard. With her back to her guest, she slipped the note out of the basket and under the edge of the embroidered cloth with which she had covered the scarred top of the sideboard.

"Anthony," he corrected. "Please, would you call me Anthony? And may I call you Rebecca?"

No! Rebecca wanted to shout. There was something in the black-haired, black-eyed lieutenant's air that made her uneasy. Something in the way he looked at her that made her wary. But if she were to glean the information she needed, she had to be on friendly terms with the soldiers.

She nodded, barely veiling her reluctance. "If you wish," she acquiesced, adding, "Anthony."

He smiled, his teeth brilliantly white in his tanned face. "Dr. Day tells me you're a widow."

"I am," she admitted.

"For long?"

"About seven months," she replied. She nodded toward the gold-framed portrait on the wall. "My husband."

Anthony glanced at the portrait. "Seven months is a long time for a beautiful woman to be alone. You must be lonely."

He took a step toward her, the brass buttons of his red-and-blue uniform jacket winking in the sunlight flooding through the window. Rebecca, a warning voice sounding in her head, backed away.

"Surely you are needed at the fort," she said, her heart racing in her breast.

"I think I may be needed more here," he replied his voice low, sly, all pretense of gallantry gone.

Rebecca tried to move away, but the edge of the high, heavy table blocked her escape. She felt Anthony's hands at her waist, grasping her, turning her. His arm snaked about her and he pulled her hard against him.

"Don't fight me," he told her, pressing her against the table, bending her back over its broad-planked top. "A woman like you needs a man in her life. Your husband's been dead six months and more. You must have missed having a man in your bed."

Rebecca's fists pummeled his shoulders, his arms, but the thickness of his jacket protected him from her blows. She tried to kick him but her skirts and petticoats imprisoned her legs.

Anthony's mouth slanted savagely across hers, bruising her lips. She felt the pain and tasted the metallic warmth of her own blood.

She struggled as his mouth ground against hers, his lips trying to force hers apart. His hand rose and closed over her breast, squeezing, kneading. Rebecca gasped and when she did, Anthony's tongue snaked into her mouth, seeking her own. Rebecca clamped her teeth down upon it. She tasted his blood as her sharp teeth pierced the soft flesh.

Anthony roared with pain. Releasing her, he stumbled backward, one hand raised to his mouth.

"Bitch!" he snarled, looking at his hand and at the smears of blood that stained it.

"Get out of my house!" Rebecca ordered, swiftly moving to the fireplace and lifting the heavy iron poker. "Get out, damn you! Is this how American men treat their women? If it is, I feel sorry for . . ." She stopped, suddenly realizing what she had said. "I feel sorry for all of us," she finished lamely. "Now get out!"

His black eyes blazing, Anthony stormed out of the house, slamming the door behind him with a force that shook the very walls.

Rebecca watched him from the window, making sure he was gone. She fastened the latch of the door and replaced the poker at the fireplace. Her hands were trembling and her anger was fading, giving way to a sickening sensation in the pit of her stomach.

Her arms wrapped protectively about herself, she sank into a chair. Gain the confidence of the soldiers, Sumner had said, charm them into giving her the information she required. Was this what he meant? Let them maul her? Rape her? Good God! What had she gotten herself into?

She remembered the note in her basket. Retrieving it from the sideboard, she sat down again and unfolded the grimy piece of paper.

The handwriting was uneven, almost childish, the spelling erratic, but Rebecca made out the message: "I am Pierre LaRoux. If you want to send any message to the fort across the water, bring it to the market tomorrow morning before nine."

Rebecca drew a deep breath. The Frenchman was the go-between who would take the information she gathered to Fort St. Joseph!

She thought of Anthony Hawkins, an American officer, carrying her basket for her. If he had known what it contained . . . If he had happened to see the note, had somehow read the message . . .

She remembered his fury when he'd slammed out of the house. He was an enemy now, she knew, and it had nothing to do with political allegiances. It went deeper than that. Having rejected him, she had wounded his manhood, his masculine vanity. If he somehow discovered her secret, he would not hesitate to destroy her, for in bringing about her downfall, he would restore his pride which she had damaged.

Rebecca felt a wave of fear engulfing her. Her rejection of Anthony Hawkins had endangered not only her mission but quite possibly her own life! She wanted nothing more in that moment than to board the first outbound ship and to run away from the dangers here.

And she would leave! She glanced down at the Frenchman's note. She would write to Sumner. She would tell him what had happened, tell him she was in danger, that she wanted to leave this place, to come back to Fort St. Joseph and safety. She would even—the thought made her frown, troubled—tell him she would marry him, for she knew that would make him work harder to extricate her from the island.

Going to her desk, she took out ink and paper. She dipped her quill into the inkwell and, bending over the desk, began to write.

Night had fallen over the island. The midnight-blue sky met the inky blackness of the water on the far horizon and the huge, glowing full moon blazed a silvery trail that seemed to Rebecca to lead in the direction of St. Joseph Island—of home.

She had hauled bucket after bucket of water from the well and had heated them in the fireplace to fill the small wooden washtub she'd found in the sloping attic. Now bathed, her black hair still damp and hanging freshly brushed down her back, Rebecca sat in her small sitting room, wrapped in a warm nightdress and robe.

A small fire burned in the fireplace of the main room, for the April nights were still cool. Its flickering glow and the warm golden lights of the candles lent the house a snug intimacy that lulled Rebecca's shattered nerves. The

horror of Anthony's attack had eased some-
what and she had even begun to have second
thoughts about the letter to Sumner that lay in
the drawer of her desk.

The knock at the door sent a bolt of fear
shooting through her. She sat frozen in her
chair until it came again, a quiet, but insistent,
rapping at the rough panels.

Rising, Rebecca went into the main room
and took a long, lethal carving knife from the
sideboard. It shook in her hand as she went to
the door.

"Who is there?" she asked, trying without
success to quell her quavering voice.

"Beau McAllister," a deep, smooth voice
replied.

Rebecca frowned. Beau McAllister? The
golden-haired lieutenant's face appeared in
her mind's eye. She had not seen him since
she'd arrived on the island and he had escorted
her to her new home and helped her open
the house. Perhaps he was here in an official
capacity. Perhaps, she thought, he was here
because of what had happened between herself
and Anthony Hawkins earlier in the day.

"What do you want?" she asked, her fingers
slipping over the door latch, making doubly
certain it was well secured.

"Only to visit with you," he answered. "I
thought we could share a glass of wine and
talk."

"I don't have any wine," she told him harshly.

Sandra DuBay

His low chuckle seemed to rumble through the door. "I brought some with me." An awkward silence followed before he went on. "Is there something wrong, Mrs. Carlyle?" Still he heard nothing from the other side of the door. "I'll leave the wine here for you, on the step outside. Keep it and perhaps one day we can share it."

Rebecca heard the muffled thud as he placed the bottle on the step outside the door. She knew he meant to leave.

I have to trust him, she thought. *I have to believe he means only to talk with me. I must take this chance if I am ever going to learn anything about this place and its weaknesses.*

"Wait!" she called, fumbling with the latch. The door swung open and she peered out into the darkness. "Lieutenant McAllister?"

A shape moved in the darkness halfway down the path leading to the street. "I'm here," he replied from the shadows.

"Come in," she invited. "Bring the wine. I'd like to talk to you."

She stepped back as he approached. Bending gracefully, he picked up the bottle and entered the house.

"Where are your glasses?" he asked as he rounded the end of the table.

"Over there," Rebecca told him, fastening the door once more. "In the sideboard."

Beau stared, then a twinkle glittered in his deep blue eyes. His lips twitched and a grin spread over his handsome, chisled features.

Rebecca was perplexed until she realized that the carving knife was still in her hand. It glinted, reflecting the flickering, orange-red flames of the fire as she used it to point to the sideboard at the opposite side of the room.

Feeling foolish, she laid the knife on the table. But Beau's smile had faded. His dark eyes were filled with curiosity and concern.

"What's wrong, Rebecca? Are you frightened of me?"

"No," she assured him. "Of course not."

"Your voice, when you answered the door . . ." He frowned at her. "You sounded terrified. Now I come in to find you holding a knife. What's happened?"

"Nothing." She busied herself arranging the glasses he had retrieved from the sideboard. "Are you going to open the wine?" she asked, forcing a lightness into her voice that sounded false to her own ears.

"Not until you tell me what's happened to you," he said sternly.

"Beau, please," she entreated, turning her back to him to hide her expression. "I'd rather . . ."

A soft scream escaped her as he came up behind her and laid his hands on her shoulder to turn her around. Rebecca backed away from him, her eyes wide, before she realized he had meant her no harm.

An embarrassed flush crept into her cheeks under Beau's relentless scrutiny.

"Tell me, Rebecca," he demanded.

Moistening her lips with a flick of her tongue, she went to the fireplace and busied herself poking at the fire. She was torn between wanting to tell him what Anthony had done and shame that she had somehow brought the assault on herself.

"Tell me," he said again, more softly, sensing that she was concealing something painful.

"Lieutenant Hawkins was here this afternoon," she said, her voice so low he could scarcely hear her.

"Anthony?" Beau frowned. "What did he want?"

Rising from the hearth, Rebecca replaced the iron poker and dusted the ashes from her hands. Slowly, reluctantly, she raised her eyes to Beau's face. The pain and shame glimmering in their amethyst depths told Beau all he needed to know. A flush of anger blazed under his sun-tanned cheeks; his fists clenched until his knuckles stood out, white and straining.

"That bastard!" he snarled. "He forced you . . . I'll kill him, Rebecca. I'll—"

"No," she cried, grasping at his sleeve as he moved to leave the cottage. "He didn't, Beau. He tried but I fought him. He didn't force me to . . ."

"Don't protect him," Beau told her. "He doesn't deserve it."

"I'm not protecting him. I swear I'm not," she insisted. "Believe me, if he had succeeded, I would not protect him."

"Even so . . ." Beau turned away from the door and gazed down at her. His temper had given way to a deep, smoldering anger. "He should be punished. I can take you to Lieutenant Hanks in the morning."

"No," Rebecca insisted. She did not want to risk having Anthony Hawkins spread vicious lies about her that could jeopardize her mission. "I don't want to bring charges against him." She held up a hand to still Beau's protests. "Not this time. But if he ever bothers me again—"

"If he bothers you again, he'll answer to me," Beau promised, returning to the table. Opening the wine, he poured them each a drink and held one out to Rebecca. "You'll tell me, won't you, if he tries again?"

Nodding, Rebecca took the glass from him. The firelight glowed in its ruby-red depths as she raised it to her lips and tasted its sweetness. Over the rim of her glass her amethyst eyes met his deep blue gaze and for the first time since William Carlyle's death Rebecca felt cared for, protected, womanly. The sudden sensation struck a warning chord deep inside her. Her eyes took on a frightened look and she set the glass back onto the table lest the rippling wine betray the trembling of her hand.

"What it is?" Beau asked, noticing her distress.

"Nothing," Rebecca assured him quickly. "Please, sit down. If you will excuse me, I'll be back in a few moments."

Before Beau could reply, Rebecca had hurried around the end of the table and disappeared into her bedroom. Closing the door, she quickly took off her robe and nightgown and pulled on her petticoat and a plain gown of pretty Indian muslin she'd brought with her from England after her marriage. Squinting into her mirror with the light of a single candle casting its dim light about the shadowy room, she pinned up her glossy black hair.

Only then did she feel she could return to the other room where Beau waited. Only then did she feel that the sudden, disquieting intimacy that had so shaken her a few minutes before had been banished.

Painting a smile across her lips, Rebecca left the bedroom. Beau rose as she appeared but Rebecca waved him back into his chair. She would be, she decided, as she sat down opposite him in the chair that flanked the fireplace, the perfect hostess. Anthony Hawkins, after all, was lost to her as a source of information. Therefore, she would do well to cultivate this man if she were to learn what she needed to know.

But as she smiled at him, as she went to the cupboard and took out the sweet, floury cakes she'd made earlier in the day and offered him one, a vague, troubling voice told Rebecca she'd have been better off with Anthony Hawkins. She could have used him without regret, betrayed his trust without compunction, charmed him with honeyed words, and laughed afterward at his credulity. But this man, this handsome, kind, admiring man, would not be so easy to deceive then forget.

Taking her place once again, Rebecca stared into the fire. She could not afford the luxury of sympathy, of softness, she told herself sternly. This man was the enemy. Of that fact she must never lose sight. This man's countrymen had captured her husband and killed him with their cruelty and neglect. She owed it to William to avenge his death; she owed it to her country to help them regain at least a part of the territory the treasonous rebels had stolen.

Fortified by those thoughts, Rebecca leaned back in her chair. She held out her glass to Beau for more wine.

"I'm glad you came to visit, Lieutenant," she said softly, her voice honeyed

"So am I," he replied, his dark eyes running admiringly over her. "And you must call me Beau."

"I will . . . Beau," she fairly purred. "But only if you will call me Rebecca."

A pleased grin split Beau's face and he lifted his glass in playful salute. "I'd like to know you better, Rebecca," he said, sipping his wine.

"And I you," she agreed. "Much, much better. You must tell me all about yourself and all about your life here. I find this place fascinating. I want to know everything about it."

As Beau smiled happily, his gorgeous sapphire eyes shining, Rebecca felt like the proverbial spider sitting in her web, waiting for the plump, juicy fly to stumble unsuspectingly into her clutches.

Chapter Three

The night deepened, the wind off the lake rattled the windows of the house, creeping through the chinks in the mortar between the logs. The candles in Rebecca's cottage burned low as she and Beau McAllister talked.

Beau leaned back in his chair, one booted foot propped against the fieldstones of the fireplace. Now and again he used the poker to prod the fire into life, stirring the glowing embers in the grate. Once or twice he added another log after promising Rebecca he would go into the forest on his first day off duty and cut her a supply that would last until it was time to begin building her winter woodpile.

Rebecca gazed into the fire. Long before winter, she knew, war would have broken out between their two countries. Long before winter's grip clamped down on the island imprisoning it in ice, Beau would know her true purpose in coming here—and he would hate her.

"Your husband?" Beau asked, startling Rebecca from her reverie.

"I'm sorry?" she asked. He nodded toward the portrait. "Oh, the painting. My husband, William."

"What happened to him? If you don't mind my asking."

He died in a guardhouse. He was a spy, like me, Rebecca thought, wryly amused at the thought of Beau's reaction should she tell him the truth.

"He died of pneumonia," she answered. "Last October."

An awkward silence fell between them. Beau considered leaving. He'd been there longer than he'd planned already. But he did not want to leave her.

"Do you ride?" he asked suddenly, breaking the silence.

"I do," Rebecca confirmed. "Though I haven't since I was a girl."

"Perhaps one day I could borrow a couple of horses from the fort and we could go riding. There are some beautiful spots, some interesting natural formations."

"I'd like that," Rebecca agreed too quickly. She told herself she'd only agreed because it would be a good way to learn the lay of the land, but in her heart she knew that wasn't the

42

entire reason. "It is a beautiful place."

"It will only get better," Beau told her. "Wait until all the leaves are out and the wildflowers bloom."

His eyes studied her as if she were some rare species of exotic animal. "You are an unusual woman, Rebecca," he said quietly.

"Unusual?" Rebecca repeated. *More than you know*, she thought to herself.

Beau continued, "Most women left alone as you have been would have gone someplace more civilized. They would not be content in a backwater such as this."

There was bitterness in his voice, an angry twist to his lips, that struck Rebecca. "Are you speaking from experience?" she teased.

To her surprise, Beau nodded. "I am," he admitted grimly. "Experience with my wife."

His wife! Rebecca felt as if an icy hand had closed around her heart. All her plans to charm him were dashed. "You're married?" She averted her eyes. "You should have told me."

"I'm not married," Beau contradicted. "I was. But my wife like your husband is dead."

"What happened?" The words were out of Rebecca's mouth before she could stop them. "If you'd rather not speak of it . . ."

Beau shrugged. "It doesn't matter. It all happened several years ago." He took a deep breath and drank the rest of his wine. "I'll tell you what happened."

His eyes took on a faraway look of remembrance. "I was stationed at Prairie du Chien on the Mississippi. My wife . . ." he paused. "Melinda . . . was from Boston, where I met her. We were married there. I took her with me to the West. She hated it. Not a day passed that she didn't miss the society, the civilization, the culture of Boston. She begged me to go back but I refused. I thought that with time she . . ." he hesitated, his golden brows drawing together. "At any rate, she was killed. By Indians."

"Oh!" Rebecca raised a hand to her lips. "I'm so sorry!"

"She was running away with my best friend at the time." Beau saw the shock on Rebecca's face and the smile that appeared on his was filled with self-reproach. "She'd convinced him to take her back to Boston, I suppose. They were both killed."

Leaning forward in her chair, Rebecca instinctively took his hand and pressed it in sympathy.

Beau's eyes met hers, and his fingers curled around hers. The rough calluses, souvenirs of long years of hard work, scratched her skin.

Then suddenly he released her hand and rose. "I'm sorry," he said, his tone almost sheepish. "I should not have told you. I don't know what possessed me. I haven't spoken about Melinda to anyone for a long time. I haven't even thought of what happened . . ." Taking his red-feathered hat from the table, he went to the door. "I'll say good night now," he told Rebecca, "as I should have done hours ago."

"I've enjoyed your company," Rebecca assured him. "I'm glad you came."

Beau nodded. "We will go riding," he promised, "one day soon."

"I'd like that." Rebecca held the door as he opened it and stepped outside. "Good night, Beau," she said softly.

"Good night," he replied, and then the darkness swallowed him.

Rebecca stood in the doorway, gazing out into the night. She was sorry to see him leave. The house already seemed empty without him. She looked around. The houses and shops nearby were all dark. The island and its inhabitants were asleep.

As she should be, she told herself, closing the door.

In the shadows of the night Anthony Hawkins stood, watching Rebecca as she shut the door of the cottage. He'd seen Beau McAllister arrive earlier, had seen Rebecca admit him. He had stood, a solitary guard, watching to see how long Beau would stay. As the hours passed, Anthony's anger and resentment had grown. His lip curled in disgust. McAllister was after the same thing he was, but McAllister couched it in pretty words and gallantry. What did it all boil down to in the end? Like himself, Beau meant to get under the pretty widow's petticoats. And if today was any indication, he was going to be successful.

45

Damn him! Damn her! She'd pay for the injuries she'd inflicted on his body. His tongue still pained him when he spoke, ate, or drank and he suspected it would go on paining him for days to come. And she'd pay for wounding his pride.

His face flushed with anger and jealous resentment, Anthony left the shadows and went off up the street toward his own house. Someday, somehow, he'd either have his way with the beautiful, black-haired Rebecca Carlyle, or see her pay for her foolishness in refusing him!

Inside the house, Rebecca banked the fire in the main room for the night.

The candles, nearly guttered in their brass candlesticks, were extinguished one by one as Rebecca circled the room.

Through the doorway, Rebecca saw her desk in the sitting room. She thought of the letter in the drawer, the letter begging Sumner to help her leave this place and return to the quiet, if dull, life she'd led before embarking on this hazardous, disturbing mission.

Odd, she thought, the difference a few hours could make. She no longer wanted to leave. She would send a message to Sumner tomorrow, but not the one she'd written that afternoon in the emotional aftermath of Anthony Hawkins's assault.

Opening her desk, she took out another sheet of paper. Taking up her quill, she wrote a letter for Sumner to pass along to Captain Roberts, his commanding officer, on St. Joseph Island.

Dear Sumner,

I have settled in here, on Mackinac Island. I am, it seems, accepted as a young widow seeking the peace and quiet of a place such as this. No one seems to question my being here.

Thus far I have made the acquaintance of Dr. Day, the post surgeon at the fort, and, through him, the acquaintance of two lieutenants—Anthony Hawkins and Beau McAllister. Of the two I like Lieutenant McAllister better than Lieutenant Hawkins. [*That*, Rebecca reflected, *is the understatement of a lifetime!*] But both seem eager to procure my good opinion. Lieutenant McAllister has offered to take me riding and to show me the island. I have accepted his offer and so should be able to give you some details of the landscape shortly. When I know more, I will be certain to send you the information *via Monsieur* LaRoux whom I met this morning.

I hope this note finds you and everyone at Fort St. Joseph well. Until I see you again, I remain,   Yours sincerely,

Signing the letter, Rebecca sanded and sealed it. She would take it to the market in the morning and give it to Pierre LaRoux.

Sandra DuBay

Her first letter, written in shock and despair, she took to the fireplace and tossed onto the banked embers. It darkened and curled, finally bursting into flames. Rebecca watched until it was nothing more than ashes, indistinguishable from the others in the grate.

Blowing out the candles in the sitting room, Rebecca went to her bedroom and undressed. She turned back the covers on the bed, then blew out the last of the candles.

Swathed in darkness, Rebecca lay in bed, remembering the story Beau had told her. His wife . . . What was her name? Melinda, that was it. That she'd been killed was bad enough. Rebecca had heard all too often of the atrocities committed by Indians against the white men and women they looked upon as invaders of their territories, despoilers of their lands and lives. But that she'd betrayed her husband with his best friend . . . Poor Beau.

Beau McAllister's handsome, tanned face appeared in her mind. What sort of woman, married to such a man, would betray. . . .

With a disgusted sigh, Rebecca leaned on one elbow and pounded her pillow into submission. Was she any different? She was here to lull someone, anyone, into trusting her. Fate seemed to have chosen Beau to be that someone. He liked her, she knew, admired her. He must be beginning to trust her, for he had confided in her what must surely be the most painful memory of his entire life. And what was she planning to do with that trust? Once he had provided her with the information she and her countrymen needed? She would betray him as surely as his Melinda had.

Tucking the quilts beneath her chin, Rebecca tried not to think of the future. She could not afford to be softhearted. Was not Beau the enemy? Had not his fellow soldiers neglected dear William during his illness and so caused his death?

"William," she whispered aloud. She tried to picture his face but the image was indistinct, as if viewed through a mist. Even as she thought of him, William's face faded and was replaced by Beau's—his golden hair, his tanned skin, the glistening smile, those deep sapphire eyes. . . .

Groaning, Rebecca turned onto her stomach. What was wrong with her? Where were her loyalties? Beau McAllister was the enemy and she was using him to help her king and country and to avenge her husband. His feelings were nothing to her and her feelings should be kept strictly under control.

But it was easier said than done. She could force thoughts of Beau out of her mind when she was awake, but once she had drifted off into sleep, her unconscious had a will of its own. Throughout the night she dreamed of Beau, troubling dreams mixed up with images of Indians and of Anthony Hawkins. She was glad when the first streaks of dawn lightened the night sky. She was relieved when, after washing and dressing, she took the letter to the market and passed it covertly to Pierre LaRoux.

The time for hesitation was past. She'd sent her first bit of information off to St. Joseph Island. Her life as a spy had begun.

Chapter Four

True to his word, Beau arrived at Rebecca's door one afternoon not many days later with two horses. Rebecca stepped back to let him into the cottage.

"Didn't you think I meant to take you riding?" he asked, seeing the surprise on Rebecca's face and the way she stared at the two horses tethered to her fence at the edge of the road.

"No, that is, I . . ." Rebecca laughed, her cheeks flushed pink. "I did not think you would manage it so quickly. Let me go change and we can go."

The skirts of her pale blue cotton dress rippled against the shining brown sides of the horse as Rebecca rode through the lush, full-blown beauty of the springtime island. Wildflowers blossomed underfoot; the leaves seemed to glow in the verdant canopy above. The air was fragrant and warm, caressing her cheeks and riffling the long black curls that peeped from beneath the wide brim of her straw bonnet.

A chipmunk, its tail standing straight on end, darted across the path causing Rebecca's mount to shy nervously. Before she could react, Beau's hand was on the horse's bridle gentling it, calming it. He smiled at her reassuringly, his sapphire-blue eyes twinkling.

Rebecca's answering smile quivered at the corners of her mouth. She had felt it—the tug at her heart, the shiver along her spine. It felt so good being surrounded by the sheer, unspoiled beauty of nature, admired and protected by a handsome man. If only. . . .

She looked away, ostensibly admiring a bed of wild violets. The truth nagged at her, taunted her. Sooner or later Beau would know she was, and had always been, his enemy. He would know she had used him, beguiled him into betraying his countrymen, lulled him into aiding an agent bent on destroying his country's dominion in this beautiful place.

"Rebecca?" Beau's tone was curious, concerned.

She looked up at him forcing a quick wan smile onto her lips. "Yes?"

"Is something wrong? You look so sad."

Rebecca shook her head, her black curls bouncing. "Nothing. Nothing at all."

They rode on, exploring the forested island,

Beau explaining the rich legend and folklore of the place. The island had figured importantly in the myths and legends of the Indians for generations and it seemed to Rebecca that every place where they stopped had some fable attached to it.

He showed her Skull Cave where, it was said, an Englishman had hidden from his Indian captors after their massacre at the old English outpost, Michilimackinac, on the mainland at the northernmost tip of the southern peninsula. It was dark when he'd taken refuge there so he had not seen much of his haven. In the morning, however, he had discovered that he had passed the night on a bed of human bones.

Rebecca shivered with revulsion. "How horrible!" she cried, stepping back from the mouth of the cave. "Whose bones were they?"

"I have no idea," he admitted. "Perhaps it was a burial place for the Indians or where they disposed of their victims' bodies."

He leered menacingly at Rebecca and she giggled. When he lifted her onto her horse, his hand lingered on the soft flesh of her calf above the low boot she wore.

"Beau," she warned, playfully slapping his hand away.

He grinned and turned away and Rebecca watched him go. The skin of her calf seemed to burn where he'd touched her.

They rode on, making their way through forests of tall cedar, spruce, and tamarack which, Beau told her, would turn golden in the autumn and lose its soft clumps of needles for the winter. Wildflowers abounded, their fragrances mingling, filling the air with a soft potpourri of delicate beauty that filled Rebecca's lungs as she inhaled deeply.

From Skull Cave Beau took her to Arch Rock where she marveled at the soaring natural rock bridge overhanging a cliff. The water lay one hundred forty feet below, its deep, rich blue framed in the craggy rock archway.

"The Indians," Beau told Rebecca as she gazed down at the water, "believed that this arch was the gateway to the island for their god, Manitou."

"It's so beautiful." She sighed. "The whole island is a paradise."

"In the summer," Beau agreed. "But in the winter it's the loneliest, most desolate place on earth. At least it was last winter. Perhaps this winter will be different." Reaching out, he touched her cheek with the back of his hand.

Rebecca smiled, trying to hide the emotions stirring inside her. Long before the bitter winter clasped the island in its cruel grasp, Beau would know the real reason she was here—and he would hate her. This blissful day, the admiration in his eyes, in his touch, would be nothing more than bittersweet memories.

"Where shall we go now?" Rebecca asked, turning from the natural beauty before her.

Beau shrugged, eyeing her curiously. "We could see Sugar Loaf, another rock formation which is supposed to be Manitou's wigwam, or Robinson's folly which is a cliff where the captain of a British outpost is supposed to have fallen to his death with his Indian lover thirty years ago." He laughed. "There's always Lover's Leap."

"It might be useful to know where that is," Rebecca murmured.

"Here, now . . ." Beau went to her side and turned her toward him. "I did not mean to make you sad with all these tragedies. They're only myths. There's probably not a word of truth to any of them."

"It's not that," she breathed, trembling.

The truth, and she did not really want to admit it to herself let alone to him, was that she wanted to touch him. She wanted to hold him, to feel his warmth, his strength, to be in his arms.

It was the height of foolishness and she knew it. He was her enemy, she ought to hate him. Instead, she yearned for him, hungered for him with an intensity she had not known even with her beloved William.

Turning away from Beau, she buried her face against the warm, arching neck of the mare, marveling at her own jumbled emotions. She had loved William with a deep and abiding love that had been between them from the start. But she had never felt this fire, this aching, ravening hunger. And yet, it was not entirely lust. There was more to it. Yes, she wanted to lie with him. The thought of his body against hers, skin to skin, flesh to flesh, made her tremble. But more than that, she wanted to talk to him, laugh with him, tell him her fears and her dreams. She was treading a dangerous path and she had to take care not to fall victim to these needs and desires.

"Rebecca." Beau's voice was worried, his handsome, tanned face etched in an expression of concern as he held her shoulders and turned her toward him. "Rebecca, please tell me. What is it?"

She shook her head. "Nothing."

"Nothing?" He touched her cheeks where a single tear glistened. "You call this nothing?"

"I . . ." She averted her eyes. "I was thinking of my husband."

"Oh." Beau looked out toward the cliff and the water in the distance. "You loved him very much."

"Yes," Rebecca agreed, thinking, *Forgive me, William, for using your memory in a lie. But how can I tell this man the truth?*

"Do you want to go home now?" Beau asked, feeling awkward.

"Perhaps we should." Rebecca nodded.

Remounting their horses, they rode back to the village in silence. At Rebecca's cottage, she smiled up at him.

"Will you come back for supper? Or do you have to be on duty tonight?"

"I don't have to be on duty," he admitted. "Are you certain you want me to come back?"

"Yes," she told him sincerely. "Please, come back."

She watched as he rode off, her mare trotting behind his horse on their way back to the fort stables. Turning toward her door, Rebecca tried not to think of tonight when they would be alone in the intimate confines of her cottage.

The evening went well until after supper when the scented warmth of the night and the wine they'd had with their meal seemed to go to their heads.

Rebecca went into the bedroom to tidy her hair. Standing at the looking glass, she suddenly saw Beau standing behind her. Her breath caught in her throat. He had taken off his blue-and-gold tunic and the muscles of his chest and arms strained at the white cotton of his shirt. His collar was opened at the throat, and the golden curls frosting his sun-tanned flesh peeked out.

Their eyes met in the mirror, their reflections wavering in the flickering candlelight. He reached out slowly and took the brush from her hand.

"So beautiful," he murmured, putting the brush aside. His fingers worked in her hair, pulling out the pins, freeing the heavy curls that cascaded over her shoulders in a shining, raven-black mass.

"Beau . . ." she whispered, the feel of his fingers in her hair making her tremble. "No . . ."

"Yes," he disagreed, his hands spanning her waist, his head dipping, his lips caressing the

57

creamy, pulsing flesh of her throat.

Rebecca moaned, her head falling back. She felt his chest against her back, felt his hands at her waist, hesitating then moving up to mold themselves to the soft fullness of her breasts.

She felt as if her heart would stop. Her knees weakened, threatening to buckle beneath her. It seemed only Beau's body behind her kept her from sliding to the floor. She felt as if a fever had seized her. Her skin burned where his lips touched it, her body ached as he caressed her. She felt a swirling, melting need deep inside her and knew that the only thing that could assuage it was the very thing that could destroy her.

"No!" she cried, pushing away from him. Whirling to face him, she crossed her arms protectively. "We can't!"

"Rebecca," Beau moaned, his own desire an urgent, demanding fire raging inside him. "It's not wrong. Your husband is dead; you are not betraying him."

"I can't," Rebecca breathed. Shaking her head, she turned her back to him. Her body quaked, still wracked with desire for him. "I can't."

"Why?" he persisted. "Won't you tell me why?"

Sniffling, she could only shake her head. And Beau, knowing he could not bear to be near her without touching her, loving her, turned without a word and left, catching up his tunic and hat on his way out.

Rebecca covered her face with her hands and wept. Damn Sumner! she raged to herself, damn this place and damn all these men and their politics! And most of all, damn her weak, woman's flesh that still burned with the fires of desire for a man who was her enemy!

Chapter Five

A week passed before Beau returned, a week fraught with worry and irritation. A week during which Rebecca had swung between sadness that she had driven him away with her refusal and anger that he should choose to stay away because she had refused him her bed.

But then, at last, he was there, standing on her doorstep, the early-summer sunshine glinting in the golden strands of his hair. As before, two of the fort's horses were tethered to her fence.

"Would you like to go riding again?" he asked when she answered the door.

Rebecca blushed. It was all too apparent that they both remembered their last time together and all too obvious that their mutual desire had not abated. Still, she wanted to be with

61

him. She had yet to accomplish her mission, she told herself primly, ignoring the fact that her "mission" was the least of her reasons for desiring Beau's company.

"I thought we could ride along the shore today. The view is beautiful."

Rebecca agreed and they were soon side by side, their horse's hooves churning the hot white sand as they rode along the shore. It was there, at the Straits, that the water of two huge lakes, Huron and Michigan, met and mingled. As they rode, Beau told her more of the history and legend that surrounded the island.

They were nearly at the opposite end of the island when Beau suggested they let the horses rest and drink at the water's edge.

They walked in the sand, silent, until Beau said, "About what happened the other night. I'm sorry, I—"

"No," Rebecca interrupted. "I'm sorry. You don't understand, Beau. Let's just forget it happened, shall we? Let's not let it come between us."

Smiling, he nodded. "Agreed. That's really what I had in mind to say to you." He laughed. "I'm glad one of us got it out. I wanted to ask you if you would come to supper with me tonight at the fort." Rebecca looked up at him in surprise and he went on; "I was telling Lieutenant Hanks about you. He's invited us to dine with him in his quarters tonight at the fort."

"Oh." Rebecca closed her eyes. It was so easy, too easy. If only she could be cold, calculating. How triumphant she should be that an officer of the fort would be escorting her to dinner with the fort's commander. Doubtless Beau would show her the fort, point out with pride, she was sure, its battlements, its blockhouses, and cannon. Unwittingly he would give her the very information she needed to help her countrymen conquer this place and tear it from the grasp of the rebellious traitors who called themselves Americans.

If only Anthony Hawkins had not accosted her. If only she could have dealt with his advances in some way that left them less than enemies. She could have taken pleasure in duping him. She could have absorbed the information he gave her and fed it back to Sumner and his commander and all the while laughed with glee at his foolishness and gullibility.

But Beau . . . She glanced sideways at him as they rode abreast. He was not like Anthony Hawkins. He had a heart—a heart that had known love and betrayal. However frequently Rebecca reminded herself that he was the enemy, some soft, womanly part of her shrank from reopening the wounds that had healed— if only on the surface—with the passage of time since his wife's death.

However hard she tried to push those thoughts aside, however desperately she clung to her principles, to the lifeline of her belief that the rebellious colonists should be brought back beneath the rule of England and her king, Rebecca found herself increasingly assailed by doubts and feelings of guilt. She could only perform her assigned task then pray that when the British flag was hoisted above the fort, she would be spared the sight of Beau's face—and the look of betrayal, anger, and doubtless loathing he would feel toward her when he discovered how he'd been used.

Twilight was giving way to nightfall when Beau and Rebecca made their way down the long, sloping ramp from the fort to the village below. Rebecca's hand, encased in the white kid gloves she had worn to complement her high-waisted, lace-trimmed gown of pale yellow silk, was linked through Beau's arm. A worsted shawl drawn around her shoulders protected her from the chill of the evening breezes off the lake.

Rebecca was lost in thought. Lieutenant Hanks, their host, had been polite and gracious. After a surprisingly elegant and well-prepared dinner, the fort commander had personally escorted his guests on a tour of the fort. Rebecca had seen the sally ports—the arched doorways built into the thick stone walls—the blockhouses, the cannon emplacements, the battlements. Flanked by Beau and his superior, Rebecca had stood on the ramparts and looked out at the straits far below.

Try though she might, Rebecca could not help thinking of the British warships that would all too soon sail into those straits. She touched the cannons that would fire upon them. She saw the men who would fight and die to protect this bastion in the wilderness, and she thought of the men of Fort St. Joseph who would also fight and die. The information she gleaned on this evening would play a vital role in the future of this place and of these people—not only the soldiers but the villagers, traders, trappers, and Indians who came to trade.

When the time came to leave, Lieutenant Hanks had bidden Rebecca good night at the fort gate—the gate nearest the guardhouse she'd noticed with a shiver—and invited her to return whenever she wished.

"You're quiet," Beau remarked when they reached the bottom of the long ramp and started along the dusty road toward Rebecca's house. "You're lost in thought."

"Lieutenant Hanks is very kind," she murmured, her face turned to hide her expression from Beau.

"He's a good man," Beau agreed. "A good friend and a fine officer. I'm happy serving under him."

"He seems very young to be in command of a fort," Rebecca said softly. "I wonder how he would perform under fire."

"God willing we'll never have to find out," Beau replied as they turned into the path leading to Rebecca's door. "But I have no doubt he'd prove a gallant and brave soldier if put to the test."

Rebecca said nothing. Could it really be, she wondered, that the men here at this remote outpost were so ignorant of the perilous state of relations between their young country and England? Did they not know that the two countries had been teetering on the brink of open warfare for months? The previous year the American government had banned the importation of British goods. Surely word of this had reached even this place. That action alone should have signaled growing hostilities. And yet here on the island life went on and the inhabitants clung to the hope—the vain hope, Rebecca knew—that peace would prevail and the serenity and beauty of this place would never be shattered by the ugliness and horror of war.

At the door Rebecca turned toward Beau. "It was a lovely evening," she told him sincerely.

"That sounds like good night," Beau said, his tone teasing.

"It is," Rebecca replied.

"I thought perhaps . . ."

Rebecca shook her head. "It's been a lovely evening," she repeated, "and a lovely day."

"There'll be others like it," he promised. "Many, many others."

"Of course," she agreed, but her heart was heavy as she turned and entered the house, closing the door behind her before Beau had moved away.

Standing in her sitting room, Rebecca peeled off her long gloves and dropped them onto the desk. She took off the pearl earrings and choker that had been William's wedding gift to her.

On the desk a blank sheet of paper lay, its clean empty surface an accusation. There was a great deal of information she could impart to Sumner concerning the fort. Though she had not yet found a landing site to recommend, she could tell Sumner that the fort itself had not changed appreciably from the days when it had belonged to the British. She could describe the condition of the battlements, the number and placement of the cannons, their size and type from which the artillery men at Fort St. Joseph would be able to determine their potential range.

She should be writing but her mind was filled with thoughts of Beau. She felt foolish that her woman's heart had softened toward him and she felt guilty that so soon after William's death she had found another man so desirable. And yet the knowledge that Beau McAllister found her desirable pleased her and frightened her.

If she spent too much time with him, if she allowed him to hold her as she knew he wanted to, to kiss her, to touch her. . . .

No! No! her heart cried. It was wrong! However handsome he was, however charming, he was the enemy and his only usefulness to her should be the information she could gain from him.

Resolute, she sat down at the desk and opened her inkwell. Without pausing to think, without risking the doubts and misgivings that lurked just outside her consciousness, she laid down in cold, factual terms the information she'd learned at the fort. She promised to send word of possible landing sites soon.

That would likely mean she'd have to spend more time in Beau's company, for he would be the best man to escort her to the more remote spots where a landing might be carried out in secret. But, she told herself, as she blotted the letter and sealed it, she could deal with Lieutenant Beau McAllister. She must only remember that he was the enemy and all too likely . . . She hesitated, a shiver of horror running down her spine. All too likely to die in the battle she was helping to set in motion.

Chapter Six

Pierre LaRoux brought no reply to Rebecca's letter. As the days passed becoming a week, then two, three, and finally four, she wondered what had happened. Perhaps, she mused, her heart filling with hope, the differences between Britain and her former colony had been settled, that some workable, if strained, armistice that would allow them to abandon these hostilities had been reached.

But then, the voice of reason whispered, would she not have been called home? If there were to be no attack, no war, would not Sumner have written to tell her to leave Mackinac Island and come back to Fort St. Joseph and to him?

Something must have happened. To Sumner? To Monsieur LaRoux? If only there was some way to find out. Rebecca sighed as she sat before her looking glass, pinning up her long black hair. Until word did arrive, there was really nothing she could do but go on with her mission. But her curiosity was piqued and would not rest until she learned the truth of this latest, worrisome development.

Luckily, she did not have to wait for long. It was late afternoon four days later when she walked in the warm golden sand along the island's wide beach that Rebecca learned the answer.

"You haven't much to say today," she told Beau who walked along beside her, his boots sinking into the sand, his hands clasped behind his back. "Perhaps you would rather see me home and go back to—"

"Not at all," he told her quickly. "It's only that . . ." He stared out at the gently rolling water, its depths reflecting the breathtaking azure of the cloudless sky above. "Oh, damn," he muttered. "I shouldn't be telling you this but we've reason to believe there is a British spy on the island."

Rebecca's heart fluttered sickeningly in her breast and she prayed the pink tinge of her sun-kissed cheeks would conceal the sudden pallor of her face.

"What makes you think so?" Rebecca asked, trying, she hoped with some success, to sound only casually interested.

"Some of the Indians who come to the fort found a dead man on the shore of one of the islands to the east. He had apparently drowned, there were no wounds on his body. He was a *voyageur* and the Indians went through the goods that had washed up near his body. In his pack there was a letter from a Lieutenant Meade at Fort St. Joseph, the British fort on St. Joseph Island. It was addressed to someone here on Mackinac Island."

"If you know to whom it was addressed—" Rebecca began, as the fear that he was in a reluctant, roundabout way going to accuse her stirred within her.

"We don't know," Beau interrupted. "The letter had been in the water several days. The ink was smeared, washed away in several places. It took quite a while even to make out this Lieutenant Meade's name and the fact that it came from Fort St. Joseph. The rest of the letter, apart from the words 'Mackinac Island,' was illegible. It could have been meant for anyone here."

"And there is no way for you to discover who the letter was meant for?" Rebecca persisted, not yet daring to relax.

"I'm afraid not," Beau admitted. "Unless someone comes forward with information, there is no way to find out where it was bound."

Although she should have been reassured that she was not going to be exposed as a British spy because of Pierre LaRoux's death, Rebecca could not quell her fear. Without LaRoux she was cut off from Sumner, from St. Joseph Island. They could not send word to her of how near they were to attacking and she could not send information to them. How, then, could she tell them the rest of the information they needed and how, she wondered, could they let her know if and when the British forces were to invade this green and peaceful island.

Her anxiety had not lessened two weeks later on an overcast afternoon when she and Beau rode through the lush forest near the far end of the island. Though she tried to appear carefree and content, she was troubled and preoccupied. She could not help wondering over and over what had been in the letter Pierre LaRoux had been bringing to her when he'd drowned. And even now, she thought, was Sumner waiting for some reply to his letter? Had there been an urgent message for her? A warning, perhaps?

"Rebecca?" Beau prompted, not for the first time.

"Hmmm?" Coming out of her musings, Rebecca realized that Beau had dismounted and tethered his horse to a tree. "I'm sorry. My mind was off in the clouds somewhere," she apologized, leaning down so he could lift her off her horse.

Beau looped her horse's reins over a branch and, taking Rebecca's hand, walked with her down to the water's edge.

"This is one of my favorite places," Beau told her.

"It is lovely," Rebecca agreed.

The shoreline stretched off unbroken as far as the eye could see. The beach was wide and sandy, the bottom dropped off quickly, deepening the water. The long expanse of trees that lined the shore was broken in this one place. It was, Rebecca realized with a shiver, a natural landing point.

"How far are we from the fort?" she asked, her breath catching in her chest.

"About two, two-and-a-half miles as the crow flies," Beau told her. "There is a road across the middle of the island that leads to the fort. There are a few farms in the center of the island. Little more. Come here, I'll show you."

Taking a stick, Beau drew a rough map of the island in the wet sand near the water's edge. He showed Rebecca where the village lay around the natural harbor, where the fort stood atop the bluff. He showed her where they stood at a spot nearly opposite the fort and village, and he showed her the path of the road that led between the two places.

As she watched, Rebecca's heart contracted. He was unwittingly spelling disaster for his friends, his comrades-in-arms, for the interests of his country.

She studied the map, knowing that, should the opportunity arise, she would reproduce it for Sumner to take to his commanding officer. She looked at Beau as he concentrated on his map and felt a sudden desire to ruffle his golden hair. She wanted to touch him, feel his arms around her, know that for this moment he cared for her even though she knew that whatever feelings he had for her were doomed, that all too soon the caring would turn to something dark and ugly.

"Beau?" she said softly.

He looked up from where he squatted on the sand. His sapphire eyes met her longing amethyst gaze and he rose slowly, carefully, as if afraid a sudden movement would frighten her.

He came to her, reaching out, and Rebecca went into his arms. Her heart pounded, tears of longing and regret welled in her eyes.

"What is it?" he asked, feeling her shaking in his arms. "Rebecca?"

She hid her face against the soft blue fabric of his tunic. What could she say? She could tell him nothing of her dilemma, nothing of her fears. She turned her face up to him.

"Kiss me, Beau?" she breathed, her hand rising to touch his face. "Please, please kiss me."

His eyes searched her face, surprise and curiosity filled his expression. "I can't," he told her simply.

"But why?" she demanded, stung by what seemed to her to be a cruel rejection. "I thought you . . . It seemed as if—"

"If I kiss you," Beau interrupted, "if I hold you and kiss you, I won't stop there. I couldn't. And you'd hate me."

"No. Oh, no, I won't hate you. I don't want you to stop."

"Are you certain? Rebecca, don't say this if you don't mean it."

Reaching up, she drew his head down and pressed her lips to his. His arms tightened around her, and she felt a shudder of desire course through his body. Then he was holding her, her body cradled in his arms, as he carried her to the edge of the forest where the grass was soft and thick as a richly woven carpet.

Lying on the soft bed of grass, Rebecca felt the warmth, the strength of Beau's body as he pulled her close, stroked her back, her hair, her cheeks. His face above hers, he gazed down into her eyes as he drew back her skirt and petticoat. His work-roughened hand caressed the smooth flesh of her thigh.

Rebecca's fingers trembled while she worked at the brass buttons of his tunic. She wanted, needed, to touch him, to feel his skin against her own. The pounding of her heart, the fire already blazing inside her drove her to boldness. She shuddered, arching toward Beau when he opened the front of her gown and lowered his head to kiss the hard, rose-red tips of her breasts.

Trembling, she tore at the white cotton shirt beneath his tunic. She moaned softly when her hands found the hard, muscled flesh of his chest.

"Beau," she breathed, pulling him closer, pressing her quivering body to his.

Beau kissed her, his mouth caressing hers, his tongue tracing her lips, parting them. His hand stroked her knee, her thigh, moving higher until he found her, touched her, teasing her moist, hot flesh until Rebecca cried out, driven near to madness with desire for him.

She reached for him as he leaned away, working at the fastenings of his breeches. And then he was above her, his strong thighs parting her softness. He pressed his body against hers, into hers, filling her, forcing a deep, shuddering moan from her.

Rebecca's fingers clutched at him, burrowed beneath his tunic and shirt to stroke the hot, flexing muscles of his back. She writhed, digging her heels into the grass, trying to get closer, ever closer to the maddening, delicious sensation building inside her. Her breath came in short, harsh gasps. Paradise seemed but a hairbreadth away but it eluded her, driving her to desperation, until at last the world seemed to shatter around her, pulsing, throbbing, taking her beyond anything she had ever known into a world of pure pleasure, sheer beauty, sweet ecstasy. . . .

Rebecca avoided Beau's eyes as they rode back through the forest to reach the road that was the quickest route to the fort and the village.

"Are you sorry?" Beau asked, seeing the way she trembled, the tears that slipped down her cheeks before she could wipe them away.

"I . . . I . . ." Rebecca could not find her voice. Part of her was sorry, for she knew that she

would never now be totally free of Beau
McAllister. Come what may—peace or war,
love or hate, life or death—he would always
be a part of her. She would never forget him,
never be completely free of the memories she
knew would haunt her forever.

Beau said nothing more. He believed she
was sorry for what had happened between
them. He thought she must be feeling she
had betrayed her dead husband, though he
thought it remarkable that so passionate, so
vital a woman had remained faithful to a
memory for so long. Still, if she wanted no
more of him, if she decided that she could not
see him again, he would accept it . . . with
regret.

They were approaching a farm when the
heavy gray clouds that had obscured the sun
all day at last released their burden. The rain
gave little warning, a drop, then two, then the
deluge.

"Come on!" Beau called, hunching against
the rain and kicking his horse into a gallop.
"We can go to Dousman's farm until it lets
up."

Saying nothing, Rebecca urged her horse forward and followed Beau toward the clapboard
house standing near the side of the road.

Chapter Seven

The farm's owner, Michael Dousman, readily admitted Rebecca to his snug, warm house while Beau went to see their horses safely stabled in the barn.

Self-consciously, Rebecca smoothed back her wet, tousled hair and wished she had a comb and a mirror.

"Tea?" Dousman asked, startling her.

"Yes, thank you," Rebecca replied.

"Why don't you sit by the fire?" he suggested. "You'll catch a chill standing there in those wet clothes."

Nodding, Rebecca went to sit before the fire that blazed in the kitchen hearth. Behind her, she heard the farmer measuring out the tea and pouring it into a cup. He passed her once and took the kettle hanging near the fire and

Rebecca heard the sound of water pouring and the clink of a spoon against the side of the cup.

She looked up with a wan smile of thanks when he brought her the cup and handed it to her. The warmth of the earthenware cup felt good against her hands and even the scalding heat of the tea when she sipped it was welcome.

Dousman went to the window and squinted out toward the barn from which Beau had not yet emerged. Turning back, he came to sit opposite Rebecca near the fireplace.

"You are Mrs. Carlyle, aren't you," he said. It was a statement, not a question.

"I am," she admitted. "Have we met? I'm sorry, I don't seem to remem—"

"No," he interrupted. "We haven't met. But I was going to come to see you."

Rebecca shifted uneasily in her seat. Had he somehow discovered her secret? Did he mean to expose her? Blackmail her?

"Why?" she asked, her mouth suddenly dry.

Rising, Dousman disappeared into another room. When he returned, he held a small, creamy packet in his hand.

"This is for you," he told her simply.

Taking it, Rebecca broke the seal and unfolded the crisp paper. Though she did not read the message, Sumner's handwriting was unmistakable even at a glance.

"But how?" she breathed, astonished.

"He wrote to me after LaRoux died. I am to be your contact now."

"But . . ." Rebecca took a long sip of her tea. She felt utterly bewildered. "But if you live here, why could you not get the information for Captain Roberts?"

Dousman smiled. "I have not the means to gain the information about the fort itself," he told her. "Somehow, Mrs. Carlyle, I doubt Porter Hanks would invite me to dinner in his private quarters and then personally show me every aspect of the fort's defenses. And despite all the years I've lived here, Beau McAllister has not once asked me to go riding and see the sights of the island."

Rebecca's cheeks glowed rosy with her embarrassment. "I suppose not," she admitted softly, then thought, *And he would not have made love to you on a secluded beach, either.*

"You know, of course, that a letter from Sumner Meade was found near Pierre LaRoux's body. The Americans know there is a British spy on the island."

"Of course they know," Dousman agreed. "But I doubt you are their chief suspect. You should not worry." He glanced again out the window. "Here he comes."

Rebecca stared at him blankly for a moment; then, suddenly realizing she still held the letter from Sumner in her hand, she quickly tucked it into the bodice of her gown.

While the rain drummed on the roof of the house, Beau, Rebecca, and the farmer drank tea and talked of the coming summer, the sudden, strange hostility of many of the Indians who had always been allies of the Americans of Fort Mackinac, and the death of Pierre LaRoux whom Dousman professed never to have met. It was a warm, congenial setting and Rebecca could not help reflecting on how different the reality was from the truth. To the unsuspecting observer they seemed casual, cordial acquaintances. One would never have imagined that two were both enemies and lovers and the other was a secret sympathizer of a foreign, hostile nation.

When an hour later Beau decided the rain had stopped and they could leave, Rebecca thanked Dousman for his hospitality and invited him to stop and visit her the next time he came to the village. Though Beau suspected nothing, both Michael and Rebecca knew the farmer's visit would be but a pretext for the passing of Rebecca's next report to Sumner at Fort St. Joseph.

Mounted again, Rebecca and Beau rode on toward the fort. Rebecca was quiet, lost in thought. War between her homeland and Beau's was imminent but Beau did not seem to know it. Part of her, the tender, compassionate womanly part that had lain with him on the soft carpet of the forest and shared those precious moments, longed to warn him, but her patriot's heart forced her to silence.

They came to a halt and Beau drew her attention with a sweep of his arm. "Beautiful, isn't it?" he asked.

Rebecca looked at the panorama before them. They were atop the heights behind the fort. Before them, the land dropped away to the fort on its bluff. Beyond that, the village was far below, near the water's edge, and then came the deep, rolling waters of Lake Huron.

"It is beautiful," she admitted. "You can see the whole fort from here, and the village and . . ." her voice trailed off and she caught her breath.

She could indeed see the whole fort, and more than that, she could see that every cannon, every single piece of artillery, was pointed off toward the water. If they were fired upon from this vantage point, they would be defeated before they could manage to turn a cannon toward the heights.

This then was the way. If the British forces landed at the spot where she and Beau had . . . She forced those thoughts out of her mind. If they landed at the other end of the island and came along the same road she and Beau had taken, they could position their cannons on the heights and take the fort's inhabitants by surprise. Lieutenant Hanks would have no choice but to surrender and the fort would fall into British hands with scarcely a shot being fired.

Rebecca closed her eyes. The loss of the fort would be a hard blow for the Americans to take, but if the British could capture it without bloodshed, she need not have the deaths of any of the men she had come to know on her conscience.

"Are you all right?" Beau asked.

"Of course," she answered too quickly. "Why do you ask?"

"You looked . . . I don't know . . . sad, troubled."

Rebecca shook her head. "I'm tired, that's all. I've been sleeping badly. Would you mind if I went home now, Beau?"

"If that's what you want."

Later that night, alone in her bedroom, Rebecca could not help remembering the afternoon. She felt again the heavy, languid warmth of the moisture-laden air. She remembered once more the long, breathless look that had passed between them just before Beau had swept her into his arms and carried her to the forest's edge.

She felt a quivering heaviness in the pit of her stomach as she thought of what had followed. Their lovemaking had been more passionate, more fulfilling, than anything she'd known with William.

In the close darkness of her bedroom she felt her cheeks flame with shame. How could she have succumbed to her desire for Beau McAllister? It was not only that she had given herself to him, had all but prostituted herself for her country, but she had reveled in it, come alive in Beau's arms in a way she had never reacted to her husband's caresses. She had betrayed William's memory.

And yet, even now, even with the guilt of having given herself to Beau weighing heavily on her conscience, images of him flashed through her thoughts. Memories of his face, his voice, his touch flitted through her mind. She found herself longing to be with him, yearning to lie again in his arms and feel his strength. She found herself wanting nothing more than to hide herself in him, to leave behind the worries and fears and know nothing but the pleasure, the pure, indescribable bliss of his love.

She was falling in love with him! Rebecca sat up in bed, her eyes wide with horror. It was true! However much she wanted to deny it, however hard she tried to tell herself she had merely been serving the interests of her country, the truth stared back at her in the darkness.

This was madness! How could she have allowed herself to be so weak, so vulnerable? There was no future for her here, no future with Beau. There could be nothing for them but heartbreak, betrayal. It was better to get this over with and try to put it all behind her.

Throwing back the coverlet, Rebecca lit a candle and went into the sitting room where she opened her inkwell and took out a fresh sheet of writing paper.

Laboriously, she reproduced the map Beau had drawn for her in the sand on the beach. She marked the spot where the British could land and traced the route of the road past Dousman's farm to the heights behind the fort.

In the letter she wrote to accompany the map, she told Sumner of her discovery, that all the fort's cannons pointed toward Lake Huron and that if the British soldiers and their allies could command the heights behind the fort, there would be little the fort garrison could do to defend their stronghold. Rebecca was convinced, she told Sumner, that if surprise was on the side of the British forces, Fort Mackinac could be taken with little or no resistance from the American soldiers.

Sealing the letter, she hid it until Michael Dousman's visit when she would entrust it to him to see it safely delivered to Fort St. Joseph and Captain Roberts.

Her heart was unaccountably heavy as she took up her candle and returned to her bedroom. She had just sealed the fate of the fort as surely as she had sealed the letter to Sumner. Fort Mackinac was as good as lost once the letter reached the British stronghold on St. Joseph Island.

And Beau . . . Closing her eyes, she lay back on her pillows. She doubted there was any way she could keep Beau from learning of her part in the fall of Fort Mackinac. She could only hope she would be spared the sight of him after the battle. She could only pray that his blood would not be shed, that she would not prove to be the cause of any injury to him—or his death.

Shuddering, Rebecca said a quick prayer for Beau's safety when the day of the invasion came. He was Britain's enemy and therefore hers, but she could not bear the thought of his suffering—or dying—because of her.

Turning on her side, she tried to force those troubling thoughts out of her mind. But it was well into the early hours of morning before she fell into a restless, fitful slumber.

Chapter Eight

"Beau, no, please don't."

Beau sighed heavily as he stepped back, the arms he'd tried to wrap around Rebecca falling to his sides.

"I'm sorry," he said, his voice tight, his face stony. "I suspected you regretted that day in the forest but I'd hoped that with time . . ." He shook his head. "I guess not."

Rebecca turned away, avoiding his accusing gaze. How could she explain to Beau her apparent coldness in the month since that rainy afternoon when they'd become lovers? How could she explain feelings she herself did not understand? She was torn between regret and desire. Her nights were equally divided between long, wakeful hours filled with self-reproach and even longer sleepless hours tortured by her yearning to feel his arms around her once more, to know again the sheer, perfect pleasure of his lovemaking.

"I'll be going," he said shortly, reaching for his hat on the table.

"Beau, don't go," Rebecca pleaded, reaching toward him as he went to the door. "Please stay, please. I need . . ."

Beau looked back at her, his sapphire eyes smoky and heavy-lidded. "Yes, Rebecca?" he asked, a chill in his voice she'd never heard before. "What do you need? Obviously not me."

"I . . ." Her throat closing, Rebecca could not say the words that sprang to her lips. She wanted to run into his arms, to tell him everything, to warn him of what must surely happen in the very near future, to beg him to forgive her for what she had done out of allegiance to her king and country.

But in the end she could say nothing and she watched, helpless, as he left the cottage and walked stiffly up the path toward the road.

Wearily, Rebecca sank into one of the worn wooden armchairs that flanked the cold, empty fireplace. All she wanted was to be away from this place, away from these conflicting, heartrending emotions. She had never thought to fall in love again after William's death. The most she had hoped for was a comfortable, placid existence with a man she could respect, perhaps even grow to admire. Love had been the last thing on her mind when she'd come here but it had found her. Now all she wanted was to flee from it.

She folded her arms on the scarred table top and laid her head on them. She had given the letter and the map to Michael Dousman. She could only trust that he'd sent it to Fort St. Joseph with yet another British sympathizer, for she knew he hadn't left the island himself. She had no idea who this other contact might be and no wish to know. She only hoped that whatever was going to happen between the two countries would happen soon so that she could put this episode and its heartbreaking conse-quences behind her.

Nor was Beau her only worry. There was Anthony Hawkins to contend with. Though Beau's threat to have him brought up on charges if he bothered her again had kept the black-haired lieutenant at a distance in the past two months, he had suddenly appeared on her doorstep the day after she had sent her last letter off to Sumner.

Rebecca could still remember the shock that had coursed through her when she'd opened the door and found him standing there. She'd been expecting Beau but instead found herself looking into the almond-shaped black eyes of the man who had tried to rape her.

Her first reaction had been to slam the door, but he put out a hand and held it open.

"What do you want?" she'd demanded, dread-ing his answer.

"Only to talk to you, Mrs. Carlyle," Anthony drawled, a sneer in his dark, silky voice.

"I have nothing to say to you," she spat.

"Then just listen to me." His black eyes narrowed and Rebecca felt like a fawn trapped by a wolf seeing its own doom in those glittering, dangerous eyes. "I suppose McAllister has told you we believe there is a British spy on the island."

"It has nothing to do with me," she retorted, feeling a sick apprehension start in the pit of her stomach.

"I'm not so sure." Anthony's stare seemed to pierce her to the heart. "You arrived here so suddenly, a widow alone, with a flimsy excuse. You've captivated McAllister and ingratiated yourself with Porter Hanks . . ."

"That is no proof," Rebecca retorted. "What proof have you?"

Anthony's eyes slitted. "If I had proof, madam, you would already be in the guardhouse."

"Then don't waste my time!" Rebecca tried again to shut the door and once again he held it open.

"Who are your contacts?" he demanded.

"I don't know what you're talking about," Rebecca bluffed. "Now, if you're finished with this interrogation, sir . . ."

"Nearly finished, madam."

"I am expecting Beau at any moment," she flung at him. "I doubt he'd be pleased to find you here."

"Your champion," he sneered. "No doubt the gallant lieutenant would challenge me to a duel. Would that make you happy?"

"Only if he killed you!" Rebecca snarled.

Anthony's already-swarthy complexion darkened, reddening. "I will leave you with a warning, madam. If I discover that you are spying for the British, I will see you punished for it. I will do everything in my power to see that you pay for it with your life!"

"Should I tremble before these threats, sir?" Rebecca scoffed, only a superhuman effort hiding the violent quaking inside her.

"Yes, madam, you should," he confirmed in deadly earnest. "If you are a spy and you bring harm to this place, you should pray that you never fall into my hands."

Try though she might, Rebecca could not stop the terrified pallor from creeping into her cheeks, banishing all color from her face. She saw the satisfied smirk on Anthony's dark, handsome face before he made her a mocking bow and, turning on his heel, strode off down the path and up the street.

She'd still been shaking when Beau arrived nearly a half hour later. He'd questioned her but she could offer no explanation. She was afraid that, if she told him of Anthony's accusations and threat, it might plant the seeds of suspicion in his mind; so she'd said nothing, refusing to answer his questions as to the cause of her agitation. In the end, though, all her reticence had done was drive them further apart. He'd been hurt by her refusal to confide in him.

Even now, weeks later, there was a distance

between them, a distance that her refusal to allow Beau to make love to her had only widened and deepened.

Rebecca pushed herself out of her chair. If only the time for the British invasion—if there was to be one—would arrive. And if there was not to be an invasion then why, in God's name, didn't Sumner send her word to come home?

A knock at the door made her start, her heart seeming to leap in her chest. Cautiously, she went to the window and peered out to see who stood there. She would not risk Anthony Hawkins entering her home.

But it was not Anthony but Michael Dousman.

Rebecca opened the door and pulled him quickly inside. "Did you see Anthony Hawkins out there?" she asked, her voice breathless.

"Hawkins?" Dousman's brow furrowed. "I didn't notice him, no. Why?"

"He suspects me of being the spy here. He demanded to know the names of my contacts. And he's threatened to have me executed if the fort is attacked."

Dousman's face reddened. "The bastard! Well, no matter—"

"No matter!" Rebecca cried. "That's easy for you to say! If's not your life we're speaking of!"

"Calm down. I'm going to St. Joseph Island. I came to bring you this letter and see if you wished me to carry back a reply."

Rebecca eagerly took the packet he offered

her. "You're going to St. Joseph Island!" she breathed, aghast, just realizing what he'd said. "Are you mad? If you go to the British—"

"Listen to me, Rebecca," he broke in, "I'm being sent there by Porter Hanks."

"The fort commander? I don't understand."

Michael laughed. "He's sending me there to spy for the Americans. He wants to know the British plans and I'm to try to find out what they're up to."

Rebecca gaped at him. A British sympathizer being sent to spy for the Americans! The situation seemed so perfectly absurd that she had to laugh.

"And are you going?" she asked, smiling.

"Of course, I'm going. I must play my part just as you must play yours. Now hurry, time is short. You must let me know if there is a reply to the letter."

Breaking the seal, Rebecca scanned the contents of Sumner's latest message. It was a sobering missive and Rebecca's smile faded.

"We're at war," she said softly, tears blurring her vision. "Captain Roberts was notified on July eighth that war had been declared. Oh, Michael, we're at war!"

Dousman nodded. "I imagined it would happen any day. What else does he say?"

Rebecca looked again at the letter. "He says as soon as they receive permission they're going to attack Mackinac Island. He says none of the island's civilians will be endangered so long as they don't fight against the British forces. And he says that I will either be put under guard or taken to safety aboard one of the British ships." Her eyes grew distant, sad. "I suppose that would be necessary. Once Anthony Hawkins realizes it was I who gave the British the information on the fort's weaknesses . . ."

"It would be just as well if you were well away from the fighting," Dousman commented. "That way, if anyone were killed . . ."

Rebecca looked up into the farmer's eyes. She knew what he was thinking. She knew most of the men at Fort St. Joseph, many had been friends of William and herself. And there was Beau, here at Mackinac. If her actions on behalf of her country resulted in the deaths of any of these men, it would be better for her not to witness it.

"Yes," she agreed, looking away. "Of course, you're right." She swallowed hard. "Well, then, we'll just have to see what happens, won't we?" She shook her head. "There is no answer to this letter, Michael. Anything I have to say to Sumner can wait until he reaches Mackinac."

"As you wish," Michael acquiesced. "I'd better be going. I plan to leave today. What is the date?"

"The fifteenth," she told him, following him to the door. "Godspeed, Michael. When next we meet . . ."

They stood on the doorstep and Michael nodded up toward the fort where the warm summer wind fluttered the American stars and stripes.

"When next we meet," he told her, his face

solemn, "there will be another flag flying from that pole up there."

Rebecca nodded as the farmer-turned-counteragent walked away. Another flag would soon be flying from the fort's ramparts, she reflected as she turned back to enter the cottage, and the man she had so foolishly fallen in love with would either be dead or would hate her. Either way he would be lost to her forever.

Chapter Nine

Rebecca was awakened at half-past two the following morning by an insistent rapping on her door. Pulling on a worn, comfortable robe, she went to the door and called, "Who's there?"

"Michael," the muffled voice answered urgently. "Michael Dousman."

"Michael!" Rebecca pulled open the door. "What are you doing here? I thought you had left for St. Joseph Island."

"I was on my way," he confirmed, entering the house. In the light of the single candle she hurriedly lit, Rebecca saw that he looked haggard, exhausted. He sank wearily into a chair. "I wasn't far from here when I met the British. They're on their way here."

Rebecca felt a sudden breathlessness. It was happening, that which she had hoped for and dreaded at the same time. Before this day was over, her country would have won a great victory—and she would have lost a great love.

"There's about six hundred of them," Michael said softly.

"Six hundred!" Rebecca exclaimed. "From Fort St. Joseph!"

"Not all of them. About two hundred are Canadians—trappers, *voyageurs*. Another three hundred fifty or so are Indians—Chippewa, Winnebago, Ottawa, Sioux . . ."

"Indians." Rebecca chewed her lower lip. "Can Captain Roberts control them?"

Dousman shrugged. "I hope so. But he's worried. He sent me back to round up the villagers and take them to the distillery under the west bluff. That way they can be guarded, and if the Indians sack the village, no one is likely to be hurt." He looked at Rebecca. "Get dressed. I'm to take you there as well."

Rebecca gazed at him. "What if some of them somehow realize it was me—"

"Don't worry, Rebecca," Michael comforted. "You'd be surprised how many sympathizers there are on this island. Come, go get dressed now. Captain Roberts must be nearly here."

Retreating to her bedroom, Rebecca pulled on her chemise, petticoats, and a simple gown. Her fingers trembled as she buttoned her gown, fumbling with her garters and the laces of her half-boots. Dragging her brush quickly through her sleep-tumbled curls, she tied them up with a cherry ribbon and pulled a black cloth mantle around her shoulders.

"I'm ready," she said, returning to the main room where Michael waited. She looked around. "I don't suppose it would do any good to lock the door."

"Not if the Indians decide to sack the town."

Returning to the bedroom, she took out the pearl earrings and choker William had given her. They were the only jewels she had brought with her and she slipped them into the pocket inside her mantle for safekeeping.

With Michael following, his guiding hand at the small of her back, Rebecca left her house and went to the distillery under the west bluff. As they walked, Michael told her more of his meeting with Captain Roberts some fifteen miles east of Mackinac Island.

"He is sailing in the the schooner *Caledonia*," he told her.

Rebecca nodded. "I know the one."

"You should have seen it. The ship was surrounded by *bateaux* filled with Indians and *voyageurs*. The Indians were shouting war cries and waving their weapons. It was a bloodcurdling sight. I—"

Rebecca looked up to see why he had stopped speaking. The farmer was looking off toward the side of the road and there she saw Dr. Day, the post surgeon, peering curiously out his door.

"Dousman!" he called. "You there, Dousman!"

"Yes, Doctor?" Michael called back, his heart sinking, knowing the doctor was not fool enough to swallow some clever tale as to why he was strolling with Rebecca Carlyle down the street at three o'clock in the morning. To make matters worse, more than one villager was hurrying in the direction of the west bluff, carting some family treasure with him.

"What the devil is going on?"

Michael glanced sideways at Rebecca. "Well, sir . . ." he began. "I—"

"Good God! They're coming, aren't they? What did you learn while you were gone? Why didn't Porter Hanks advise me that attack was imminent?"

Not replying, Michael simply propelled Rebecca along the street, hurrying by the doctor's house and moving swiftly toward the distillery.

"Dousman!" the doctor called after him. "What did you tell Porter? Did you tell him we were about to be attacked? Did you? Damn you, you varlet, answer me!"

"He's going to go to the fort and warn them," Rebecca told him.

"I know," Michael agreed. "But it won't do any good. It's too late. And, anyway, Porter Hanks will muster the men and set his lookouts to watch for attacks from the water. By now, Captain Roberts and his men must be on their way across the middle of the island. They're dragging two pieces of artillery with them. They're going to position them on the heights above the fort as you suggested."

As she'd suggested. Now that the attack was underway, now that she thought of the soldiers at the fort unaware that their outpost was about to be taken from them by a force that outnumbered them nearly ten to one, she wished more than ever that she had never come to this place. She had been the daughter of a military family, the wife of a soldier, but war had always seemed something distant, something in which women played no part except to worry about their loved ones, to nurse them if they were wounded and mourn them if they were killed. The enemy was a nameless, faceless evil to be despised. But now. . . .

Now the enemy had a face, a voice, a heart . . . She closed her eyes. *Please, God*, she prayed silently, *keep Beau safe. Even if he is going to hate me forever after tonight, even if his loathing burns the memory of my face from his heart, don't let him be harmed.*

They reached the distillery and found most of the villagers already there. Many of the men were armed, having heard of the hoardes of Indians who were coming with the British. Some of the women were weeping, frightened that what they'd thought would be a relatively bloodless battle might well turn into a bloody massacre. Of the children, some of the boys were vowing to take up arms against the enemy, though they seemed confused about who precisely the enemy was. A few of the older girls giggled among themselves over the

imminent arrival of British officers, resplendent in their scarlet coats.

They were not there long before a half-dozen
British soldiers arrived, led by a young sergeant
in his red coat with its blue-and-crimson sash
and a tall stovepipe hat.

"Mrs. Carlyle?" he called as he entered the
distillery.

"Yes?" Rebecca answered, stepping forward.

He tipped his tall hat with its brass plate and
red-and-white plume. "Captain Roberts sends
his compliments, ma'am. He asks that you
stay here until the fort is captured. Lieutenant Meade will come then to escort you into
the fort."

"Is that necessary?" Rebecca asked, dreading
the ordeal of being paraded as a heroine before
the vanquished men she'd helped to defeat.

The sergeant looked at her curiously. "Your
help has been invaluable, ma'am. You deserve
recognition for your bravery."

Rebecca wanted to argue, to refuse to be
paraded before the defeated soldiers as a loyal Englishwoman who had duped them into
taking her into their confidence. But before
she could think of a way to decline without
arousing suspicion, the privates who formed
the guard summoned their sergeant.

Near the distillery's entrance, Rebecca
saw a young American officer she recognized, Lieutenant Archibald Darragh, speaking earnestly to several of the villagers.

His eyes swept over the townspeople

lingering on Rebecca and Michael Dousman who stood together. Then, abruptly, he turned to leave.

The British sergeant, Ambrose Kelton, and his men moved swiftly to block the retreat of the American and his two companions. But the Americans drew their pistols and, their eyes fixed on the British soldiers, backed away up the street, retreating toward the fort to make their report.

"Sergeant," Rebecca said, going to the tall, portly man, "will there be much of a battle, do you think?"

"I shouldn't think so, ma'am," he replied. "This Lieutenant Hanks is, by all accounts, an intelligent man. He'll know better than to fight in a hopeless cause."

Rebecca could only pray it was so. But the hours of darkness, the dawning, and the morning passed at a snail's pace.

By noon nerves had frayed, friendly discussions became shouting matches, fussy children complained of hunger and fatigue. Sergeant Kelton's announcement that Lieutenant Meade was approaching sent a wave of excitement rippling through their ranks.

He appeared in the door, tall and straight, his scarlet coat and white breeches immaculate, his cocked, feathered hat resting on his wavy dark hair, the crescent-shaped brass gorget worn by the officer gleamed, and the fringe of the scarlet sash banding his narrow waist rippled as he walked.

The young girls sighed as he marched straight to Rebecca and, taking her hand, lifted it to his lips.

"I've missed you," he said softly.

"Is it over?" she asked, her voice anxious, her hand trembling in his.

"All over," he replied. "The terms of capitulation were just signed."

"Was anyone hurt?"

Sumner shook his head. "Not a shot was fired. I don't think it was the cannons that convinced Hanks to surrender; I think it was the Indians. There are hundreds of them and he knew that if even one was shot they would swarm over the fort and no one would escape. Doubtless they would have burned the fort and the village as well."

"What will happen now?" Michael wanted to know.

"The Americans will be held as prisoners until they can be sent to an American outpost. The American villagers will have a month to pledge allegiance to the king or get out of British-held territory."

From outside came the growing, insistent booming of cannons and the firing of rifles. Rebecca looked at Sumner for explanation.

"The Indians and Canadians went back to their canoes. They're going to accompany the *Caledonia* around the island to the harbor. They're going to fire the fort's cannons in salute when she enters the harbor." He smiled down at her. "Are you ready to go? Captain Roberts is anxious to see you."

With a weary smile at Michael Dousman, Rebecca left the distillery on Sumner's arm. But before they were halfway along the street leading toward the fort, she asked, "Could we stop at my home for a little while, Sumner? I've been at that distillery since three o'clock this morning. I'd like to wash and change before we go to the fort. And I'm starving."

"So am I," Sumner admitted. "Perhaps Captain Roberts won't miss us if we don't go up to the fort for a little while."

Rebecca unlocked her door and let Sumner into her cottage. He laid his tall hat on her table, where Beau had left his when he'd come here, she thought. And he draped his scarlet, long-tailed coat over the same chair where Beau had draped his blue tunic. He came to take Rebecca into his arms, but she moved quickly out of his reach.

"Let me freshen up first," she said lightly, hurrying out the back door to the well to draw a pail of water.

"Let me get that for you," Sumner offered, but Rebecca shook her head and, going into her bedroom, shut the door in his face.

Pouring a basin of water, Rebecca undressed and washed. It was over, she kept telling herself. The moment she had longed for and dreaded had come. Beau was safe, unscathed. Soon he and his fellow officers would be sent to another American outpost far away. She need never see him again.

Never see him again . . . Never hear his voice, never see him smile, never feel his touch, know his love. . . .

While the British lieutenant, the victor of Mackinac, waited outside, Rebecca sank onto the edge of her bed and wept for her vanquished lover.

Chapter Ten

Knowing she could not stall the inevitable forever, Rebecca washed away the traces of her tears and fatigue, pinned up her hair, and pulled on a walking dress of white muslin with a flounce of lemon lace trimming the hem and sleeves. She had a creamy shawl embroidered with yellow Chinese flowers that she would drape around her shoulders. With a straw bonnet and her cream kid half-boots she supposed she would meet with Sumner's approval.

Bonnet in hand, she took a deep breath and opened her bedroom door. The main room was empty but, having heard the bedroom door swing open, Sumner appeared from the sitting room.

"Rebecca," he said, his eyes running over her approvingly. "How I've missed you."

Coming to her, he took her by the shoulders and leaned down to kiss her. Chastely, Rebecca turned her cheek toward him. After a moment's hesitation, Sumner pecked at the cool, smooth cheek. Straightening, he regarded her with a mixture of curiosity and concern.

"I had hoped you would have missed me more than that," he said quietly.

"I'm sorry," Rebecca replied, laying her bonnet aside and moving to the sideboard. "Of course I've missed you. But I've been . . . under a great strain lately. Surely you must realize . . ." She shrugged, letting the sentence trail off. "Let's have something to eat before we go to the fort, shall we? There's not much but I have some cold meat from last night's supper. And there is a loaf of fresh-baked bread."

"That's fine," Sumner agreed, coming to sit at the table. He studied Rebecca as she got out the food, the plates, knives, and glasses for the wine she placed on the table.

In near silence they ate their meal, each lost in their own thoughts. For Rebecca's part, she wondered where Beau was, how he was faring, if he had any inkling that she was the one who had sent the British commander the information that had allowed him to capture the fortress with almost insulting ease.

Sumner sat opposite her, watching her eat. There was a closed air about her, a secretiveness that hadn't been there before she'd left Fort St. Joseph. What, he wondered, had happened to her here? What was she hiding from him? He had hoped this time apart would bring them closer together. He had hoped she would miss him and would realize that he was the logical man to step into the void left by William's death.

But apparently that had not happened. He saw no sign that she had longed for him, had missed him in the months they had been apart. If anything, she was cooler, more distant than she had been before. Where before he had not quite dared to court her, fearing he would meet with discouragement, now he was almost certain that if he pressed his suit he would meet with complete and utter rejection.

"Tell me about your life here," he said conversationally. "You mentioned several of the fort's officers in your letters. What sort of men are they?"

Rebecca rose and turned to get a glass of water. "They are like men anywhere," she said vaguely. "Some are good, some bad."

"You must have been a breath of fresh air to them. I saw few young, lovely, unattached women in the streets or at the distillery."

"I was sent here to gather information," Rebecca said stiffly. "I could hardly do that by being churlish and unfriendly."

"The question is, how friendly were you?" Sumner countered, his tone light and teasing but his eyes, his expression, in complete earnest.

Rebecca laid aside her knife and fork. "What is it you're asking me, Sumner?" she snapped.

"Why don't you come out and demand to know if I slept with any of them!"

Sumner's already ruddy complexion pinkened. "Of course I would never imagine such a thing!"

"Wouldn't you? Come now, Sumner, I can't believe you haven't wondered exactly how 'charming' I was to our enemies."

Rising from the table, Sumner went to the window and gazed out, his hands clasped behind his back. "I admit," he said softly, "that I was jealous when your letters arrived full of information you had learned from this lieutenant . . . What was his name?"

"McAllister," Rebecca supplied, her voice scarcely above a whisper.

"Yes, McAllister. But you can't blame me for that. You know I care for you, Rebecca. I had hoped, once this business was finished and once your grief for William had lessened, that you and I might find happiness together."

Rebecca was silent and Sumner turned toward her. "Your silence is hardly encouraging," he told her.

"I can't make any promises," Rebecca replied. "These past months have had an effect on me. I've come to know these people, Sumner. For all that they are our enemies, they are not all bad people. Like us, they care about their country. They befriended me, put their confidence in me. To know, day after day, that I was living a lie, that I was turning their kindness against them has been a great strain.

It will take time for me to get over it."

Sumner nodded, disappointed, disheartened, but not willing to give up his quest to make her his own.

"I understand," he said. It was not entirely true. Before Rebecca had left St. Joseph Island, she had been a rabid monarchist, an almost fanatically loyal Englishwoman dedicated to king and country. Now she was less than three months later finding it hard to reconcile herself to the fact that she had accomplished her mission spectacularly and helped to win a great victory without a single drop of blood being shed.

Tying on her bonnet and draping her shawl around her shoulders, Rebecca said, "I suppose we should go to the fort now."

"I suppose so," Sumner agreed, picking up his cocked hat and buckling on his sword.

Without speaking, they walked up the street and up the long ramp leading to the south sally port. Looking ahead, Rebecca saw that the Union Jack had replaced the American stars and stripes on the fort's flagpole. She remembered Michael Dousman's prediction and shivered, thinking she had never imagined how quickly it would come true.

"What will be done with the prisoners?" she wanted to know.

"They'll be sent to Chicago, I suppose," Sumner answered. "Fort Dearborn is the nearest American outpost."

"I mean for now."

"Ah. The soldiers will be placed under guard. The officers will likely be housed together in one of the blockhouses."

The scarlet-clad privates standing guard at the sally port snapped to attention as Sumner and Rebecca passed through the arched entrance. They passed the guardhouse and walked along the path toward the stone officers' quarters where Captain Roberts was settling in Porter Hanks's former rooms.

"The description you gave in your letter was remarkably precise," Sumner said. "When we came in, I almost felt I had been here before."

"I came to supper here," Rebecca told him. "Beau . . ." She caught her breath. "Lieutenant McAllister brought me to dine with Lieutenant Hanks."

Sumner laughed. "You played your part masterfully," he complimented her.

"It was not entirely a role," she admitted. "I found Lieutenant Hanks a charming host. I felt . . ." she hesitated, wondering how much she was willing to admit to him. "I felt guilty writing that letter."

"Guilty!" Sumner stared at her. "These men are our enemies, Rebecca. Had we not had the element of surprise on our side, thanks to you, they would have fired upon us. They would have tried to kill us."

"And you would have tried to kill them," Rebecca countered.

"Of course. We are at war," Sumner reminded her.

They reached the officers' quarters and Sumner took her inside. To her relief, she found that the rooms he had been alotted were not those formerly occupied by Beau. She could not have borne knowing that Sumner was living in the rooms, sleeping in the bed, Beau had called his own.

Piles of belongings were heaped on the floor in the hall outside various doors. Rebecca looked questioningly at Sumner who told her, "Their belongings. They will be packed and sent with them when they go to Chicago."

A private came up to them and saluted. He told Sumner, "Captain Roberts wishes to see you in his quarters, sir. He asks Mrs. Carlyle to excuse him for a few minutes."

"Go along, Sumner," Rebecca told him. "I think I'll wait outside in the sunshine."

Sumner left her and Rebecca wandered down the hallway toward the back door which led to the parade grounds. As she passed Beau's door, she glanced down at the crumpled pile of clothing and effects waiting to be packed. On top, a small leather case lay half-buried beneath one of Beau's uniform tunics.

Glancing around, Rebecca stooped and snatched it up. She found the catch and opened it, revealing a small, gold-rimmed miniature painted on ivory. It was a perfect, lifelike likeness of Beau in civilian dress. He wore a coat of deep wine-red with a high rolled collar that framed his head and made his golden hair look almost flaxen. His shirt collar was high, his neckcloth tied intricately. He was faintly smiling and the artist had caught the deep, sapphire twinkle in his eyes. Rebecca's heart thudded in her breast, she felt a quivering deep in the pit of her stomach, a weakness in her knees. This man, this handsome, brave man had been her lover, had taken her to heights she'd never dreamed existed. But he was lost to her, she harbored no doubts on that score. Their love had been doomed. From the moment the first of the British forces had set foot on this island, Beau had been lost to her.

Glancing once again behind her, Rebecca closed the little leather case and slipped it into her bodice where her chemise and the tight, high waist of her gown would keep it safe until she was at home. If she could not have Beau, she could at least have this likeness to remind her that he had truly existed, to remind her of what had all too briefly been hers.

Stepping out into the sunshine, she looked around. The British soldiers were moving into their enemies' former barracks. The Canadians who had come with the British and Indians of several tribes milled around. They were, Rebecca imagined, disappointed that there had been no bloody battle. They would very likely remain on the island until it was made clear to them that they would profit very little from staying here.

Rebecca deliberately avoided looking at the blockhouses, the tall square structures that pierced the ramparts on the four sides of the fort. She did not know which one held Beau and his fellow officers and she did not want to risk seeing him, a prisoner, with her to thank for his captivity.

"Rebecca?" Sumner appeared behind her, stepping through the door closely following his commanding officer.

"Mrs. Carlyle," Captain Roberts said, smiling.

The captain had aged visibly since she'd last seen him. He was thinner, his complexion an unhealthy shade of gray.

"Captain," she replied. "It's good to see you."

"I wanted to see you as soon as possible after we took command of the fort," he went on. "You did a marvelous job. You deserve a medal for your actions. Rest assured I will include a full report in my next letter to General Brock."

"I'm glad no one was hurt," she said simply.

"As are we all," the captain agreed.

Taking her hand, he bowed over it, his lips pressed to her soft, golden skin. Unbidden, Rebecca suddenly glanced up and her eyes met a pair of sapphire-blue eyes.

In the window of the west blockhouse, Beau stood staring at her. His face was a picture of stunned surprise. Rebecca gazed at him, unable to tear her eyes away and, as she watched, Anthony Hawkins stepped up beside Beau. He said something to Beau and his expression was partly malicious triumph, partly black hatred.

Rebecca longed to tear her hand out of Captain Roberts's grasp and run to Beau, try to explain what she'd done and why. But as she stood, her eyes riveted to the blockhouse window, Beau turned away. She was left staring at Anthony Hawkins, who glared at her with such evil loathing that Rebecca knew her life would not be worth a tuppence's purchase if he'd had access to a weapon at that moment.

Chapter Eleven

During the ten days that followed the British invasion, the fort was a beehive of activity. Its storehouses of weapons, ammunitions, and other supplies were a godsend to the British, who had brought little with them from St. Joseph Island. Captain Roberts put men to work assessing the value of the goods, for, as was the custom, the common soldiers would be given payment as a reward in proportion to the value of the prize taken.

A few days after the attack, Porter Hanks was brought to his old quarters to meet with Charles Roberts.

"I have a report, Mr. Hanks," he said after inviting the lieutenant to sit, "stating that you have, among your men, three deserters from the British army."

"It's not true!" Porter Hanks cried, half rising from his chair.

Captain Roberts consulted a paper on his desk. "You have among your men a Redmond McGrath, a Hugh Kelly, and an Alexander Parks?"

"I have," Lieutenant Hanks admitted. "They are good and loyal Americans."

"Redmond McGrath, my dear Lieutenant, deserted from the fifth Regiment of Foot some fifteen years ago. Alexander Parks deserted from the Royal Regiment of Artillery and Hugh Kelly from the forty-ninth Regiment of Foot. I must advise you that these men will be detained along with those of your men found to be British subjects."

"British subjects!" Porter Hanks breathed. "Impossible!"

"Not at all," Captain Roberts assured him. From his desk top he took another, much longer list and handed it to the former commander. The British commander was quiet as his American counterpart scanned the long list. "There are twenty-two of them," he said at last.

"These men are nearly all FrenchCanadians," Porter Hanks argued. "They enlisted in the American forces. We consider them naturalized citizens."

"We do not recognize their 'naturalization,' " Charles Roberts told him calmly. "They will have to remain behind when the rest of you leave for Chicago."

"I will register a strong protest through General Hull, my commanding officer," Porter Hanks informed him. There was nothing else he could do. Certainly he could not force the British to release the men they claimed as citizens. It was all so frustrating, maddening. He felt weak, helpless, impotent. "Is there anything else?"

"Nothing," Captain Roberts admitted. "We will be administering the oath of allegiance to the island's inhabitants."

"If they refuse?"

Captain Roberts shrugged. "Any who refuse will be dispatched to Chicago with you. But I doubt many will refuse."

"Not knowing that if they do their property will be forfeit to the British Crown," Lieutenant Hanks agreed.

"Exactly so. Now, Lieutenant, if you will go with the sergeant, he will take you back to your fellow officers."

Reluctantly, Rebecca climbed the long, sloping ramp to the fort. Though she tried her best to avoid it, she'd been summoned to help in the infirmary and she felt she could hardly refuse.

Passing through the sally port, she saw immediately that the American officers, under guard, were being allowed out onto the parade ground for fresh air and exercise. Averting her eyes, she hurried along the walk toward the infirmary building at the far end of the fort.

"There she is!" an all too-familiar voice cried out. "English bitch!"

Rebecca lifted her chin. She could feel Anthony Hawkins's hate-filled glare boring into her. She knew that only the guns in the hands of their British guards kept him from attacking her.

"Whore!" he shouted after her. "You're nothing but—"

Rebecca glanced up as Anthony's voice was abruptly cut off. Beau was beside him. His golden hair was tousled, his uniform rumpled from having slept in it. He said something to Anthony, who tried to pull away from him, snarling.

Quickly, not wanting to see any more of their confrontation and unwilling to hear any more of Anthony's vile abuse, Rebecca hurried to the infirmary and ducked inside.

She busied herself changing the bandages of an English corporal, who'd been injured in a fall from the ramparts during night watch.

"What was all the shouting?" the corporal wanted to know.

"One of the American officers," Rebecca told him, taking the old bandages to the basin where they would be washed to be used again. "He did not appreciate my efforts on the Crown's behalf."

" 'Twas a brave thing you did," he said. "You shouldn't listen to these bloody Americans, pardon my French. We're all proud of you, ma'am, and if you don't mind my sayin' so, Lieutenant Carlyle would have been proud as well."

Rebecca stared at the basin where she was to wash the bandages. "Thank you, Corporal," she replied softly. "I hope he would have been."

"Mrs. Carlyle?" a voice said from the doorway.

Rebecca turned. Two British privates flanked Beau in the infirmary doorway. "What's happened?"

"Bit of a fracas among the prisoners, ma'am. We think this one's broke his hand."

"It's not broken," Beau protested. "It's perfectly all right."

"Let the lady look at it," the other private ordered. "We can't have you claiming we treated you badly when you get to Chicago, can we?"

Scowling, Beau crossed the floor and sat down on a hard wooden bench not far from Rebecca. Extending his arm, he displayed a red and swollen hand, his knuckles raw and bloody.

"Who did you hit?" she wanted to know, bringing a pan of water and a cloth to wash away the blood.

"Hawkins," Beau answered shortly, drawing a hissing breath as Rebecca began to wash his scraped knuckles.

"I would not have expected you to defend my honor after—"

"I wasn't," he interrupted grimly. "I just don't appreciate an American officer making a jackass of himself in front of the enemy."

"I see." Rebecca rose and went to the cupboard for fresh bandages. Coming back to him,

123

she sat down. "Move your fingers," she commanded.

Obligingly, Beau waggled his reddened fingers. "I told you it's not broken," he reminded her.

Rebecca's hand shook as she held his and began winding the bandages around it. "Do you agree with Anthony Hawkins?" she asked, not daring to look at his face.

"Does it matter?" Beau countered.

Rebecca hesitated. "Yes," she admitted. "It matters."

"If you expect me to applaud you for a fine performance, I will," he told her. "Some moments, of course, were more convincing than others. I particularly remember one afternoon at the other end of the island."

"Please, Beau . . ." Rebecca said, her voice quavering. "You would have done the same—"

"I doubt it," he interrupted. "You took this masquerade of yours to extremes, Mrs. Carlyle."

"It wasn't all a masquerade," she insisted, aware of the injured corporal and the two privates in the room. Though her voice was hushed, the earnest expression on her face, the obvious distress in her voice and air, made them understandably curious.

"Spare me," Beau snarled. "We're to be taken to Fort Dearborn in a few days, madam," he said, rising. "You and I will never see one another again. So you don't need to go on with this farce of yours."

"Beau," she said as he walked back to his

guards, "I don't want us to be enemies."

He looked back at her, his sapphire eyes stormy. "What else could we be?" he demanded, then turned to his guards and preceded them out of the infirmary.

Turning her back to her patient, Rebecca hid the pain Beau's anger caused her. She had expected bitterness, disillusionment, even loathing but somehow the reality was far more painful than she'd imagined.

She drew a deep, shaking breath. As he said, they would soon be going to Fort Dearborn and in all likelihood they would never meet again. In time, she prayed, the pain would fade. In time she would let go of the feelings she had for Beau; they would wither and die like a beautiful flower deprived of sun and water. In time she might even turn to Sumner. It was obvious that he wanted to marry her. Might that not be the wisest course? She did not love him but then again he could not hurt her. That seemed very attractive to her just then, when the pain of Beau's bitter disdain was still fierce and burning inside her.

She thought again of Sumner and the painless, if dull, future she could have with him on the afternoon of July twenty-sixth when the American soldiers and those of the islanders who refused the oath of allegiance set out aboard the *Mary* and the *Selina*, two captured American ships.

She stood on the ramparts of the fort, watching as the ships sailed west into Lake Michigan. Her heart was heavy, her spirits low. She felt as if a part of her had been torn away and she wondered if Beau was there, among the passengers crowding the decks of the ships, gazing back at the fort that had been his home and thinking of her.

He probably was, she told herself, biting her lower lip. He was probably wishing her every calamity that could befall a human being. He probably wished her disease, poverty, and unhappiness if not worse.

She sighed, a heartrending sigh wrenched from the very heart of her, as the ships rounded the tip of the far peninsula and disappeared from sight. Beau was gone—gone forever—and her life stretched before her, an unending promise of wistful, futile regret.

"Rebecca?" Sumner was striding toward her. He was tall and attractive in his scarlet and white, his gold braid and brass buttons and gorget winking in the July sunshine. "What are you doing up here? I was looking for you in the infirmary."

"There's no one in the infirmary," she replied. "I was just enjoying the view."

Sumner looked out over the panorama of water and land stretched out before them. "It is beautiful," he admitted. "Are you sure there's not more to it than an admiration for the scenery?"

"What else could it be?" she countered evasively.

Sumner gazed at her. The two privates, who had accompanied Beau to the infirmary after his countretemps with Anthony Hawkins, had told Sumner that the American lieutenant and Mrs. Carlyle had spoken in quiet, earnest tones. They could not hear what was said, but McAllister had seemed angry and Mrs. Carlyle upset. Sumner burned to know what there had been between Rebecca and the American officer. McAllister had been the source of her information, Sumner knew, so they must have gotten close during the months Rebecca had been here. But how close? And how involved were her feelings?

Sumner felt a sharp pang of jealousy. He knew that Rebecca was fond of him. He also knew she did not love him. Her heart was like an elusive butterfly, tantalizing, beautiful, but always just out of reach. Had the American, McAllister, managed to touch her heart?

The thought stung Sumner but he took what comfort he could in the knowledge that the ship that had just left the island was taking McAllister far away, out of Rebecca's life. With the American gone, perhaps she would turn back to him, perhaps he could at last capture the prize that had eluded him for so long.

Chapter Twelve

For the fourth time, Rebecca straightened the silver place settings on her table. A ship had come from St. Joseph Island bringing the personal effects of the men and women who were abandoning Fort St. Joseph and moving to Mackinac Island. Rebecca's cottage was now furnished with her own belongings. Her family pictures hung on the walls, the lovely things she had brought from England with her after her marriage were positioned on her sideboard and tables.

Sumner was coming for dinner and he was late. The succulent stew of venison and vegetables simmered in the pot hanging in the fireplace, and she frowned as she stirred it. She wondered what could be keeping him. Usually when she invited him to dinner, he was at her door early. It was generally a chore to keep him away, not to get him here on time.

Leaning over the table, she blew out the candles to save them. Those that remained burned on the mantel and in the sitting room, casting a dim, golden glow enhanced by the fire in the grate.

She sighed, idleness and boredom causing her to lower the guard she kept on her mind and heart. If only she were expecting Beau. If only the knock that would eventually sound on the door meant that Beau had arrived. If she could open the door and see him standing there, so tall and handsome in his brass-buttoned blue and white. . . .

Pushing herself away from the table, she went to the fireplace and stirred the stew with a vengeance. She wouldn't think of Beau, she wouldn't! Doubtless he'd forgotten her by now. No, she didn't believe that, but he likely thought of her with disdain and anger. Another, less welcome thought occurred to her. Perhaps there was another woman in his life now. Perhaps at his new post he had met some beautiful American woman who would help him forget the treachery of the last two women in his life. Though he'd left with his comrades less than a month ago, he might be more anxious to put the past behind him than she was.

The thought that Beau might be somewhere tonight smiling at another woman, laughing with her, loving her, made Rebecca want to weep. She wanted to blow out the rest of the candles and go to bed. She wanted to bury her tears in the softness of her pillow and try to shed Beau from her heart, wash him from her mind with a flood of hot, salt tears. How long would it take, she wondered bleakly, before she could put all this behind her? How long would this aching, this yearning last?

If only she could leave. Then she wouldn't be reminded day after day by the sight of this cottage, the island, the white fort. But she feared it was impossible. Britain and America were at war. How could she, an Englishwoman alone, find her way to the east coast? Every day brought word of battles, of Indian attacks. And even if she did somehow reach the east, what American ship would take her home? What British ship would dock in an American port? It was hopeless.

The knocking at the door took her by surprise. She started, nearly knocking over one of the last two crystal glasses that had survived the long journey from England to St. Joseph Island to Mackinac Island.

"Sumner," she said, stepping back to let him enter. "You're late."

"I know," he admitted. "Forgive me, Rebecca. I was called to Captain Roberts's quarters just as I was about to leave."

Rebecca took his hat and coat and draped them over the chair in the sitting room. "What did he want?" she asked, returning to the main room where Sumner was pouring himself a glass of the wine that had been found in the fort commissary. Some three hundred fifty gallons of wine and over two hundred fifty gallons of whiskey had been there, and Sumner had brought Rebecca several bottles of both.

Sumner sighed. "I don't know if I should tell you," he replied cryptically as he sat at the table. "Then again, I suppose you'll find out eventually anyway."

"Find out what?" Rebecca demanded impatiently as she ladled stew into the bowls on the table.

"It's about Fort Dearborn."

The ladle in Rebecca's hand rattled noisily against the china bowl. "Fort Dearborn," she repeated softly. Images of Beau filled her mind. "What about it?"

"According to the report Captain Roberts received, General Hull of the American forces ordered Fort Dearborn evacuated due to hostile Indians in the area. While the occupants were leaving, the Indians attacked. There was a massacre."

"Massacre . . ." Rebecca breathed.

Sumner nodded. "There were nearly a hundred people in the fort. Some fifty-four military men, a dozen civilian men, nine women, and eighteen children. Of those, twenty-six of the soldiers died in the massacre and another five afterward, all the civilian men, two of the women, and twelve of the children."

"My God," Rebecca whispered, her face pale.

"Yes, it's horrible. The survivors were sent on to Detroit. It fell the next day to our forces."

"Detroit surrendered!"

"It did. Now, so the report said, some of those soldiers taken prisoner when Detroit fell will be sent here to be held." His eyes watched her closely as he continued, "Most of them were from here to begin with."

Rebecca swallowed hard, her eyes trained on the untouched bowl of stew before her. "From here?" she asked.

"Darragh, Hawkins, Simmons, Dyer . . . Mc-Allister."

"Beau?" Rebecca could not keep the mixture of relief and dread from her voice. "Beau survived the massacre?"

"He is wounded, I understand. I don't know how seriously."

"And what of Porter Hanks?" she asked, forcing herself to sound as interested in the fate of the fort's former commander as in that of Beau.

"He is dead," Sumner answered bluntly.

"I'm sorry," Rebecca murmured sincerely. "He seemed like a good man and a good soldier. Was he killed in the massacre?"

"No, a cannonball killed him in the battle for Detroit." Sumner drank deeply of his wine. "Are you really so concerned for Porter Hanks, Rebecca? Or is is just that you don't want me to think there is any one of them in particular you worry about?"

Rising, Rebecca turned her back to him. "Don't you ever tire of these insinuations?" she said tightly.

"No," he admitted, "particularly not when I find you so changed after our being apart. You're not the same woman who left Fort St. Joseph last spring."

"I am the same," she argued, knowing it was a lie.

"You're not," he disagreed. "Before you left, you know how I felt about you. You knew that once your year of mourning was finished I intended to court you."

"I knew what you intended," Rebecca admitted. "But I was not sure of my feelings for you. I don't love you, Sumner."

"I knew that," he surprised her by saying. "I know that you loved William. I did not really expect you to fall in love with anyone after he was taken from you."

Rebecca closed her eyes. She hadn't expected to fall in love again either but she had. The only trouble was that the man she loved was not Sumner.

"Sumner," she said softly. "Please, try to understand. It is not that I don't care for you but I am not in love with you. I don't know what would have happened had I stayed at Fort St. Joseph rather than come here. Perhaps, had there not been a war, I might have chosen simply to return to England. I don't know. But I must ask you please, please, don't try to force me to love you. It would only destroy those feelings I do have for you. And I don't want them destroyed."

"Neither do I," Sumner agreed. "But you must

try to understand that it is difficult, very very difficult, to love someone and know that they don't return your love."

Rebecca nodded, her face averted to hide the quick tears that scalded her eyes. "I'm sorry," she said simply, thinking that she understood better than he could have imagined what it was like to love someone who did not love her.

"Perhaps I should go," Sumner offered, starting for the sitting room where his coat and hat were.

"Only if you want to," Rebecca said softly. Sumner stopped and looked back at her. "I said I care for you, Sumner," she told him, "and I meant it. I enjoy your company. Please stay and have dinner with me."

Nodding, Sumner returned to the table and sat down, but dinner was a quiet affair. Sumner was lost in his thoughts of how he could possibly win this beautiful, impossible woman. And for Rebecca's part, all she could see in her mind were images of Beau, greviously wounded, being shuttled from one battleground to another. What condition might he be in by the time he reached Mackinac? Perhaps he would die on the way.

No! she hissed to herself, sending a little prayer heavenward for his safety. *Let him live,* she prayed, *let him come here. And I will nurse him back to health, even if he curses me every step of the way!*

Chapter Thirteen

The prisoners taken after the fall of Detroit arrived at Fort Mackinac a few days later. Most were wounded, some superfically, some seriously enough to be put directly in the infirmary.

Rebecca knew that she was needed at the fort. She had always helped the post surgeon, Dr. Mitchell, at Fort St. Joseph and she knew he would be needing her help now. But Beau was among the wounded, and not knowing how grave his condition might be, she could not find the courage to make her way up the ramp to the fort to offer her services.

From the drawer in her bedchamber, she took the leather-bound miniature she had taken from among Beau's belongings before he'd left the island. She'd tried to keep from looking at it all this time. That handsome face, those twinkling eyes, those chisled, smiling lips, brought back too many painful memories.

A knock at the front door brought her out of her reverie. Quickly, she tucked the miniature back in the folds of her linen, fearing it might be Sumner at the door and unwilling to risk his seeing the tiny portrait.

Smoothing her gown, she went to the door and opened it. A young corporal stood there.

"Good afternoon, Philip," she said. "Won't you come in?"

"Thank you, ma'am," the young, brown-haired soldier replied, "but I've come from Dr. Mitchell. He asks that you come to the fort. He needs you in the infirmary."

Rebecca sighed. She could, of course, refuse, but there would be questions asked, questions for which she had no answers, none at least that would not cause controversy.

"Very well, I'll come. Tell Dr. Mitchell I'll be there directly."

The young corporal bowed and, with a smart, quick turn, strode off down her path and turned into the street to return to the fort.

Returning to her room, she changed into an old, serviceable gown of printed cotton. Braiding her hair, she wrapped it in a coronet around her head and pinned it in place. Wearing her kid half-boots and a cambric pelisse pulled over her gown, she left for the fort.

Outside the infirmary building, Rebecca paused. The plain truth of the matter was that she did not want to go inside. She didn't want to see Beau lying in pain, perhaps dying. It would be doubly hard to have him come back into her life only to have to stand by and watch him die of fever or infection.

Finally, noticing a few of the British soldiers eyeing her curiously, Rebecca hissed to herself under her breath, "Coward! Get inside and stop dallying out here like a child!"

Squaring her shoulders, she marched into the infirmary where the bright sunlight outside was muted by curtains at the windows. At the far end of the long room, she saw Dr. Mitchell emerge from behind one of the cloth-covered screens that separated the beds.

He looked up as her shadow fell across the scrubbed wooden floor. "Ah, Rebecca, here you are, thank God. As you can see, we've half a dozen patients."

As she walked toward the doctor between the double row of cots, she saw several faces she recognized. At the foot of the next to last cot on the right, she stopped. The man in the bed thrashed and moaned, his wrists and ankles were tied to the posts at the corners of the narrow bed.

Dr. Mitchell came to stand beside her. "Sad case," he murmured. "Thomas Roe, a private. There's nothing I can do for him, I'm afraid. Gangrene."

"But couldn't you—" Rebecca began.

"Amputate?" The doctor shook his head. "Would do no good. The poison was all through him before he ever got here. All I can do now is ladle whiskey down his throat and keep him senseless until the end."

"How horrible," Rebecca murmured, feeling sick to her stomach.

"As for the rest, they'll mend with care and time. Except for that man on the far side at the end. I'm afraid the same thing may happen to him as is happening to poor Roe."

Her stomach churning with fear, Rebecca walked to the end of the long room. Peering around the screen, she saw Beau lying on his back, the sheet pulled up under his arms. His skin had none of the golden, healthy glow she remembered, but a flushed, moist look that bespoke fever. His eyes were closed, the lids sheened with perspiration, his golden hair damp and dark against his head and the thin pillow.

"Know him, do you?" Dr. Mitchell asked, coming to stand at the foot of the bed. "McAllister, his name is. Lieutenant McAllister."

"Yes," Rebecca agreed. "I knew him when he was here before. How is he wounded?"

"Come." He led her to the side of the bed. Tossing back the sheet, he revealed Beau's right leg. A large pad of gauze nearly covered his thigh. Gingerly, the doctor removed it.

"Dear God!" Rebecca breathed. The flesh beneath had been slashed. The gaping wound, hastily stitched in Detroit, was obviously infected, festering and red, and ominous crimson streaks were beginning to radiate from it.

"It's a mess," the doctor agreed dispassionately.

"But couldn't it be cleaned and restitched?" Rebecca wanted to know.

"Certainly," he said. "But the cleansing would take time and patience. See there, those white threads deep in the wound?"

"Yes," Rebecca confirmed. "What are they?"

"Pieces of his uniform, I'd guess. Bits of his breeches driven into the flesh by the same knife that inflicted the wound. They all have to be gotten out or else the wound will not heal."

"If I can clean the wound, will you take out the old stitches and put in new?" Rebecca asked. "If those old stitches stay, the wound will heal raggedly, if at all."

"If you can get it cleaned and bring the infection under control, you will have saved this man's life," he answered, pulling the sheet over Beau. The man in the other bed moaned and strained at his restraints. "You'll have saved him from the agony that poor devil's going through. Excuse me, I've got to pour more whiskey down him."

Rebecca gazed down at Beau. Dr. Mitchell had placed his life squarely in her hands, and if she could do it, she would see that he did not die.

From the bucket in the corner, she poured a basin of tepid water. Taking a cloth, she went to Beau's bedside and pulled the sheet off him.

He stirred restlessly as she washed his feverish face and throat. His lips were cracked and dry, and she pressed the cloth against them to wet them. Slowly, gently, she bathed him, removing the grimy perspiration.

When she'd bathed him, Rebecca refilled the basin with warm water and took a clean cloth. Returning to his bedside, she took away the gauze pad and pressed the warm, wet cloth to the wound.

Beau stirred, moaning, and Rebecca murmured softly to him, meaningless, comforting sounds meant to soothe and reassure. He frowned, as if some part of his unconscious mind heard her and was confused. His hand groped on the sheet, then, finding her hand, squeezed it tightly.

Rebecca looked up at Dr. Mitchell as he came around the screen. "He knows I'm here," she said softly, her heart thudding.

"I doubt it. Likely it hurts when you touch the wound. Perhaps it would be a mercy to take the leg off now and not risk gangrene."

"No!" Rebecca cried, the thought of Beau's being maimed or even dying while the doctor plied his saw was too much to bear. "I'll take care of him," she promised. "You won't need to take the leg."

"I'll leave him to you, Rebecca," the doctor said, "but if it shows signs of gangrene, I'll take the leg off. I won't have him suffering like Roe over there."

"He won't," Rebecca vowed fiercely, trying to block the pitiful moanings of the other man from her mind. "He won't!"

* * *

It took nearly a week before the wound, plied with poultices, disinfected with whiskey, was healed enough for Dr. Mitchell to think it worthwhile to take out the old stitches. He then neatly sutured the gaping, ragged wound into a clean, if jagged, line that would eventually heal, leaving only a long white scar.

Afterward Rebecca sat on a chair beside Beau's bed. He would live, she knew now, he would regain his strength and be the same healthy, handsome man he had been before.

Well, perhaps not the same man, she thought sadly. The old Beau had loved her, trusted her. She feared that once he recovered his strength, once the fever that kept him unconscious broke, he would realize who had bathed him, changed his bandage, and spooned broth down his throat. The same British spy who had gained his trust—and his love—and betrayed both in the service of a tyrant across the sea. And, she feared, he would not want her near him.

Automatically, she moved to pull back the blankets as he kicked them off. The night was warm and his skin still held that moist, unhealthy heat which had to abate before he was truly out of danger.

Tucking the blankets in around him, she reached up to smooth back a lock of the golden hair she'd washed and brushed the last time she'd bathed him.

"Rebecca?"

Gasping, she thought for a moment Beau had spoken, but he hadn't. Sumner stood at the foot of the bed.

She blushed, wondering how long he'd been standing there. Had he seen her touch Beau's hair? Had he noticed the sad, wistful look on her face as she sat there, gazing at her patient?

"Sumner," she said coolly. "How long have you been there?"

"Just for a moment," he replied. "I went to your cottage. I did not think you'd be here so late."

"Dr. Mitchell is exhausted," she told him evasively. "Private Roe died this afternoon."

"From what I've heard, it was a blessing," Sumner commented.

"It was. There was nothing the doctor could do. It was difficult for him to stand by and watch helplessly as the man suffered. He deserves an early evening."

"I agree," Sumner admitted. "But what about you? You've been here more than you've been home since these men arrived."

"Someone has to help Dr. Mitchell. He can't do it all alone, you know."

"I know, but . . ." Sumner gazed at Beau lying on the bed. "This is McAllister, isn't it? The man who gave you information?"

Rebecca looked away, busying herself tidying Beau's blankets. "Yes, he did," she admitted.

"Dr. Mitchell says your diligence saved his life. He says that without your care, the man

144

may well have developed gangrene and died."

"He's not out of the woods yet," Rebecca said grimly. "His fever has yet to break."

"And when it does?" Sumner wanted to know.

"What do you mean?" Rebecca countered.

"You know damned well what I mean. Once he's well, what will happen?"

"He is a prisoner of war, Sumner. Once he's well, he'll be put under guard like the other prisoners."

"And that's all?"

Rising, Rebecca led Sumner away from Beau's bed. "Yes," she snapped, "that's all! And do you know why? Because he hates me! He loathes me because he trusted me and I betrayed him! Once he's well, once he's aware of his surroundings, he won't want me near him."

"And what about what you want?" Sumner persisted. "Will you want to be near him?"

"He's an enemy, Sumner, of yours, of mine, and of the king's. No doubt we'll be ransoming all these men to the American government soon. He'll be gone from our lives and that's that. For now, let me get on with the business of trying to get him well!"

Turning on her heel, she disappeared around the screen that hid Beau's bed. Sumner stood in the dim light that illuminated the infirmary, and prayed with all his strength for Beau's recovery. There was a look in Rebecca's eye, a catch in her voice, when she spoke of Beau

McAllister that did not bode well for Sumner. The sooner the American was well and shipped back to his own country the better as far as Sumner was concerned!

Chapter Fourteen

It was late at night the following day when Beau's fever at last broke. Bathed in sweat, he lay beneath the soaked sheets, alternately shivering and trying to push away the blankets that seemed to be smothering him.

Rebecca washed him with warm water, sponging away the rivulets of perspiration that ran down his body, his limbs, and his face and soaked the mattress and pillow. When at last he was quiet, the unhealthy flush gone from his skin, his breathing deep and regular, Rebecca sank into a chair and took what seemed to be her first peaceful, relaxed breath in days.

Feeling a hand fall on her shoulder, she started. Dr. Mitchell stood beside her.

Rebecca laughed weakly. "I didn't hear you. You surprised me."

147

"I'm sorry," the doctor apologized. Circling the bed, he laid a hand on Beau's forehead. "He's nearly cool to the touch. I don't think we've anything to worry about now. His leg is healing well. He'll limp for some time; he'll need a cane for a while. But he'll live. He owes his life to you, Rebecca."

"I wonder if he'd thank me for it," she murmured.

"What was that?"

Rebecca shook her head. "Nothing. Doctor, do you think you could help me change his sheets? They're soaked. By morning, they'll be cold and clammy."

While Dr. Mitchell helped to shift Beau's body, Rebecca stripped the damp sheets from the bed and replaced them with others that, while of coarse cloth, were at least dry and clean. That done, she tucked the blankets around him and stepped back.

"You've done everything you could," the doctor told her. "He'll be all right now. Go home and get a decent night's sleep. You're worn out."

Suddenly Rebecca felt the weight of all the sleepless nights, the worry, the strain. She felt as though lead weights were dragging at her arms and legs, her eyelids drooped as though she'd taken some soporific potion.

"You're right," she admitted, taking her shawl from the peg on the wall. "Suddenly I feel so tired. Exhausted."

"Then go home. Doubtless your charge will sleep for hours."

The doctor left and Rebecca drew her shawl around her shoulders. As she was about to leave, she heard a soft sound from Beau.

His head turned on his pillow. His tongue ran over his dry, fever-cracked lips. Rebecca went to the pitcher and poured a cup of water.

"Here," she said, sitting on the edge of the bed and lifting his head. "Drink, Beau. Try to drink a little."

Raising a hand, he covered hers as it held the mug. He sipped thirstily once, twice, a third time, then lay back against his pillow. His shadowed sapphire eyes opened and he looked up at her as she rose to stand beside the bed, the mug cradled in her trembling hands.

"Rebecca," he said quietly, his voice raspy. He scowled. "What the hell are you doing here?"

Rebecca swallowed hard, stepping back. "Leaving," she managed before her throat closed painfully. "Just leaving."

Dropping the mug on a table, Rebecca fled from the infirmary. Scarcely acknowledging the greetings of the men she passed, she left the fort and hurried as quickly as she dared down the long ramp to the village and to the safe haven of her cottage.

Taking her bucket, Rebecca went out into the dark garden and drew water from her well. In the house she built a fire in the grate and warmed the water, for she had not taken the time to care for herself since Beau had arrived at the island infirmary.

While the water was warming, she went into

her bedroom and, from the depths of a trunk, dug out the last sliver of fine, French-milled soap that was all that remained of what she'd brought with her from England. She hadn't been able to bear seeing it used up but now she felt the need of a little pampering, of the creamy, thick lather, and the rich, rose scent.

In her bedroom she set her largest basin on the floor. Then, standing in it, she sponged the warm water over her naked skin, scrubbing until it glowed with ruddy health. Her hair, too, she washed, lathering it and rinsing it.

When she was done, she felt revived. Pulling a nightdress over her head, she took the soapy water to the back door and dumped it outside. In her bedroom she kindled a small fire in the fireplace, banked the fire in the main room, then climbed into her bed.

Beau's face danced before her closed eyes. The look on his face when he recognized her, the disdain in his voice when he'd spoken to her . . . She tried not to think of it; she turned her mind from it, drew a curtain across those memories, allowed her exhaustion to overtake her and draw her down into the blissful nothingness of sleep.

The fire was out by the time Rebecca awoke, but it did not matter, for the bright sunshine was glowing behind the drawn curtains of Rebecca's bedroom. Feeling groggy, she pushed herself up. With her fists, she rubbed her eyes.

She felt stiff, sore, as if in her exhaustion she had not moved from the position in which she had fallen asleep.

Through the closed bedroom door she heard a muffled thudding. It sounded once, then again, and Rebecca frowned, wondering what it could be.

"Rebecca?" The voice was distant, definitely masculine. "Rebecca?"

Beau! Kicking back the blankets, Rebecca hurried to the front door and flung it open. Sumner stood there, his expression concerned.

"Sumner," she said softly, realizing all at once how foolish her first thought had been. Beau was a prisoner at the fort. He would not be in the village and she was probably the last person he would seek out if he could get out.

"Come in," she invited, running a hand through her tousled hair. "What time is it?"

"Nearly six. What time did you leave the fort last night?"

She shook her head, sighing. "I don't know. It must have been nearly midnight."

"I brought you some supper from the fort mess," he told her, showing her the tray of covered dishes he carried. "I brought some soup, roast venison, and fresh-baked bread."

"Thank you," she said, taking dishes, silver, and glasses from the sideboard. "Open some wine, will you, while I do something with myself."

In the bedroom, she dressed and dragged a comb through her hair. She was hungry, she realized. She hadn't eaten since midday of the day before. She'd neglected herself lately. There were dark circles under her eyes and her dress hung loosely on her. She'd worn herself to a frazzle nursing Beau and for what? The moment he had opened his eyes he'd been hostile to her.

Returning to the main room, she found Sumner filling her plate.

"I want you to eat all of this," he said. "You're getting thin."

"I was just thinking the same thing," she remarked, sitting down opposite him. She ate some soup, some meat, and some bread, savoring the taste as she ate and washed the food down with wine. "I've been so busy in the infirmary lately I haven't had time to think of myself."

"Well, you won't have to worry about it any longer," Sumner told her. "All the patients in the infirmary are gone now."

"Gone?" Rebecca stopped, her fork poised in midair. "What do you mean? Beau McAllister . . ."

"He's been released. Dr. Mitchell thought he should stay another day but McAllister insisted he wanted to join the other prisoners."

"It's too soon, surely," she mused, more to herself than to Sumner. "He should have stayed. His fever only broke last night."

Sumner chewed a mouthful of meat and drank some wine before he answered. "You're wasting your concern, Rebecca. The man's an ungrateful wretch."

"What are you talking about?"

Sumner studied her as he answered, "McAllister told Dr. Mitchell he wanted to rejoin his fellow prisoners because he didn't want you nursing him any longer."

Rebecca averted her face. "I see," she said softly, trying her best to hide her hurt. "Well, he needn't have left the infirmary. I would have stayed away."

"Would you?" Sumner asked. "Could you?"

"Of course," she insisted, feigning a coldness she was very far from feeling. "I only nursed him because Dr. Mitchell was busy with the other men."

Sumner could have argued the point, he could have reminded her that the last of Dr. Mitchell's patients had left the infirmary two days before Beau's fever had broken. He could have pointed out that Dr. Mitchell could easily have tended him. But he knew McAllister was a vulnerable subject with Rebecca. He did not know precisely what had happened between them. At this point he was not sure he wanted to know. All he knew was that negotiations were underway to ransom the Americans, and the sooner he saw them marched onto a ship and taken away from Fort Mackinac, the happier he would be!

It was three days before Rebecca returned to the fort. She went back to the infirmary, quiet now, its beds empty of patients. The long room was speckled with the late-afternoon sunshine filtering through the windows. Rebecca worked tidying the freshly made beds, straightening Dr. Mitchell's collection of lethal-looking instruments.

A scalpel slipped from her hand and clattered to the scuffed floorboards. Sinking to her knees, Rebecca searched for it under the bed that had been Beau's.

As she looked for it, she heard footsteps enter the infirmary. They passed down along the long aisle between the double row of beds and approached Rebecca.

"Dr. Mitchell?" she called, not looking up. "I've dropped one of your instruments. As soon as I can reach it, I'll see that it's washed and—"

She glanced up and froze. Instead of Dr. Mitchell standing there, Beau watched her. He held a wooden cane in his hand, but did not lean on it as he stared down at her.

Slowly, warily, Rebecca got to her feet. "How did you get in here?" she demanded.

"The guards are a little lax," Beau replied. "So long as I don't go near the magazine, they don't care where I wander. I'm not likely to go far with this . . ." He tapped his leg with his cane.

"Does it pain you?"

"Does it matter?" he countered.

"Not at all!" Rebecca snapped. "I nursed you for weeks because I wanted you to die!"

She turned her back to him and he said softly, "Dr. Mitchell said you saved my life."

"I did," Rebecca stated without pretense.

"Why?"

"Would you have preferred I let you die?"

"I wouldn't have thought you'd give a damn either way. We are enemies."

"And you hate me," Rebecca said quietly.

"Yes," he agreed. "I hate you."

"Because I betrayed you," she murmured.

Beau laughed and Rebecca smelled the whiskey on his breath. "You've been drinking," she accused.

"They're generous with the whiskey we left for them," he said, amending, "or should I say the whiskey we left for you since you are one of them."

"Why are you here, Beau?" she demanded, the look in his sapphire eyes making her feel uneasy.

"For retribution," he replied. "I gave you what you wanted, however unwittingly. Now you're going to give me what I want."

Chapter Fifteen

Rebecca felt a shiver of sudden fear shoot through her. "Dr. Mitchell will be coming soon and—"

"No, he won't," Beau said, smirking. "I saw him leaving the fort to go down to the village. I presume you know he's taken over Dr. Day's house."

He reached out and his hand, strong and callused, closed about Rebecca's upper arm. She tried to pull away but he held her fast.

"I wondered," he said, his voice low and harsh, "why we were together only that once, in the forest."

"It was a mistake," she breathed, feeling trapped as he loomed over her.

"Why a mistake?" he demanded. "Because you thought you shouldn't take your spying quite so far? Wasn't lying with your enemy part of your plan? Or was it just that you'd gotten the information you needed so you didn't need to play the whore for your country any longer?"

Rebecca's eyes blazed. "Damn you! It wasn't like that!"

"No?" Beau sneered. "How was it then? Was it love, Rebecca? Was it passion? Or was it merely lust? Perhaps Anthony Hawkins was right. You were a young widow who missed having a man in her bed."

Tears burned Rebecca's eyes. Those precious moments they'd shared in the forest had been all she'd had to remember that was good in this whole dreadful situation. Now he'd sullied that memory with his insinuations.

"I hate you, Beau," she murmured, her voice trembling.

"I know you do," he agreed. "I'm the enemy. And yet, if I touched you—"

"Don't!" she gasped, jerking away, breaking free of the grip he held on her arm.

"Why not?" he asked. "Because you hate me? Or because of something else?"

"I don't know what you mean!" she hedged, backing away from him.

"I think you do, Rebecca." He moved toward her. "I think it was more than mere duty to your country that brought you into my arms that day. I think there was desire, passion, and I think they're still there, however you might want to deny it."

"You're wrong," she insisted, hiding her shaking hands in the folds of her skirt.

"Am I?" he asked doubtfully. "Why don't we put it to the test?" He advanced with the swiftness and grace of a great, tawny jungle cat.

Rebecca whirled, intending to flee, but it was too late. Beau's arm snaked about her waist and he pulled her against him. His body was like a rock wall at her back and his arm was a band of iron, imprisoning her in his embrace.

His free hand cupped her chin and held her face as he bent his head and kissed her slowly, lingeringly, in the hollow of her throat where her pulse fluttered wildly. She squirmed in the cage of his arms but her strength was nothing against his.

"Please, Beau," she whimpered, knowing that the pounding of her heart and the whirling of her senses had to do with his nearness, with the warmth of his breath on her skin, the rough caress of his hand on her throat, and the long, slow, hot kisses he trailed along her throat, her jaw, her ear.

"It wasn't only for the information, was it, Rebecca?" Beau purred in her ear, his hand sliding sensuously across her breasts.

Rebecca felt her knees turning to water. It seemed that only Beau's arms about her kept her on her feet. She closed her eyes, her body aquiver, and tried to will herself not to feel his caresses, tried to force away the heat of desire rising inside her.

"Rebecca," Beau prompted, turning her in

his arms. "There was more, wasn't there? There was desire just as there is now."

"No." She shook her head, tears blurring her vision. "I hate you. Hate you!"

"Perhaps," he agreed, his arms around her, his hands working at the laces of her gown, "but you want me now, don't you?"

"No! No!" she hissed, writhing as he held her fast, one hand pulling the bodice of her gown from her shoulders, leaving her clad only in her thin cotton shift. "I don't want you!"

"You're lying."

Slipping a hand behind her knees, he tipped her back onto the bed in which he'd spent so many hours as a patient. His body, so much larger than her own, pressed her deep into the straw tick. The ropes, threaded through holes in the wooden bedframe, creaked in protest at their weight.

"All I have to do is scream," she reminded him, her voice breaking with tension as she felt his hand creeping beneath her petticoat, finding the warm, smooth flesh of her thigh, "and half the fort will come running. They'll have you before a firing squad by nightfall."

Beau's face, his sapphire eyes glittering, paused above hers. He arched a golden brow. "Then scream," he told her. "Go ahead. Scream. Bring half the fort in."

Rebecca hesitated. If she screamed, the soldiers within earshot would come to her aid. They would rescue her and Beau would be executed for assaulting her. But the thought

160

of seeing him standing before the fort walls, of hearing the crack of the rifles, and seeing his body torn and bloody, perforated by musket balls, stilled her tongue.

"Scream, Rebecca," he goaded.

Rebecca turned her face away, unable to stifle a moan as his hand found her, touched her, caressed her. She felt as though she were burning, as if her flesh was scalded by the heat of the desire he forced her to feel. She was lost, lost, and they both knew it.

When Beau pushed back the ruffled cotton of her petticoat, when he moved over her and took her, she arched against him, hating herself, wanting him more than she'd ever wanted anything in her life.

Tears of frustration, of self-loathing, trickled from the corners of her eyes even as her body shuddered, as the beginnings of ecstasy began building inside her.

"Beau," she breathed, grasping for that rapture that seemed just out of reach, "please, oh, please!"

She clutched at him, her fingers digging into the cotton of his shirt and the hard, straining muscles of his arms. Her muscles tautened, she pressed her body to his. Her flesh, her senses were betraying her, but at that moment nothing mattered but the strength and the heat and the punishing rhythm of Beau's body against her own.

And then, in a moment, it was over. Beau's body shuddered. His face, strained, sheened with perspiration, was buried in Rebecca's shoulder as he pulled her hard against him for a moment, then two, before he left her poised maddeningly on the edge of ecstasy.

"Beau!" she protested, feeling as if she'd been drenched with icy water. She reached toward him but he eluded her outstretched hand.

At the bedside, he gazed down at her as he adjusted his clothing. Under his relentless stare, Rebecca felt exposed, indecent. Pushing herself up on the bed, she tugged down her petticoat and struggled to close the bodice of her gown. Where a moment before she had been lost in the pleasure of his flesh and hers, now she felt sullied and ashamed, as though her surrender to passion had been something disgraceful.

"The last time this happened," Beau told her coldly, "I gave you information. I have no more information for you but I'll give you something else for your trouble."

From the pocket of his jacket, Beau took a gold piece. He flipped it to her and, when it landed on the bed beside her, picked up his cane, and left the infirmary.

Rebecca sat on the edge of the bed, her gown rumpled, her hair in wild disarray, her senses still ajumble. Her body ached, her stomach roiled. And her heart felt as if it had shattered like fine crystal in her breast.

Rebecca walked up the long, sloping ramp to the fort, her hand linked in the crook of Sumner's arm. She wore a pelisse of scarlet kerseymere over a gown of pearl-gray silk. She had been invited to dinner by Captain Roberts and could hardly refuse.

Still, it would mark the first time she had returned to the fort since Beau had found her alone in the infirmary. That had been three weeks ago and she had not been able to force herself to return. But when Sumner had come with the invitation from the captain, Rebecca had known she could not refuse without offering some explanation. But what could she say? Could she admit to Sumner that Beau had seduced her? Could she admit, even to herself, that in the heat of those moments she had wanted him so desperately she had been willing to abandon all morals, all scruples, all pride, to have him? She could not and so she said nothing.

And in truth, she did not know why she maintained her silence. Of course Sumner would at the very least demand a duel with Beau, and Sumner was an excellent shot. Did she protect Beau because she was afraid Sumner would kill him? He did not deserve her protection. What he'd done, turning her own senses against her, taking her merely to prove that he could, had been cruel, vicious. He was angry with her, bitter, disillusioned, but even so. . . .

She turned her thoughts from Beau as they passed the sentries at the sally port. The September night was cold. Winter came early in the north country and Rebecca knew, having spent the winter on St. Joseph Island, that it could be a cruel, hard time of bitter cold and scarcity of supplies. There would be few more nights like this one, few more times when food would be plentiful enough to allow for social dinners at gracious tables.

In Captain Roberts's quarters, Rebecca and Sumner sat down with the captain and Dr. Mitchell. Over wine after dinner, Dr. Mitchell said, "I've missed you, Rebecca, at the infirmary."

"No one's been sick, have they?" she asked, concerned that her feelings about what had happened between her and Beau might have made her neglectful of her duties.

He shook his head. "Nothing out of the ordinary. I've had to change a few bandages, stitch a few cuts. Nothing serious. But it is nice to see a pretty face once in a while."

Rebecca smiled but said nothing. She'd enjoyed helping in the infirmary both here and on St. Joseph Island. She'd felt useful, even when it only meant cleaning or organizing the infirmary's supplies. But now . . . The thought of returning to that building, of working alone as she'd done so often, was repugnant to her. She had no reason to suspect that Beau might try to catch her there alone again; he had proven that he could master her senses at will. He'd had his revenge, he'd hurt her, humiliated her. It was unlikely he'd feel the need to repeat it.

She forced her mind away from those

thoughts and concentrated on what the captain was saying.

"I've had orders," he said, "to send them to York for trial."

"Who?" Rebecca broke in, wondering instinctively if he meant the American prisoners.

"Parks, McGrath, and Kelly," the captain repeated, "the three deserters we found with the Americans when we took the fort."

"Will you send them?" Dr. Mitchell inquired.

The captain shook his head. "Kelly, perhaps, but Parks and McGrath are in no condition to be reinducted into service. And, as they can function on fife and drum, I intend to keep them with us."

"And the others?" Sumner asked. "The Indians and the Americans? If they're still here this winter, we'll be desperately short of supplies."

"The Indians are leaving," Captain Roberts replied. "Some are going home to begin preparing for the winter, some are going south to join in the fighting. As for the Americans, negotiations are nearly complete. I doubt they'll be with us much longer."

They all professed themselves eager for their prisoners to leave, none more fervently than Rebecca who longed with all her heart to see Beau step onto a ship and sail out of her life.

Less than an hour later, she and Sumner bade the captain and doctor good night and left the officers' quarters.

As they walked along the path that bordered the parade ground, Sumner said, "I wonder if it's wise to let those men have so much freedom."

Rebecca looked to see who he meant and her eyes focused on four of the American prisoners sitting on the grass. In their center Beau leaned back, his arms propped behind him. He stared as she and Sumner made their way toward the sally port.

"Isn't that McAllister," Sumner asked, "the big blond one who's watching you?"

"Yes," Rebecca admitted, refusing to look in his direction.

Beau's voice rang out clear and strong on the night breezes that swept in off the lake and whirled about the fort. "Good night, Mrs. Carlyle."

Sumner looked down at her when she made no reply. "Aren't you going to answer him?" he asked, curious.

Rebecca shook her head, her expression stony. "No," she answered shortly.

"Do you want to stop to speak to him?"

"No!" Rebecca snapped. "Come on, Sumner, I want to go home!"

As they reached the sally port, Rebecca ventured a glance over her shoulder. Seeing her, Beau blew her a kiss and grinned as his companions burst out in loud laughter.

Rebecca's cheeks flamed as she descended toward the village. Her hand trembled in the crook of Sumner's arm and she vowed that nothing—nothing!—would get her back to that fort until Beau was well away from the island.

*   *   *

She got her wish less than two weeks later when the American prisoners were brought down to the docks to board a ship that would take them to some far-flung American outpost. Rebecca watched as the boats were rowed back and forth, taking one man at a time and the British guards who accompanied them to their ship. Her feelings were mixed as she watched them board. The anchor was raised, the sails hoisted.

On the one hand, she thought, analyzing her feelings, she was relieved at the departure of Beau McAllister, her tormenter, the man who had turned her own body against her in his desire for revenge. On the other hand, she was apprehensive because he was the father of the child she suspected she carried—the child she would carry and bear on this isolated island amidst the questions and accusations she did not know if she could honestly answer.

Chapter Sixteen

Autumn was a time of blustery winds and warm sunshine, brilliant colors, breathtaking scenery, and sudden, biting cold. The beauty of nature was never more apparent than when the forests turned to blazes of red, gold, and orange.

But all too soon the leaves lost their color, turned brown, withered, and fell. The winds that had been warm in October froze the blood in November and rattled the shutters that had been closed against them on the windows of the houses on Mackinac Island.

Behind the closed shutters of her cottage, in the main room where a log fire blazed in the stone fireplace, Rebecca hugged her secret to herself. She had told no one. Who was there to tell? Sumner? He would have to know eventually but she would not tell him now. Dr. Mitchell?

What could he do but tell her to take care of herself, to rest, to eat as well as she could, considering the limited resources of this place in the winter. Among the women on the island she had a nodding acquaintance with a few but they were not the sort of friendships where she would confide such a secret to them.

And so Rebecca said nothing to anyone. She sat before the fire, solitary, living in the future, thinking of the child nestled within her. Would it be a boy? she wondered. Beau's son. She pictured a small child with golden hair and sapphire eyes, a sturdy, healthy child, who would grow up never knowing the circumstances surrounding his conception.

At other times, when she could not so easily lose herself in dreams of the beautiful child she was certain she would have come springtime, the reality of her situation frightened her.

If the war were over—damn the war! she cursed each and every day—she would go back to England. No one there would know of the events leading up to her child's conception. She could even say she'd remarried after William's death and that her second husband, like her first, was killed in the struggle against the Americans.

She was not without resources in England. William had had an inheritance, not an enormous sum to be sure, but one that would provide his widow with a comfortable, if modest, living. And there was her family. They would never turn their backs on her. On the contrary, they would welcome her with open arms, for they had tried to convince her to remain in England while her young husband completed his duties in the wilds of America. If only she had listened. . . .

But, no, she would not give in to regrets and self-pity. Her one real regret when William died was that they had had no child. They had been married such a short time and both had agreed it would be wiser to wait until they had returned to the safety and civilization of home. Now she would have the child she'd longed for in those dark days after William's death. But it was not William's child but the child of a man who despised her.

If only she could go home, but it was impossible. She had to plan for the here and now. She could spend her pregnancy in this isolated place, made more so by the coming of winter. Thank God that when the time for the child's birth came the weather would be warm and food once more plentiful.

Rising from her chair, Rebecca laid another log on the fire. There was a great pile of firewood behind the cottage, though most of it had been cut the previous summer and so was not as dry as it ought to be. Still, with care it would last her the winter. She could not depend on Sumner to provide her with more. Once he learned of her pregnancy, he might well be done with her. Heaven knew he already suspected there had been more between Beau and herself than she'd admitted. Even if she told him this child's conception was not an act of passion but of revenge, would he believe her?

Returning to her chair, Rebecca tucked her feet beneath the folds of her heavy petticoats and skirts. She positioned the corners of her blanket over her lap and tried to ignore the cold wisps of wind that blew beneath the front door. Deny it though she might, even to herself, the thought of spending her pregnancy all alone, of giving birth in this remote place, daunted her. She had every confidence in Dr. Mitchell and there were children aplenty on the island, but those women had husbands to comfort them, to reassure them. They had friends and relations to help them and advise them. She had no one.

Then she thought of Beau and she caught her breath. What would she tell her child of its father? Could she tell her son, her sturdy, golden-haired boy, that his father was dead? In a sense it would be true. Beau was dead to her, to the child he did not even know he had given her. Should she tell her child the truth? The entire truth? How could her child ever trust her if she told him that his parents had been brought together through a lie, a masquerade? And how could he be taught to respect a father who had taken a woman out of hatred and a desire for vengeance?

No, she decided, she would tell her child none of it. The baby was innocent of its parents' treachery. Whatever lies and subterfuge had brought Rebecca and Beau together, whatever act of revenge had resulted in the child's conception was not the child's fault. Why should a child be troubled with such matters?

She sighed, folding her hands protectively over her still-flat belly. She would go back to England at the first opportunity. She would make a life there for herself and her child, a happy life, a serene and secure life, away from this place with its hunger and danger, with its wars and wild animals and Indian attacks.

Beau, she knew, would prefer that his child be raised an American with no allegiance to England and her king, but what did that matter? Would Beau be there to comfort her in the long, cold days ahead? Would Beau be there to hold her hand, to comfort and help her when the time came for the birth? Would he be there to help her raise the child? No, no, and no! So what did his wants and opinions matter? Since he had left her with all the responsibility, he had also left her the authority. The decisions were hers to make and she would make them according to the dictates of what she believed was best.

She thought of England, green, lush, with bustling cities and polished society. Her child would be raised to take his place in that society. He would be an English gentleman, educated, cultured. He would remember nothing of this place, these times. If only this damned war would end!

Her secret was still her own on Christmas Eve when Sumner came to her door. He stamped the snow from his boots and shook it from the cape of his woolen greatcoat before entering Rebecca's cottage.

"Let me hang that by the fire to dry," she offered, taking his coat from him. "Is it still snowing?"

He nodded, setting his hat on the table. "There's no sign it's going to stop. Do you know how glad I'll be to get back to England and her mild winters when all this is over?"

"Not half as glad as I'll be," Rebecca responded, pouring him a mug of mulled wine. "I've been wishing this war were over so I could go home."

"Alone?" Sumner asked.

Rebecca knew what he meant. Her year of mourning was long since over, her sojourn as a spy had ended, and Beau McAllister was gone. It seemed unlikely their paths would ever cross again. So now Sumner had apparently decided it was time to begin his courting in earnest.

She sighed. "Sumner," she murmured, not meeting his eyes. "I have to tell you—"

"No," he interrupted, "don't say anything more. Not now, not tonight."

Rebecca knew he thought she meant to reject him, to once and for all spurn his affections and end the hopes she knew he cherished. But she hadn't been going to do that at all. She knew that he would learn of her pregnancy soon. Only the weight she had lost before becoming pregnant made it possible for her clothes to conceal the recent expansion of her waist and the rounding of her belly. She'd meant to tell him the truth and at last share the secret she'd kept so scrupulously.

"You don't understand, Sumner," she persisted. "I have to tell you—"

"I love you, Rebecca," he blurted. "I know you don't love me but you do care, don't you?"

"Of course I care for you," she admitted honestly. "If things were different . . ."

"If what was different!" he demanded. "Rebecca, I know you loved William but he's been dead a year and more. Is it McAllister? What was there between you? What happened when you were with him? You nursed him until you were half-dead yourself; you saved his life!" Sumner stared at her, an expression of dread in his eyes. "Are you in love with him, Rebecca? Are you in love with that American—"

"No!" Rebecca cried. "No, I don't love him! I hate him!" She stopped, her breath catching in her throat. Tears prickled her eyes, hot salty tears that threatened to spill down her cheeks. "I hate him," she whispered, sinking into a chair.

She buried her face in her hands and Sumner watched, at a loss to understand her tears. Her sorrow moved him despite his jealous

175

resentment of her obvious feeling for Beau McAllister.

"Rebecca?" Going to her side, he knelt beside her chair. "Don't cry. I didn't mean to make you cry. It's only that I love you, and I want you to be mine. The thought of your loving Beau McAllister drives me mad."

"I told you," she insisted, lifting her face from her hands. "I hate Beau McAllister."

"Very well." Sumner nodded, not wishing to press the point but thinking how closely related love and hate could be. "I brought you something. A Christmas gift."

"You shouldn't have," she told him. "I have nothing for you."

"That doesn't matter." From the pocket of his greatcoat Sumner took a small parcel. Opening it, he held out to Rebecca a delicate gold chain from which hung an exquisite enameled locket.

"It's lovely." She sighed, taking it from him.

"I had it sent from England. Last spring, before all this began. It arrived not long after you left St. Joseph Island. Let me clasp it around your neck."

Rebecca lifted her hair as Sumner slipped the cool gold chain over the standing collar of her dull red woolen gown. The locket rested against her breast, shimmering in the firelight.

"It belonged to my mother," Sumner said.

"Are you sure you want me to have it?" Rebecca asked. "It's a family heirloom and—"

He waved aside her objection. "I want you to have it," he insisted.

"Thank you," she said softly. "It's beautiful."

Sitting down opposite her, Sumner gazed at her. "Not half as beautiful as you," he whispered. "If we were married, you could move to the fort. My quarters are large. We'd be comfortable there. I'd do everything I could to make you happy; you must believe me."

"I do believe you," Rebecca replied.

"Then why won't you let me make you happy? You say you care for me."

"You don't understand," she insisted wearily.

"Make me understand."

Lifting her head, Rebecca gazed into Sumner's eyes. "There is someone else to be considered."

"Beau McAllister," Sumner said harshly.

Rebecca shook her head. "No, not Beau." Taking a deep breath, she burst out, "I'm pregnant, Sumner. I'm going to have a child."

Chapter Seventeen

"You're . . ." Sumner's face seemed unnaturally pale despite the rosy glow of the fire blazing in the fireplace. "But—"

"A child," Rebecca repeated. "I've known for nearly two months."

Backing away from her, Sumner groped behind him for his chair and, finding it, sank into it. His eyes seemed glazed as he stared at her. "A child," he murmured, his gaze straying to her still-slender waist. "When will it . . ."

"June," she answered. "The baby will come in June."

Sumner shook his head, not listening to her, lost in his own shock, his own disillusionment and disappointment. "No wonder you were evasive when I asked you about McAllister!" he growled. "It is McAllister's child, isn't it?"

"Yes," Rebecca admitted.

"McAllister." The image of the tall, broad-shouldered, good-looking American lieutenant taunted Sumner. "An American. An American, Rebecca! The enemy! And there I was, on St. Joseph Island, longing for you, missing you, while you . . ."

He frowned, staring at her. "When did you say it was due?"

"June," Rebecca supplied.

"June," Sumner repeated. "Then it happened when he was here . . . after . . ."

Rebecca nodded. "After the surrender of Detroit," she confirmed. "When he was a prisoner."

"Under my nose!" Sumner cried, his pale face reddening with anger. "Good God, what a fool I've been! What a bloody, credulous fool!"

"Sumner . . ." Rebecca tried to cut in.

"I admired you for helping Dr. Mitchell in the infirmary! I admired you for devoting long hours to helping him care for those men. Now I understand! It was a ruse, wasn't it? All that selflessness, all that compassion. It was all an excuse so you and your lover could be together!"

"It wasn't like that," Rebecca defended. "I didn't offer my help to Dr. Mitchell simply to—"

"No wonder you nursed him so tirelessly!" Sumner went on, too lost in his own hurt and anger to hear Rebecca. "So long as McAllister was in the infirmary the two of you could be together! Good God, Rebecca! Did you lie with that bastard there? In the infirmary? Did the two of you—"

"It wasn't like that," Rebecca insisted more loudly. She was beginning to quake but was helpless to stop the emotions overwhelming her.

"And you acted so cold to him the night we went to dinner with Captain Roberts. I remember he called to you but you ignored him as if he were so much rabble. He seemed so disdainful, so sarcastic! What a charade the two of you were acting out! Did you get together and work out your lines like actors in a play? Did you laugh at the way you were fooling us all?"

"It wasn't like that!" Rebecca screamed, tears glistening on her cheeks. "Damn you, Sumner, listen to me!"

Sumner glared at her, his eyes filled with fury and pain. "How was it then?" he demanded, his tone rife with skepticism.

Rebecca wiped her cheeks with shaking fingers. "It happened after Beau left the infirmary, after his wounds had healed. I was working alone one evening, tidying up. All the patients had been released; the infirmary was empty. I heard footsteps. I thought it was Dr. Mitchell. But it was Beau. He . . . I . . . ." She shuddered, wrapping her arms around herself. "I tried to stop him, Sumner, I swear I did not want him to . . . to . . ."

Covering her face, she gave in to the tears she had suppressed ever since that night. She wept for herself; for her intolerable situation; for the

181

remembered humiliation of that horrible night when the man she had loved had taken her without love, without affection and shattered her emotionally; and she wept for the fatherless child she would give birth to in this desolate place.

"Rebecca," Sumner breathed, trembling with outrage. He came to her and knelt beside her chair. "Are you telling me that he ... that McAllister raped you?"

Rebecca hesitated. Technically, she knew, it was not true. At the moment he had taken her, she had wanted Beau with a burning, urgent desire she could not deny however much it shamed her. But she was not prepared to admit that to anyone, least of all Sumner. And, anyway, even if Beau's assault had not been a physical rape, hadn't he raped her emotions? Her senses? Hadn't his attack on her heart been as brutal, as violent as any physical assault would have been?

"Rebecca?" Sumner prompted, trying without success to pry her hands away from her face. "Did McAllister force himself on you?"

He had forced his will upon her, had forced her to feel emotions, desires, she had not wanted to feel, had forced her to humiliate herself by forcing her to surrender to a passion that had nothing to do with love. Wasn't that a kind of rape?

She allowed Sumner to draw her hands away from her tearstained face. He was so concerned, so angry for her sake. She depended on Sumner for so much now and she and her child might well have to depend on him for more in the months to come. It was likely she would never see Beau again; he would not come looking for her. It would be better for herself and for her child if she simply allowed Sumner to believe that her pregnancy was the result of something other than her own misplaced desires. After what Beau had done, he did not deserve her defending him.

Avoiding Sumner's gaze, she nodded, affirming his fears.

"He took you," Sumner said dully, "and left you with his child." Sighing, he took her hands into his own. "Why didn't you tell me? Why didn't you tell anyone?"

"I . . ." She closed her eyes. "I was ashamed," she whispered, her voice soft and breathy, almost inaudible. That much of it was completely true. She was ashamed of her own weakness, of the ease with which Beau had inflamed her desires, of the passion he had evoked in her with a few caresses, a smattering of kisses.

"Rebecca," Sumner said, his face grimly serious, "there is no reason for you to be ashamed. You should have come to me. If you had told me, or Dr. Mitchell, or anyone while McAllister was still here, we'd have seen him punished for what he did to you."

"I could not tell anyone," she insisted. "It was my fault that it happened."

"No, that's not true," Sumner argued. "He came looking for you. It was not your fault."

Sandra DuBay

"But it was," she disagreed. "Don't you see, Sumner? He knows. He knows I was spying for the British. He knows I sent the information as to where to attack the fort. He showed me the island. He took me to the other end, to the landing, and that was when I realized the potential of the place as a landing site. I used him, Sumner. He trusted me, cared for me, and I betrayed him. I used him to betray his country. What happened in the infirmary was his vengeance, his punishment against a spy for her treachery."

"And this?" Sumner asked, laying a hand on the gentle swell of her abdomen. "Is this part of his vengeance as well?"

"He couldn't know . . ." she began.

"That's no defense. Damn it, Rebecca, don't you realize that if I had known I would have seen him hanged for it? By God, I would have shot him like the dog he is!"

Rebecca said nothing. The truth—and she hated herself for feeling this way—was that she had known that if she told anyone what had happened they would have tried and executed Beau. Why, in heaven's name, she asked herself, should she care? She should be glad to see him hanged or stood before a firing squad for what he'd done to her. But even now, even after what had passed between them, she could not bring herself to be the cause of his death.

She had told Sumner that she hated Beau. But that was not the truth. She hated what he'd done. She hated the way he'd used his

184

maleness and her femaleness as a weapon to punish her for her betrayal of his trust. But Beau himself . . . No, try though she might, she could not hate the man she'd fallen in love with during those golden, warm days and nights last summer. It was that Beau she thought of when she remembered those nights. She remembered the look in those sapphire eyes when he gazed at her, she remembered the strength of his arms, the hardness of his body against hers when he held her, the warmth of his hands as they caressed her skin. She did not want to remember him as the angry, vengeful man who had forced himself upon the woman who had duped him into betraying his comrades and country.

She could not remember that Beau without remembering, with a pang of guilt, her own actions. She had tricked him, after all. She had gone on with her spying even after she knew she was falling in love with him. Not that that excused him for what he'd done, but she could understand his rage, his desire for revenge.

Torn from her reverie, she looked up at Sumner, who paced before the fireplace.

"I tell you, Rebecca," he was saying, "if I ever have the chance, I'll kill McAllister for what he's done to you. I swear to you, I'll kill him!"

But though Sumner vowed to avenge Rebecca, and swore she would not suffer because of her situation, he did not persist in his attempts to persuade her to marry him and to come live with him at the fort. He was perfectly willing, she reflected, to avenge her honor but not willing to save her from the dishonor of bearing a fatherless child by marrying her and giving the child his name.

Not that she would have accepted his marriage proposal. She had loved William, and she had been in love with Beau. She would not, could not, marry a man she did not love simply for convenience's sake.

The winter dragged on, cruel, bitter. The soldiers were reduced to wearing coats made of Hudson Bay blankets and the style was soon copied by the islanders and *voyageurs*. Supplies dwindled. Food was doled out in carefully measured amounts.

At last, when it seemed it could get no worse, an epidemic of whooping cough struck. Unable to sit idly by, Rebecca helped Dr. Mitchell, though the tearing, violent coughs that nearly suffocated its victims broke her heart. Hardest hit were the children. As she held them, as she felt their small, frail bodies being wracked, saw their little faces turn red, heard the gasping *whoop* that followed a fit of coughing as they tried to force air back into their tortured lungs, it seemed to Rebecca she could feel her own child shuddering in her womb.

She walked home beside Dr. Mitchell one freezing night in February after a little girl they'd nursed had died. Rebecca, exhausted, drained physically and emotionally, leaned heavily on the doctor's arm as they walked up the path to her cottage.

"Will you come in?" she asked as she opened the door. "Warm yourself for a moment before you go on to the fort."

"You've talked me into it." Dr. Mitchell laughed. "You wouldn't happen to have a sip of whiskey to warm these old bones, would you?"

Rebecca laughed. "I just may. Come in."

After pouring the doctor his drink, Rebecca built up the fires she had banked while she'd been gone. The fire in the main room blazed as she went into the bedroom and put logs into that grate. It was while she was prodding the logs into place that the pain took her by surprise.

Gasping, she sank to her knees, the iron poker clattering to the floor. She heard Dr. Mitchell speaking, but his words did not penetrate the haze of pain and sudden fear that swept over her. Wrapping her arms protectively around herself, she crouched on her knees, trying to will the pain away.

"Rebecca?" the doctor called, having received no reply to his repeated questions. "Did you hear me?"

She said nothing, did not hear him set his mug aside and come to the bedroom door. She did not hear him call her name, did not realize he had come to her until he took her arms and tried to raise her.

"The baby," she breathed, tears stinging her eyes.

"Baby?" He stared at her. It was cold in the bark and log cabins where they'd tended their patients, and the doctor had not seen Rebecca without the voluminous woolen cloak she wore to ward off the cold. "What baby?"

"My baby," she whispered. "I'm losing my baby, David."

"My God," the doctor murmured. "Come, try to get to the bed."

With his help, Rebecca moved to the bed. She felt the weight of her cloak slipping from her shoulders as Dr. Mitchell unfastened it and let it fall to the floor. Gratefully, she sank onto the edge of the bed.

"How far along are you?" he asked as he helped Rebecca lie back onto the bed and pushed up her skirts and the heavy petticoats beneath.

"Five months," she told him, trembling.

"Why in God's name didn't you tell me?" he demanded, angry at her and at himself for not noticing. Had he not been so preoccupied with the epidemic he surely would have realized her condition.

"I wanted to help you," she defended, "I wanted to help the children."

"And you've exhausted yourself," he told her.

"I don't want to lose my baby, David," she said fearfully. "Please, please help me."

But it was already too late. Rebecca, like too many mothers during that bitter, freezing winter, watched, weeping as a tiny body was temporarily interred until the spring thawed the ground enough for a pitifully small grave to be dug.

Chapter Eighteen

July 1814

A year and more had passed since Rebecca had
lost her child. The war dragged on and each
winter that found her still on Mackinac Island
seemed more cruel than the last and made her
long even more keenly for England and sweet
forgetfulness.

Captain Roberts, whose health had eventually worn down even his proud warrior's
spirit, had been replaced by Captain Richard
Bullock. Between Captain Roberts's departure
for Montreal and Captain Bullock's arrival,
Sumner had been in command of the fort.
He'd acquired a taste for command during his
brief tenure and it seemed to Rebecca he found
it hard to relinquish the post when his former

commander's replacement arrived.

Throughout the bitter winters of 1813-1814, Captain Bullock commanded a garrison that seemed constantly on the verge of starvation. Added to that, the tide of the war seemed incredibly to be turning in favor of the Americans.

The fledgling American Navy had met and defeated the British on the Great Lakes. General Henry Procter, the commander of the British forces at Detroit, had been forced to withdraw into Ontario where his forces had been pursued and soundly routed by William Henry Harrison and his men. It was no secret among the troops of the Great Lakes that an attack was soon to be mounted to regain Mackinac Island. The British garrison and the villagers were in a state of permanent tension.

As the winter gave way to the spring of 1814, orders were issued to strengthen the fort's defenses. The well within the fort was to be reopened to allow the men to withstand a seige by the invading Americans. And the heights—the famous heights which had allowed the British to capture the fort so easily—were to be fortified.

From May until July every person, soldier and villager, who was strong enough to hammer or chop or carry, was put to work building the fortified blockhouse and surrounding earthworks which, when finished, was named Fort George after the king.

Captain Bullock, under whose command the

plans for the new fort had been drawn up, had been replaced in May by Lieutenant Colonel Robert McDouall. A bluff veteran of nearly twenty years service, the Scot took command and spent much of his first few weeks reassuring both his own men and their Indian allies that they were firmly ensconced on the island and no band of miscreant American rebels would roust them.

To Rebecca, it all meant very little. The loss of Beau's child had killed something inside her. She went through the motions of living but took no joy in it.

After a period of awkwardness, Sumner resumed his visits. It was as if, in his mind, the loss of the child marked the end of an era. Beau McAllister, he seemed to believe, had been swept from Rebecca's heart as well as her life.

It was not true, of course. Few days or nights passed when Rebecca did not take out the miniature of Beau she had stolen and gazed into those painted blue eyes. She wondered where he was, if he was in the midst of the fighting. She would not consider the possibility that he, like so many men on both sides of the dispute, might have been killed. Somehow, she felt she would have known if he'd been killed. The ache she felt in her heart when she allowed herself to think of her lost child would surely have grown sharper had Beau been killed in some bloody skirmish somewhere.

She thought of Beau when she rode beside

Sumner up to the heights where Fort George now overlooked both Fort Mackinac and the straits beyond. From its blockhouse the sentries could keep watch for approaching attacks from the island's inland forests.

They sat there on the heights, gazing out toward the straits and the mainland beyond and Sumner spoke softly and urgently, "Word has come from Detroit. An American expedition left on the third. They're coming to attack us."

"The third?" Rebecca thought quickly. "It's the twenty-fourth. Surely they should be here by now!"

Sumner nodded. "We think they've gone to St. Joseph Island to destroy the fort there."

"It's abandoned," Rebecca reminded him.

"I know. But that will keep us from retreating to it if we're driven from this place."

"Could that happen?" she asked.

Sumner laughed. "I doubt it. There's nothing for you to worry about, Rebecca. Nothing at all."

But as they rode back to the village, back to Rebecca's cottage, she was not worried. She was only anxious, tense, wondering whether one of the men embarking for Mackinac Island might be a certain golden-haired, sapphire-eyed lieutenant she had once vowed she hated.

At dawn two days later the American force was sighted. The ships anchored near Round Island but after the cannon fire from the fort seemed perilously near their targets, they raised anchor and moved to Bois Blanc out of the reach of the British guns.

By nightfall the village was deserted. The villagers had not needed to be told twice when Lieutenant Colonel McDouall had ordered them to come to the fort where they could be protected when the attack came. Crowded together in the white-walled fort, they gritted their teeth and waited. . . .

And waited and waited. One day became two, three, a week, two weeks. Confused, bored, the villagers began drifting home, confident that there would be time enough for them to retreat to the safety of the fort when—and if—the attack finally occurred.

Over Sumner's objections, Rebecca too returned to her cottage. She was bored with the confined, crowded life in the fort and tired of Sumner's constant company.

Wrapped in her oldest cotton nightgown, her hair brushed and tumbling down her back, she lay in her bed, covered by a light sheet, reading by the light of a single candle. It was peaceful, quiet, unlike the overcrowded fort where she had spent the past two weeks. The silence seemed like a precious luxury.

Somewhere in the darkness a dog barked. Rebecca heard a man's voice shouting at the animal to be quiet. She smiled. Only a few miles offshore, the pride of the new American Navy was anchored, planning an attack, but life here seemed to be resuming some sort of guarded normalcy.

The knocking on the door seemed like thunder in the silent cottage. Rebecca started, dropping her book.

"Sumner," she whispered to herself, frowning as she pushed back the sheet and swung her legs over the side of the bed. She rolled her eyes. She had seen enough of Sumner during her stay at the fort to last her quite a while.

Opening the door to the main room, she stepped through the doorway as the knocking sounded again. Puzzled, Rebecca looked at the back door. Why the back door? she wondered.

Unfastening the latch, she swung the door open. But it was not Sumner who stood there. Instead, she found herself face to face with a tall *voyageur* in the unofficial "uniform" of corduroy trousers and brightly colored shirt. A gray wool togue was pulled low on his brow.

"Who are you?" Rebecca gasped, grasping at the open neck of her cotton nightdress. "What do you want?"

"Rebecca," the man said, and his voice was like a lightning bolt through her heart.

"You," she breathed, stumbling backward. "My God, it's you!"

Beau stepped into the room, pulling the wool togue from his blond hair. He seemed like a ghost in the shadowy candlelight spilling through the open bedroom door. His sapphire eyes seemed shadowed, fathomless in the darkness, and his face was leaner, sharper than before.

Rebecca turned away from him. It was as

if a ghost had appeared before her, as if her thoughts had somehow taken form and crossed the line from dream to reality.

She reached out for the support of a chair, her hand trembling, her body quaking. Their last meeting, that night in the infirmary, replayed in her mind in painful detail. She remembered the horror, the humiliation, the guilt she had endured. And she remembered, most of all, the pain of bearing a dead child and of seeing him lain to rest in a tiny grave in the forest.

Her hands, still shaking, curled into fists. All her pain seemed to change in that instant to pure, unreasoning fury. Whirling toward him in a flurry of white ruffled cotton and glossy black curls, she attacked him, pummeling him with her fists, kicking him with small bare feet.

"Damn you!" she cried, tears of rage blurring her vision. "I'll kill you!"

Beau bore it all wordlessly, making no effort to defend himself, not trying to ward off the blows that caused him little actual pain. It was only when her fury began to abate, when her rage gave way to tears and tremors, that he raised his hands to touch her.

"Don't touch me!" Rebecca screamed, backing away. "Why have you come here?"

"I wanted to see you," he said softly. "Lieutenant Colonel Grogan sent some of us ashore to look around. I had to come."

"It did not occur to you I might not want to see you after—" she broke off, looking away.

"Yes," he admitted. "It did occur to me. There

195

have been times since then that I wanted to write. But I didn't know how to say what needed to be said."

"Nothing needs to be said between us," she told him, forcing a bravado that had its source deep inside her quaking body. "We are enemies. I betrayed you. You took your revenge in the way men usually avenge themselves on women."

"I'm sorry," he said softly. "That is all I came to say. The attack will happen any day now. I did not want to die without telling you I was sorry."

"Die?" The very real possibility of his death shook her.

Beau shrugged his shoulders. "There's no use fooling ourselves. You know we're here. You know we're going to attack. This is not going to be the same sort of bloodless rout it was when the British took the island two years ago."

"I suppose not," she admitted, a sudden sick feeling blooming in the pit of her stomach.

"I should go," he said, his reluctance to leave evident in the very posture of his body. "I am truly sorry, Rebecca. And . . ." He twisted the woolen togue in his hands. "I'm sorry about the child."

Rebecca gasped, the color leaving her face. "How did you know?" she demanded.

"The British are not the only ones with spies," he told her. "We get reports from here. One of them mentioned the cough and also mentioned that Mrs. Carlyle, the former British spy, had miscarried a boy child." He swallowed, his golden brows drawing together. "Was he mine, Rebecca?"

Wordlessly, she nodded, tears of remembrance stinging her eyes.

"From . . ." Beau hesitated. "From that night in the infirmary?"

Again, she nodded and Beau sighed heavily, his shoulders sagging.

"I never meant to cause you pain," he told her, adding, "well, perhaps I did because I was hurt and angry and . . ." He passed a hand over his brow. "But not like this, Rebecca, you must believe me."

"I . . ." Rebecca started to speak but a sharp rapping on the front door made both her and Beau jump.

Glancing at Beau, she went to the front door. "Who is it?" she called, her heart pounding in her breast.

"Sumner," the muffled voice called back from the other side. "Let me in, Rebecca!"

Her eyes wide, her pulse fluttering, she looked back at Beau, who stood rooted to the floor between the table and the fireplace.

Chapter Nineteen

"Just a moment," she hissed to Sumner through the door.

Beau moved toward the back door but Rebecca reached a hand toward him. "Please, don't go!" she whispered.

Beau glanced toward the front door, knowing Sumner Meade, the British lieutenant he'd met while he'd been a prisoner at the fort, was waiting impatiently on the other side.

"Wait in the bedroom," Rebecca asked. "Please, Beau."

After a moment's hesitation, Beau went into the bedroom. Rebecca followed him and, snatching up the single candle burning there, took it back into the main room, and pulled the bedroom door nearly shut.

Taking a deep breath to calm herself, she

unfastened the latch and opened the door. She stepped back as Sumner entered.

"What's going on?" he asked, glancing around the shadowy room.

"Nothing," she insisted. "You woke me. It's a warm night, Sumner. I had to put something on before I could let you in."

He smiled, his eyes skidding over her in her flowing white cotton gown. "A pity," he said softly.

Rebecca blushed, knowing Beau was in the bedroom, well within earshot of their every word. "What brings you here so late, Sumner?" she asked, anxious for him to state his business and be gone.

Sumner sighed, wishing she would be more welcoming. "There've been reports of activity among the American ships anchored off Bois Blanc," he told her. "Someone said they thought they saw a pair of canoes headed toward the island from that direction. I thought if there are Americans skulking about I should come and take you to the fort."

"I don't think that's necessary," Rebecca demurred. "I'm perfectly all right as you can see."

"Rebecca," Sumner argued, "the Americans know you were the informant before we captured the fort. It's not impossible that they mean to capture you and put you on trial for spying."

Rebecca thought of Beau and of how easily she'd allowed him into her cottage. What if it was true? What if he had come to capture her, to take her back to one of the ships to face charges for her espionage? But, no, she could not believe he could hate her enough to want to destroy her. If that had been the case, surely he would have seized her the moment she'd opened the door and even now would be taking her back to his superiors.

"I'll come in the morning," she promised. Seeing him open his mouth to argue, she rushed on, "I'll keep my doors and windows locked tonight, I swear, and first thing in the morning I'll come to the fort."

"I can't talk you into coming now?" he persisted, exasperated.

She shook her head. "No, truly, Sumner, I'll be all right tonight."

Sumner sighed. "I know how stubborn you can be, Rebecca. I know it's useless to stand here arguing. But don't open your doors to anyone for the rest of the night. Swear to me you won't."

"I swear," she obliged. "Now if you don't let me go back to sleep, it will be noon before I'm awake enough to report to the fort."

Obviously reluctant, Sumner allowed her to propel him to the door. He tried to think of some argument that would convince her to come with him but could not.

As the door closed in his face, he was left with no choice but to return to the fort, trusting Rebecca to honor her promise to come in the morning. Sighing, frustrated by his failure,

Sandra DuBay

he started back to the fort, ever watchful for Americans skulking in the shadows.

"He's right, you know," Beau said, standing in the bedroom doorway. "You should have gone back to the fort with him."

Rebecca smiled mockingly. "Well why didn't you tell me that while he was still here, sir?"

Beau smiled thinking of Sumner Meade's reaction had he appeared from the bedroom to help the British lieutenant argue his case.

"Seriously, Rebecca," he said, his smile fading. "Anthony Hawkins is aboard the *Niagara*. He swears that once the battle is over and the island is ours he'll see you tried and executed for betraying us to the British."

Rebecca laughed wanly. "Yes," she admitted, "I betrayed you to the British. Tonight I have betrayed the British by hiding you when Sumner came."

Beau gazed at her, understanding her dilemma. "Why did you betray me?"

"For my country, my king," Rebecca answered honestly. "To avenge my husband's death."

"And why did you betray Sumner Meade tonight?"

Rebecca hesitated. "For you," she admitted. "Sumner would have wanted to kill you. At the very least he would have tried to take you back to the fort as a prisoner."

"You loved your husband," he observed, glancing at the portrait of William Carlyle that still hung on the wall.

By Love Betrayed

"I did," Rebecca admitted.

"So you spied on us for love?"

Rebecca nodded. "Yes," she said softly.

"And tonight?" His voice was low, urgent. "Did you protect me . . ."

"For love," Rebecca said, so quietly he could scarcely believe he'd heard her.

His heart pounding, Beau reached out and touched one of her tumbled curls. He'd loved her and had hated her; he'd taken his revenge on her and had regretted it. He'd grieved for the loss of the child they'd created in those terrible, violent moments and had wished he could make amends. He'd believed she would surely hate him forever for what he'd done and now he'd heard her admit she loved him. And here they stood on the eve of a battle that could cost one—or both—of them their lives, on opposite sides. Enemies in love.

They gazed at one another, his eyes, glittering, sapphire-blue in the candlelight, her own deep amethyst, shimmering with unshed tears of some undefinable emotion. There was so much to be said but somehow this moment defied explanation. It was not time for words, and yet neither could be the first to reach across the months and years of turmoil toward the other.

Beau's fingers itched to touch her, his arms ached to enfold her, but he could not forget the pain he had caused her. He did not know if any amount of love could ever erase those tortuous memories.

"I should be going," he said softly, making a move toward the door.

Rebecca's fingers touched his sleeve, stopping him. "Must you?" she asked almost shyly. "Must you leave now?"

"If I stay . . ." Beau began, swallowing hard. He wanted her, his body ached for her. "If I stay, Rebecca . . ."

She went to him. "Yes," she breathed, reaching up to twine her arms about his neck. "If you stay . . ."

She pulled his head down and her lips brushed his softly, invitingly. "Stay," she whispered, her breath warm and sweet on his cheek. "Please, stay."

Beau's arms went about her, pulling her close. Rebecca held him, her arms about his neck, her body stretched on tiptoe pressed against his. She was trembling, her body aquiver with desire, afire with pure, primal passion that could be buried no longer.

Parting, Rebecca took Beau's hand and led him into the bedroom. The light of the candle burning on the table in the main room cast a dim, golden glow that spilled through the open doorway.

Rebecca stood, her back to Beau. Her fingers shook as she unbuttoned her nightdress. Slipping it from her shoulders, she let it fall to the floor and puddle around her feet. She heard Beau's soft intake of breath as her beauty was revealed.

She held her breath as he moved up behind her. His clothes, like hers, lay on the floor and his skin was warm against hers as their bodies touched. His hands lingered at her waist, then slipped up over her ribs to cup her breasts. She leaned back against him, her eyes closed, her head cradled in the warm, pulsing hollow of his shoulder, as he caressed her soft flesh, teased the tight coral tips. She could feel his body against hers, hot, hard, his desire as urgent, as demanding, as her own.

Beau turned her in his arms. His fingers sank into the ebony silk of her hair as he lowered his head and kissed her tenderly, searchingly, thirstily like a man too long deprived of the fresh spring dew that moistened her tender lips. Rebecca clung to him, letting him guide her to the bed.

Beau lay her across the tousled sheets but as she raised her arms to him, he knelt beside the bed. His hands caressed her legs that dangled over the side, stroking them down to her toes that barely touched the rough boards of the floor.

He kissed the smooth flesh of one thigh, then the other, his fingers teasing the sensitive backs of her knees. With soft, fluttering kisses he worked his way up until he found her, tasted her, explored her sweet, honeyed secrets.

Rebecca gasped, her eyes wide. She shuddered, her fingers laced in Beau's hair. It was like nothing she'd ever known, ever dreamt of.

She watched him, her small pearly teeth worrying her lower lip, as he loved her. The pleasure, the sheer, golden sensation, built inside her, sweeping from peak to peak, until her body arched, until she cried out, writhing against him.

Her body still quaked as Beau rose above her. She welcomed him, her arms slipping about him, drawing him down, eager to feel his flesh against her, within her.

Moving together, their passion built, blossoming like some rare, night-blooming flower that burst into beauty, leaving them breathless, awed into silence, as they lay in one another's arms and the flame of the single candle flickered then died.

Dawn was not many hours away when they finally parted. Wrapped in a sheet, her black curls falling like a shining cloud about her shoulders, Rebecca walked Beau to the door.

"I wish you could stay," she whispered, snuggling against his chest. "Just a little longer."

Beau held her. Her soft, warm body nestled in his arms, relighting the fires of desire inside him.

Sighing, he stepped a little away from her. "So do I," he admitted wistfully. "But it's impossible." He smiled. "The men I came ashore with are doubtless certain I've been taken prisoner. I'll be lucky if they haven't gone back to the ship without me."

"If they have," she teased, "come back to bed." She smiled up at him, then nodded, resigned. "I know, you can't." Her smile faded to be replaced by a worried frown. "Beau, you will be careful, won't you, when the time comes? I couldn't bear it if—"

"Shhh," he hushed her, one gentle finger brushing away the tear that glistened on her cheek. "I'll be as careful as I can. Promise me you will go to the fort. It's the safest place for you during the fighting."

Rebecca nodded. "I promise."

Beau pulled her close and kissed her, a gentle kiss, a lover's kiss, filled with longing. And then he was gone, swallowed by the night, leaving Rebecca with the darkness—and the fear of what the dawn might bring.

Thrill to the most sensual, adventure-filled Historical Romances on the market today...

FROM ▉ *LEISURE BOOKS*

As a home subscriber to the Leisure Romance Book Club, you'll enjoy the best in today's BRAND-NEW Historical Romance fiction. For over twenty years, Leisure Books has brought you the award-winning, high-quality authors you know and love to read. Each Leisure Historical Romance will sweep you away to a world of high adventure...and intimate romance. Discover for yourself all the passion and excitement millions of readers thrill to each and every month.

Save $5.⁰⁰ Each Time You Buy!

Six times a year, the Leisure Romance Book Club brings you four brand-new titles from Leisure Books, America's foremost publisher of Historical Romances. EACH PACKAGE WILL SAVE YOU $5.00 FROM THE BOOKSTORE PRICE! And you'll never miss a new title with our convenient home delivery service.

Here's how we do it. Each package will carry a FREE 10-DAY EXAMINATION privilege. At the end of that time, if you decide to keep your books, simply pay the low invoice price of $14.96, no shipping or handling charges added. HOME DELIVERY IS ALWAYS FREE. With today's top Historical Romance novels selling for $4.99 and higher, our price SAVES YOU $5.00 with each shipment.

AND YOUR FIRST FOUR-BOOK SHIPMENT IS TOTALLY FREE!

IT'S A BARGAIN YOU CAN'T BEAT! A Super $19.96 Value!

▉ *LEISURE BOOKS*   A Division of Dorchester Publishing Co., Inc.

Get Four Books Totally FREE— A $19.96 Value!

▼ Tear Here and Mail Your FREE Book Card Today! ▼

PLEASE RUSH
MY FOUR FREE
BOOKS TO ME
RIGHT AWAY!

Leisure Romance Book Club
PO Box 1234
65 Commerce Road
Stamford CT 06920- 4563

AFFIX
STAMP
HERE

Chapter Twenty

True to her word, Rebecca set out not long after dawn for the fort. Glancing toward Round Island and Bois Blanc beyond it, she could see that the American ships had moved, some had sailed away apparently in the direction of the opposite end of the island.

Nor was she the only one making her way to the protection of the fort on the hill. Most of the other villagers who had returned to their homes when the attack did not happen were now returning.

"They're going to land at the other end of the island," a woman said to Rebecca as they climbed the ramp to the sally port. "Their cannons can't reach the fort and they won't risk attacking from the harbor."

As they entered the fort and Rebecca saw that

Lieutenant Colonel McDouall had left only a handful of soldiers to hold the fort while he and the rest of the garrison had gone to meet the attack from the far end of the island, she wondered at the wisdom of the American strategy. Surely they must know the British would expect them to copy the plan the British, themselves, had used in capturing the fort two years before. The Americans should, she thought, have sent a token number of men to the far end of the island, then landed their main force on the shore below the undermanned fort.

She smiled at the thought. She had spent too much of her life surrounded by military men, she told herself. She could not hear of a battle without planning her own strategy for attack.

Not knowing what else to do, Rebecca went to the infirmary to see that everything was in readiness for the inevitable casualties. She dreaded the thought of the bloodied, wounded men who would be brought in half-dead or dying. She shrank from the thought of Beau lying somewhere in the forest wounded, perhaps dying. Unless he were brought to the infirmary, she would never know he was hurt. If the Americans took their wounded back to their own ship, he could die and she'd never. . . .

But, no, she told herself sternly. Beau would not be harmed. He would be safe, safe. She closed her eyes and breathed a prayer for his safety, adding one for Sumner as well to ward off the bad luck of praying for the safety of a man she should think of as the enemy.

Dr. Mitchell looked up as Rebecca's shadow fell across the floor. "Ah, Rebecca, I was hoping you'd come. We've a patient already."

Rebecca's heart thudded. "What? Has the battle already started?"

"Not that I know of. I haven't heard any artillery fire. No, this man was brought ashore by the Indians. Apparently, the Americans sent a squad of men ashore on Round Island. Commander McDouall sent some of the Indians to drive them away before they could set up any guns. This man was left behind. The Indians captured him and brought him back, intending to kill him. McDouall sent men down to rescue him but I'm afraid the Indians' knives got to him first."

Rebecca went around the screen shielding the man's bed. She gasped. Though he seemed swathed in bandages, half his face was visible. He was pale, hardly breathing, and only the shock of raven-black hair seemed alive.

"Know him, do you?" the doctor asked, coming to stand at the foot of the man's bed.

Rebecca nodded. "His name is Anthony Hawkins. He's an American lieutenant. I knew him when he was here before. He was a very handsome man."

Dr. Mitchell pursed his lips. "Well, if he lives, he won't be handsome any longer, I'm afraid. His wound runs the length of his face. He's lost his left eye."

"Poor man," Rebecca murmured. She did not like Anthony Hawkins; she knew he hated her with a passion and had vowed to see her pay with her life for her actions against the American garrison at Mackinac. Still, for a man so handsome, such hideous wounds would scar his mind, his soul, just as horribly as they would scar his flesh.

Both Rebecca and Dr. Mitchell jumped as the first volley of cannon fire rumbled across the island.

"It's begun," Rebecca whispered. She closed her eyes. "Oh, please, please, keep him safe," she breathed.

"There, there, now," Dr. Mitchell comforted. "I don't think you have to worry about Sumner. McDouall left him in command of Fort George on the heights. I doubt the Americans will even get that far."

"I'm sure you're right," Rebecca agreed. She could not tell him that her prayer was not for Sumner or for any member of the British garrison.

The American attack was ill-starred from the first. Outnumbered, outflanked, and outmaneuvered, it seemed their every move was met and repulsed by Lieutenant Colonel McDouall's men and the three hundred fifty Indian allies who were all too eager to join in the battle.

American casualties were heavy and it was soon obvious that there was no point in pressing their attack. The battle was lost and to persevere would only mean more wounded and dead men.

The American commander, Lieutenant Colonel Grogan, ordered his men to retreat to the ships, fleeing the British and their allies. By sunset the Americans were once more aboard their ships and the British were nursing their wounds, counting their dead, and reveling in the ease of their victory.

In the infirmary, Rebecca dressed wounds, some serious, most a matter of bayonet wounds or musketballs lodged in arms or shoulders.

She went about her tasks automatically; her mind, her thoughts, were elsewhere. Was Beau safely aboard one of the American ships, she wondered, or was he even now lying dead in the forests of the island's interior? If only there was some way of knowing.

She looked up from bandaging a young private and saw Sumner enter the infirmary. He was immaculate, his scarlet and blue-and-white uniform was spotless. Rebecca smothered a smile. How he must resent these happy young men who could show off their battle scars and boast of their bravery under enemy fire.

"Are you all right, Sumner?" she asked, baiting him.

He shot her a disgusted look. "I should have taken a book!" he groused.

Rebecca laughed. "It was quite a battle."

"It sounded like it," Sumner agreed. He watched resentfully as a young corporal with a minor wound entertained his friends with his version of how he'd been wounded.

"Come now, Sumner," Rebecca soothed.

"You don't truly wish you'd been in the battle, do you?"

"Of course I do!" he insisted. "Do you think I was happy sitting at Fort George? The fighting never came near us! I didn't even see an American, at least not clear enough to get a shot at him."

"How sad," she murmured. Unlike Sumner, the Americans were no longer nameless, faceless enemies to be hated simply because they owed no allegiance to England and her king. She had known many of them, had loved one, and she could take no pleasure, share in none of the glory, of the bloody battle and its high toll of American lives.

Sumner caught sight of Anthony Hawkins in the bed behind the screen they were passing.

"Isn't that . . ." he began.

Rebecca nodded. "Anthony Hawkins. An American lieutenant. Apparently some of the Indians captured him on Round Island."

"Oh, yes. He had to be rescued. Good Lord, I didn't realize he'd been so badly wounded. Will he live?"

Rebecca shrugged. "If his wounds don't become infected. Do you think the Americans will want to take him away with them now? It wouldn't help to move him in this condition."

"If he were given his choice, he'd doubtless prefer to remain here and be nursed by a beautiful woman." Reaching out, Sumner touched Rebecca's cheek.

"I doubt it," she stated flatly, turning away.

"What do you mean?" Sumner asked.

Rebecca glanced back at Anthony. "If you remember my letters back to Fort St. Joseph, Lieutenant Hawkins was one of the first men I met when I came here. After the fort fell, he vowed to see me punished for spying. He's sworn he'll see me die for it, Sumner."

"I wouldn't worry about it," Sumner told her, casting a disdainful glance at the unconscious man in the bed. "There's nothing he can do to you. I think we've proven today that the Americans will never take Mackinac back from us."

Washing her hands, Rebecca left the infirmary and, with Sumner at her side, made her way to the sally port.

Darkness was falling and in the distance the lights of the American ships were clearly visible. Was Beau aboard one of those ships? she wondered. She hoped so . . . She prayed. . . .

"Do you want me to see if I can find out the names of the American dead?" Sumner asked suddenly.

Rebecca glanced up at him. His face was tight, his expression stony. "What do you mean?" she asked softly.

"You're wondering, aren't you, if he was there? If he was wounded . . . or killed?"

"Sumner . . ." she began.

"Damn it, Rebecca!" Sumner swore, his voice hushed to keep the soldiers nearby from hearing. "After what he did to you! You should pray he's lying somewhere in the forest bleeding his life away! You should hope the Indians

215

got to him and cut him to pieces! You should wish—"

"Enough!" she hissed. "I'm tired of it, Sumner, I'm tired of being torn this way and that! You sent me here! You! And I did what I was sent to do. You have your damned fort! Now leave me alone!"

With a toss of her head, Rebecca stormed out through the sally port, ignoring the sentry who snapped to attention as she passed. She hurried down the steep ramp, moving as quickly as she dared, wanting only to put the fort and the cheerful victors as far behind her as possible.

By midmorning of the following day the American ships had hoisted anchor and sailed away, leaving only two ships, *Tigress* and *Scorpion*. The American dead, some sixty men, had been buried on the island. Six more had died aboard the ships. The attack had been an ignoble failure and Rebecca, like most of the island's inhabitants, believed it impossible for the island to be torn out of British hands.

Rebecca went about her business trying to avoid facing the inevitable fact that she did not know if Beau were dead or alive. And there seemed no way she could find out. She would simply have to live with the suspense, the torture of not knowing, until Beau managed to get some message to her.

The thought of living from day to day in perpetual suspense, waiting for a message that might never come, made the future seem grim. She gazed out the window toward the water, toward the two American ships still riding at anchor on the calm blue lake. Would they know? she wondered. Would the men aboard those ships know if Beau had survived the battle?

With a self-mocking smile, she turned away. What did it matter if they knew? There was no way for her to contact them, and even if she did, why should they tell her anything? She was a British subject, a former spy who had been instrumental in their loss of this stronghold. If she tried to contact them—if she were so foolish as to slip out to one of the ships under cover of darkness—it was unlikely she would be allowed to escape unscathed.

Chapter Twenty-One

The reason for the two American ships remaining behind when the others withdrew soon became clear. A blockade was being mounted. If the British could not be driven off the island, perhaps they could be starved into submission.

For Rebecca's part, she tried to keep busy, tried to fill her hours to keep from brooding about Beau. She went to the fort, to the infirmary, where Anthony Hawkins lay, slowly recovering, kept nearly insensible most of the time, until the wound that so disfigured him had healed enough for the danger to pass.

She saw Sumner now and again but he seemed eager to avoid her. He was angry, she knew, that in spite of all that had passed between them, in spite of the pain he'd caused her, she still cared if Beau McAllister lived or died.

Leaving the infirmary, Rebecca caught sight of Sumner. His eyes met hers but he quickly turned away. She sighed. She had never meant to hurt him but she could not help the way she felt about Beau. She had not asked to be sent here; she had not asked to be put in such close quarters, such intimate contact with Beau. Had she been allowed to remain at Fort St. Joseph, she would still look on the Americans as the enemy and Beau McAllister would simply be another damned, treasonous colonial to be brought back under the auspices of the Crown.

Deep into the night, she lay awake, pondering her dilemma. She had risked everything, including her life, to serve her country and had found love. Then she had nearly lost everything—and had lost a child—because she had succeeded too well in her task. There seemed no way she could win. If she was loyal to England, to the king, she would lose Beau. And because of her love for Beau, Sumner had withdrawn his friendship.

But in Sumner's case, it was more his pride than anything else that was wounded. He had intended to court her, to make her his own, once her sojourn among the enemy was ended. Never in his wildest dreams had he expected her to find love and certainly not with one of the very men she had been sent to spy upon.

But she had found love. And though the war came between them, threatening to tear them apart, threatening their very lives, she knew there was a bond between them which neither distance nor politics could sever.

Sighing, Rebecca rolled onto her side. The moon had hidden behind gathering storm clouds; thunder rolled in the distance. Rebecca listened to it rumbling hollowly. It was a lonely sound, echoing across the miles of water that lay between herself and. . . .

Rebecca sat up in bed. In the silence that followed the thunder she thought she'd heard a rattling, as if someone were climbing over the cedar fence surrounding her back garden. Perhaps Sumner . . . But, no, he would simply have come to the front door. One of the Indians? It was not unheard of for the Indians to take whatever was growing in anyone's garden. Occasionally, even a cow or sheep disappeared only to have its butchered remains found after the meat had been taken.

Holding her breath, straining to hear any more sounds, Rebecca waited. Then, finally, she heard a soft rapping at the back door.

"Beau!" she whispered. But it couldn't be, could it? It was impossible, and yet. . . .

Throwing back the coverlet, she hurried to the back door. "Who is it?" she asked, her fingers toying with the latch.

Her heart leapt when a familiar, loved voice replied, "Open the door, Rebecca. It's Beau."

Flinging the door wide, she launched herself into his arms, nearly knocking him off his feet. Laughing, Beau swept her up and carried her into the cottage. He kicked the door shut and set her unceremoniously on the long table before the fireplace.

Their lips met hungrily in a long, searching kiss. Rebecca wound her arms about him, her hands spread across his back. As their lips parted, she laid her head on his shoulder.

"I was so worried about you," she murmured. "I didn't know where you were. I didn't know if you'd been wounded or . . ." She drew a deep breath. "There was no way for me to find out if you'd been killed in the battle. The thought of waiting and waiting to hear from you when all the while you were . . ." She shivered with horror at the thought.

"I'm sorry, sweetheart," he said, holding her close. "If there had been a way to get word to you earlier, I would have. As it happens, I never got off the ship. I remained aboard to fire upon the island."

"I would have felt much better knowing that," she told him. She toyed with the buttons of his shirt. "You know, don't you, that Anthony Hawkins is in the fort infirmary?"

"How is he? The Indians didn't kill him?"

Rebecca shook her head. "He may wish they had. They cut him dreadfully, Beau, all over. Most of his wounds have healed but his face . . ." She wrinkled her nose. "The scar is hideous and he's lost one eye."

"Good God. And you're nursing him? A bit ironic considering he's vowed to see you dead."

"He doesn't know I'm nursing him. We ladle him full of whiskey to dull the pain. I suppose once he's well enough to know what is happening around him there'll be hell to pay. The first time he catches sight of me . . ."

"That's the day to ship him back out to us," Beau laughed. "Not that I'd be particularly happy to see him." He ran gentle fingers along Rebecca's jaw. "Now, I think we'd do better to forget about Anthony Hawkins for the moment, don't you?"

Rebecca shivered as his fingers worked at the tiny buttons fastening the front of her nightdress. "Yes." She sighed as he parted the soft, white cotton and bent his head to kiss her breast. "Oh, yes."

Beau kissed her, fondled her, aroused her to something akin to madness. He held her face cupped in his hands and kissed her lips with little, teasing kisses until she laughed aloud. Finally, lifting her as though she were made of eiderdown, he carried her into the bedroom and lay her on the bed.

Rebecca watched him, silhouetted in the darkness, as he undressed. She sighed as he slipped into bed and gathered her into his arms. She reveled in his lovemaking and scarcely heard the storm which broke over the island in the wee hours of the morning.

By dawn both the storm and Beau were gone. But in the days that followed she scarcely noticed Sumner's coldness or the growing scarcity of food as the American blockade took its toll. She lived for the nights when Beau would come to her whenever he could slip away and row himself to shore, slipping into the sleeping village, then back again before the dawn broke on the eastern horizon.

The situation with regard to the blockade remained static for nearly a month. No supplies could reach the island. The American schooner, *Scorpion*, prowled the waters around the island like a hungry cat waiting for a mouse to emerge from its hole. The other schooner, *Tigress*, retreated to the Detour Passage to prevent supplies being sent down into Lake Huron from upper Canada.

It was not long before food was being rationed on the island. The salt pork and beef that formed the basis of the soldiers' diet was soon gone. The few merchants who had food to sell raised their prices to exorbitant levels. The Indians who had remained after the battle left, seeing little to gain by remaining. More and more the diets of the villagers consisted mostly of fish that could be caught in the shallow waters near the shore. When there began to be talk of killing the horses at the fort and salting the meat, it became clear that desperate measures were in order.

An officer of the Royal Navy, Lieutenant Miller Worsley, managed to slip past the blockade late one night along with seventeen seamen. He and his men had escaped when the *Tigress* had attacked and destroyed their schooner, *Nancy*, bound for Mackinac Island with desperately needed supplies.

Reporting to Lieutenant Colonel McDouall, Lieutenant Worsley outlined a plan for ending the blockade. The commandant agreed and, with a force of volunteers, the young lieutenant slipped away under cover of darkness, heading for *Tigress* and the Detour Passage.

Rebecca knew none of this. Without Sumner, she was not privy to all the comings and goings, all the plans and movements of the garrison. She went about her daily tasks, helping in the infirmary, living for the nights when Beau would come to her.

"We're leaving in the morning," he told her one night when by candlelight they ate bread he had brought with him and maple syrup she had purchased in the summer when it was plentiful and cheap.

"Leaving?" she said, pausing as she was about to lick a drop of the syrup off one finger. "Why?"

"*Tigress* was supposed to return the day before yesterday. We're going to see if something's happened to her."

"When will you come back?" she asked anxiously.

Beau smiled, twining a curl of her hair about his finger. "I don't know. This war keeps tearing us apart. Why don't you tell Lieutenant Colonel McDouall to surrender and then we can be here together?"

"Wretch!" She laughed, slapping him. "Why don't you tell your commanders to surrender? Then we can go back to England and live in a civilized country."

Beau's smile faded. "Is that what you want to do?" he asked sternly. "Go back to England?"

"I had planned to," Rebecca answered honestly. "Oh Beau, if only you knew what it was like . . ."

"I know what it's like," he replied. "Toadying to men whose only claim to superiority is that their ancestors have been sitting on their arses in the House of Lords for two hundred years. People living in squalor and poverty with no chance of improving their lives or their childrens' lives because some high and mighty 'milord' owns everything and will give them no chance to earn an honest living."

"It's also a beautiful country of literature and art and music," Rebecca argued.

"And we here in America, by contrast, are ignorant, illiterate, and uncultured," he growled. "And certainly there is no beauty hereabouts."

"If you mean forests and lakes and wilderness, yes, there is beauty," she admitted. "But in England there are cathedrals and opera houses and parks. And, yes, to be honest, many of the Americans I have met have been ignorant and crude."

"And what Americans have you met?" he demanded. "Rough, unschooled soldiers living a dangerous existence in a remote, isolated place during a war! What did you expect to find here, Rebecca, concerts? Balls? Did you have those on St. Joseph Island?"

"Of course not," she admitted, wanting only to put this argument behind them. "Please, Beau, I know you love this country. I know you believe in America and her government, but—"

"But England with its ruling class is better," he finished for her.

"That's not what I was going to say!" she argued.

"But that's what you think." Shaking his head, Beau left the bed and began pulling on his clothes. "It's no good, Rebecca. I had thought once this war was behind us that you and I could make a future together."

"We can!" Rebecca insisted.

"Where? Here or in England? I'm an American, born and bred. You're an Englishwoman, a monarchist. How could we be happy together?"

"We could make it work!" she argued. "I know we could!"

"Perhaps," he admitted, "perhaps not. In any case, I have to go."

"Stay until morning," she pleaded, not wanting him to leave in the middle of an argument.

"I can't. We're sailing well before dawn. Good-bye, Rebecca."

"Beau. Beau!" Wrapping a sheet about herself, Rebecca ran after him. But his long legs took him swiftly to the door and the night took

227

him away as surely as his ship would bear him far away before the morning light had broken over the island.

Returning to the bedroom, Rebecca climbed back into bed and lay limply across the tousled sheets. Tears shimmered in her eyes. They could resolve their differences, she knew they could. But would fate give them the chance?

Chapter Twenty-Two

Rebecca was still wide awake, red-eyed and headachy from weeping, when dawn broke over the island. Dressing, she walked down to the shore. Shading her eyes, she scanned the horizon. She looked for Beau's ship but there was nothing. *Scorpion* had sailed and the hard feelings between them would go unresolved until she saw him again—if she saw him again.

Weary, unhappy, she returned to her cottage and did her morning chores. The scene the night before in her bedroom replayed again and again in her mind. Their differences seemed insurmountable but there must be a way. There must be! If they truly loved one another. . . .

But did they? Nagging doubts ate at her. She loved Beau—there was not the shadow of a doubt in her heart that that was true. But what of his love for her? He desired her—that went without saying. But love? If only she knew. . . .

She jumped, startled, as a sharp rapping came at the front door. Curious, she opened the door. A dark-haired young private stood there.

"Mrs. Carlyle?" he said, belatedly jerking his stovepipe shako from his head. "Dr. Mitchell would like to know if you could come to the fort, ma'am. The infirmary's full of wounded men."

"Wounded men!" Rebecca's heart leapt. "Has there been a battle?"

The private's blue eyes sparkled. "A victory, ma'am! The American schooner, *Tigress*, has been captured!"

"*Tigress!*" Rebecca cried, thinking of Beau and his shipmates sailing away to see why *Tigress* had not returned from the Detour Passage. "When did this happen? How?"

"Could we talk while we're walking, ma'am?" the private asked. "Dr. Mitchell did say he needed you most urgently."

"Oh, of course. Just a moment."

Retreating to her bedroom, Rebecca changed into the pale calico dress she often wore in the infirmary and pinned her hair securely up so it would not hang down and get in her way. Taking up a shawl, she and the private left the cottage and started toward the fort.

"Tell me," Rebecca urged as they walked swiftly along the dirt road.

"Well, ma'am," the private began. "You knew that the Americans captured and destroyed the schooner *Nancy*."

"No, I didn't know that," Rebecca answered.

"Why, yes, ma'am. The ship was bringing supplies to us but the Americans captured her and sank her. Lieutenant Worsley and some of his men escaped and came here. He and Commander McDouall worked out a plan and Lieutenant Worsley and some of his men went to capture *Tigress*."

"And they succeeded?" Rebecca breathed, amazed.

"They did!" The private swelled with pride at the accomplishment of his countrymen. "They took the ship and captured her crew. Lieutenant Worsley sent the Americans here. All the officers and some of the sailors were wounded."

"And where are Lieutenant Worsley and his men now?" Rebecca asked.

"Still aboard *Tigress*," the private replied. "He means to capture *Scorpion* as well! He learned that *Tigress* was to return and meet her sister ship. He knew when they did not return the others would come looking for them. He's got the American signal codes. When *Scorpion* arrives, *Tigress* will signal her. The commander aboard *Scorpion* will think everything is normal. By the time he realizes his mistake, it will be too late!"

Rebecca's stomach twisted. She felt sick, dizzy. Beau and his comrades were sailing into

231

a trap! How could all this have happened without her hearing a word of it? But she knew the answer. Sumner was angry with her and so he had told her nothing of what was happening at the fort. Without him, she was as uninformed as any of the villagers.

She closed her eyes, scarcely able to believe she could still walk, still talk, still act as if the earth had not dropped out from beneath her feet. What a time for her to quarrel with Sumner! If only they had been on friendly terms! If only she had known about Lieutenant Worsley and his plans, she could have told Beau, warned him, saved him and his ship from the ambush awaiting them in the Detour Passage! She could have. . . .

"Mrs. Carlyle?" the young private beside her asked, his voice alarmed. "Is anything wrong?"

"No," she murmured in reply. "Nothing at all."

But her thoughts whirled in her head. *I told the Americans' secrets to the British; now I would have told the British secrets to the Americans. How can my loyalties be so torn? I feel as if I'm being pulled apart and the worst of it is that neither of the two men responsible for my problems want to have anything to do with me!*

She wanted to laugh to keep from crying. But in the end she did neither. She lost herself in helping Dr. Mitchell treat the wounded Americans and prayed that Beau and his shipmates would somehow survive the enemies lying in wait for them.

* * *

As it turned out, her hopes were partially realized. Beau survived the ambush as did his comrades but Lieutenant Worsley and his men succeeded in capturing *Scorpion*.

He and his men sailed the two ships into Mackinac Island harbor to the cheers of both the soldiers and the villagers. The seige was over; supplies could reach the island. The almost certain starvation they'd faced during the coming winter would not happen.

Rebecca was at the fort when the American prisoners were marched through the sally port. She saw Beau, tall, strong, handsome, glancing about the fort. Stepping into the infirmary doorway, she waited, breathless, for him to notice her. But when, at last, he did, he merely glared at her and looked away.

Surely, she thought, he was not still furious with her over their quarrel the night before he'd left! Their loyalties were different, it was true, but even so. . . .

No, she told herself, it was only his anger at having seen his ship taken out from under him, at having to stand by and watch while his commanding officer surrendered a fine ship to the enemy without a fight. His anger was understandable.

She waited and watched, hoping for a moment when she could speak to him in something approaching privacy. Her opportunity came a few days later when he stood near the well, drinking a cup of the sweet, fresh water.

Sandra DuBay

"Beau?" she said softly, dipping a cupful of water for herself. "I'm sorry about—"

"About what?" he demanded, his tone cold, furious.

"About what happened with *Tigress* and *Scorpion,* of course. If I had known—"

"Are you going to tell me you didn't know?" he snarled. "Are you actually going to try to tell me you knew nothing about Worsley and his plan to capture *Tigress?* Are you going to pretend you did not know we were sailing into a trap?"

"I didn't know!" Rebecca insisted. "I'd heard nothing—"

"Stop it!" he ordered. "There's nothing that goes on here that you don't know about. You and your pet lieutenant discuss everything!"

"Not any longer!" she replied, her anger growing apace with his. "Sumner and I do not speak! And do you know why? Because of you! Of you!"

"I don't believe you," he told her bluntly, turning away.

"My God!" she breathed. "Do you believe, do you truly believe I could be with you, make—" She fell silent waiting for a sentry to pass by before continuing, her voice hushed. "Make love with you and see you sail off, knowing you were sailing into a trap, and say nothing?"

"Why should you betray your beloved England?" he asked, his sapphire eyes slitted.

"You do believe it!" she whispered. "What kind of woman do you think I am?"

234

"An Englishwoman," he answered flatly. "And a spy."

"And you," she hissed, her eyes blazing, "are a coldhearted, bigoted son of a whore!"

"An American son of a whore," he corrected, a sneer in his voice, "which is better than being king of your precious England!"

With a toss of her black hair and a swirling of cotton skirts and petticoats, Rebecca stormed off, leaving Beau to stare after her.

He watched her go, his certainty of her guilt shaken by her anger. But then, he told himself, leaving the well and returning to his fellow prisoners, she was a consummate actress. Hadn't she played the part of the lonely widow to perfection when she'd come to the island as a spy? Why should he believe that her current guise, that of a woman in love, was anything more than merely another act in her play? He wasn't sure what game it was she was playing now and the doubts that nibbled at the corners of his mind bothered him more than he cared to admit. But whatever her game might be he wanted no part of it.

Trembling, fighting back tears of anger and frustration, Rebecca returned to the infirmary. Most of the wounded prisoners had been treated, then sent to join their countrymen. Only a few remained and they seemed to be asleep.

Trying to drive the scene at the well out of her mind, Rebecca busied herself tidying the infirmary. She noticed as she was straightening Dr. Mitchell's instruments, that one of his scalpels, a long, lethal piece of equipment, was missing.

Rebecca looked around, stooping to check under the table and the nearby furniture. It could have been knocked on the floor, she supposed, but surely someone would have heard it striking the wooden floor. Or it might have fallen onto a pile of soiled linen and that would have muffled the sound. But if that were the case, she would have to search through the linen to find it. She wrinkled her nose, thinking of the piles of old bandages waiting to be buried and the mounds of dirty bedding waiting to be washed. The thought of sorting through it all was not an appealing one. Perhaps she would wait for Dr. Mitchell. There was always the chance that he had accidentally taken the instrument with him when he'd left the infirmary. If he had it, or knew where it was, that would save her the unappetizing task of rooting through unwashed laundry and old bandages to find it.

She circled the infirmary, checking on the patients, pulling up a blanket here, checking a forehead there. She came to Anthony Hawkins who lay on his back, his face composed. The fever that had wracked his body in the early days after his wound was gone. The bandages that had swathed his head had been reduced to a single strip covering his missing eye. The angry, puckered red of the wound had faded to a bright pink; but to a man who had once been as handsome as he, the change in his looks would be a difficult thing to accept.

Going to his bedside, Rebecca bent over and laid a hand on his forehead. It was cool and dry, a good sign. The whiskey that had been given to him to dull the pain of his wounds was no longer doled out in hefty amounts. He had been quiet, sleeping most of the time, and steadily improving. Dr. Mitchell said he might be released in time to return to Detroit when the prisoners from the two captured ships were sent back.

As Rebecca straightened Anthony's bedding, his remaining eye opened. He stared at her, a savage glitter in his eye, and his hand moved beneath the blanket.

"English whore!" he hissed. "You're to blame for the deaths of many good men! And you're going to pay for it!"

With a speed she would not have thought him capable of, Anthony whipped his hand from beneath the blanket. Rebecca saw the dangerous glitter of the scalpel in his hand as it arched toward her, but surprise slowed her reaction. Though she moved away, the blade of the knife tore through her dress just above her left breast. She felt it bite into her skin, saw the quick, warm flow of red blood.

Screaming, she stumbled back. Her hand, pressed to her torn flesh, was wet with the blood that oozed between her fingers and soaked into the cuff of her sleeve.

Anthony pushed back the blanket and rose
from the bed, the bloodied scalpel still clasped
in his hand. He moved toward Rebecca like a
black panther stalking its prey.

Feeling waves of giddyness stealing over her,
Rebecca staggered back toward the door. As
Anthony lunged toward her, the scalpel slashing
the air scarcely a foot from her face, Rebecca
screamed again.

This time her screams brought a pair of soldiers on the run. They overpowered Anthony
and disarmed him, but by then Rebecca had
slumped to the floor, fainting from the shock of
Anthony's attack and the pain of her wound.

Chapter Twenty-Three

The shouts of the two soldiers restraining Anthony Hawkins brought more men. Dragging a still ranting Anthony with them, three soldiers bore him out of the infirmary and toward the guardhouse where he could be locked in the single, windowless cell there.

"Go and find Dr. Mitchell!" one of the soldiers in the infirmary commanded the others who crowded around him as he knelt beside Rebecca. He looked at a private kneeling nearby. "I hope he hasn't gone down to the village. She's bleeding fast."

"What should we do?" the private asked. Mrs. Carlyle had bandaged all their wounds, nursed them through influenza and dysentery. And now she lay here, her lifeblood pooling about her, and they felt helpless to save her.

Sandra DuBay

Mercifully, Dr. Mitchell was in the fort. He appeared in the infirmary doorway and froze, gaping at the scene before him.

"Sweet heaven!" he breathed. "What in hell happened here!"

"One of the patients, the one-eyed American, attacked her with a knife," the soldier at Rebecca's side told him. "Please, Doctor, she's bleeding something terrible!"

"Everyone out!" the doctor commanded, "except you, Kelton, and you, Sims. Sims, fetch me bandages from that cabinet."

When the private had complied, Dr. Mitchell packed the slashed flesh as best he could. The bleeding was staunched for the moment and he ordered, "Pick her up, Kelton, take her to Lieutenant Meade's quarters. She can't stay here with all these American prisoners. I'll bring what I need to stitch the wound."

As gingerly as he could, Sergeant Kelton gathered Rebecca into his arms. Her skin felt cold, clammy against his arm as he touched her cheek; her body was limp as he raised her off the floor. She was pale, too pale, and he wondered if he had waited too long before sending someone for the doctor.

The commotion in the infirmary had attracted the attention of the men, both American and British, who had been on the parade ground. A collective gasp rose from them as Sergeant Kelton appeared with Rebecca in his arms.

"Stand back there!" a British sentry ordered as Beau attempted to approach the path that led from the infirmary to the officers' quarters. "I said stand back!"

"Keep him away!" Sumner called, appearing in the doorway of the officers' quarters. "Get back, McAllister! Or do you mean to finish what your friend began?"

"What are you talking about?" Beau demanded, trying to push his way past a line of British soldiers. "What happened to her?"

Striding up to the line of sentries, Sumner snarled at Beau, "Your friend, Hawkins, tried to kill her! He stabbed her with one of the doctor's instruments."

"Good God, no!" Beau groaned, paling beneath the sun-kissed tan of his face. "Will she live?"

"What do you care?" Sumner sneered. "If she does, do you mean to try again?"

"Damn you!" Beau growled, launching himself at the wall of sentries that separated him from Sumner. "You'll pay for that!"

"Come on, then!" Sumner taunted. "How will you make me pay, you bloody bastard?"

Beau reached past the sentries, struggling, trying to reach Sumner who stood just out of his reach. With the encouragement of his own countrymen urging him on and the jeers of the British soldiers nearly drowning them out, it took several attempts before Lieutenant Colonel McDouall managed to get Sumner's attention.

"Mr. Meade!" he boomed, his face nearly as red as his scarlet coat.

"Sir!" Sumner whirled to face his commanding officer and snapped to attention.

"You'd better clear some of your belongings out of your quarters. Mrs. Carlyle is going to be there for some time."

"Aye, sir," Sumner agreed. With a last smirking glance at Beau, he strode off toward the officers' quarters.

Meanwhile, Rebecca lay on Sumner's bed. Dr. Mitchell had peeled away the blood-soaked bodice of her gown and chemise. After cleaning the wound, he was relieved to see that it was not as deep as he'd thought. It was serious enough—a long, ragged slash—but not as life-threatening as he'd feared.

Sumner appeared in the doorway of the small bedroom. He stopped and gaped, shocked by the ugly red line of stitches that marred the creamy flesh of Rebecca's shoulder and ran down to the upper curve of her breast.

Dr. Mitchell glanced over his shoulder. "Oh, it's you, Sumner. Have you a spare nightshirt we could put on her when I've finished?"

"Yes, Doctor," Sumner replied, going to the chest against the wall. From it he took a long white cotton nightshirt. "Will she be all right?" he asked, coming to the bedside.

"Barring infection. What was all the rumpus outside?"

"McAllister, one of the Americans, attacked me. The bastard. Of all the casualties of this benighted war, why couldn't he have been one of them?"

242

Rebecca stirred, her head tossing on the pillow. Her tongue darted out, moistening her dry lips. "Beau," she breathed, "Beau, help me . . ."

Sumner's face turned to stone, his eyes were like chips of ice. The doctor paused in his stitching and cast a glance toward him.

"McAllister?" he asked.

Sumner nodded silently and, laying the nightshirt down on the edge of the bed, turned away to begin his packing.

Finishing his stitching, Dr. Mitchell used a scalpel to slice through the cotton of her gown and chemise. Tossing the ruined fabric aside, he called to Sumner, "Will you help me get her into the nightshirt and into bed?"

Sumner turned back toward the bed. He stared, drawing a sharp breath. Rebecca's eyes were closed, her body pale and perfect, marred only by the fiery-red cut and the coarse black stitches holding its ragged edges together. Sumner swallowed hard, moved by her beauty; then a raging jealousy overtook him. He had never seen her creamy flesh, her exquisite beauty, while McAllister—that damned bastard— had seen her, touched her, loved her, given her a child.

The thought of her beautiful body nurturing that wretch's child made Sumner want to run his sword through McAllister and watch the lifeblood run out of him to stain the ground.

"Sumner?" Dr. Mitchell prompted, smiling gently, not realizing the fury raging inside

243

Sumner. "I know she's very lovely but we must get her into bed."

"Of course," Sumner agreed, grateful that the doctor had mistaken the reason for his inattention.

As gently as they could, Sumner and Dr. Mitchell pulled the cotton nightshirt over Rebecca's legs and hips. They guided her arms into the too-long sleeves and eased it up and over her injured shoulder.

"There now," Dr. Mitchell said, buttoning it almost but not quite up to the pristine white bandage.

The doctor tucked the blanket around Rebecca's waist, then stood away from the bed. "She should sleep now," he said. "She's lost a lot of blood and the shock of the wound will make her sleep. When she wakes up, she'll be in a lot of pain." He clapped Sumner on the shoulder as he prepared to leave the room. "She is going to need a great deal of care, my boy. She's going to be scarred and that will be difficult to accept. She'll need your reassurance that she is still a beautiful, desirable woman."

"My reassurance?" Sumner asked bitterly. "Perhaps we should bring McAllister in here to reassure her."

"Now, don't despair. McAllister is an enemy. Rebecca was only playacting with him to convince him to give her the information the regiment needed."

Sumner wanted to believe it was true. He reminded himself that the child she'd lost—

McAllister's child—had been the product of rape, not love.

"Perhaps you're right," Sumner admitted. "I'm letting my jealousy get the better of me. I hate the thought of the time she spent with . . ."

"It's over now," Dr. Mitchell counseled. "And by the time Rebecca is ready to return to her own home, the prisoners will have been sent back to Detroit. McAllister will be gone and you'll have her all to yourself."

Sumner picked up his bundle and followed the doctor out of the bedroom. He could share the quarters of another officer until Rebecca felt well enough to return home. Until then, he'd feel better knowing she was sequestered in the officers' quarters, in the very heart of the fort, safe from McAllister. Though the American prisoners were free to roam the parade ground so long as they kept well away from the powder magazine, there was no way that any of them could venture into the officers' quarters.

Sumner glanced once more through the bedroom doorway before leaving. Rebecca lay still, her black lashes like sooty fans on her cheeks.

"Rest well," he said softly, "heal quickly but not before we manage to ship those damned Americans back to their own country!"

With careful nursing by Dr. Mitchell and daily attention from Sumner, Rebecca mended rapidly. Her wound healed cleanly with no infection and no fever. She was left with a long, jagged red line to mark the path the scalpel's blade had taken through her flesh.

"I'm not an invalid," she protested to Sumner one afternoon when he brought her dinner from the officers' mess.

"I know you're not," he said, setting the food down before her on the table in his small sitting room. "Can't you let me spoil you a little? After all I—we came near to losing you."

Rebecca shuddered. "I can't bear to think of that day. I see it at night in my dreams— the flash of that blade, the pain, the blood, Anthony's face . . ."

"Try not to think of it," Sumner soothed. "Come, eat something."

"I'm going to ask Dr. Mitchell when I can go home," she said as she buttered a piece of bread.

"What again?" Sumner teased. "Don't you ask him that every time he comes to visit you?"

"Nearly every time. And every time I do, he says the same thing. Soon."

"Well, he's the doctor. He knows best."

Sumner watched her as she ate. It was he who had convinced Dr. Mitchell to keep Rebecca here as long as possible. The return of the American prisoners was being negotiated and Sumner wanted Rebecca kept safely in his quarters until Beau McAllister was away from Mackinac Island. He'd explained to Dr. Mitchell about Beau's rape of Rebecca and had convinced him the wretch was likely to try it again.

And so the two men had conspired to keep Rebecca safe in Sumner's quarters and they hoped that by the time she felt well enough to demand to go home, Beau McAllister would be far, far away.

Chapter Twenty-Four

July 1815

Rebecca was packing. Carefully, tenderly, she wrapped a quilt around William's portrait and laid it in the bottom of one of the trunks she'd retrieved from the attic.

The war was over. The previous December the Treaty of Ghent had been signed in Ghent, Belgium, much to the disgust of Lieutenant Colonel McDouall and many others who still believed the Americans could be beaten with time and proper provisioning.

But the aspect of the peace treaty that had infuriated the fort's commander was the clause that stated that all territories conquered during the war must be returned to their respective nations. And that, of course, meant that

Mackinac Island and the fort must be handed over to the Americans.

"Our negotiators," he had commented over dinner in his quarters one night not long after the news arrived, "have been egregiously duped."

He made no secret of what he thought of the notion of handing over the most important stronghold on the Great Lakes, but there was nothing he could do. He had his orders and preparations for the departure of the British garrison had begun without delay.

It had been thought at first that they might return to St. Joseph Island, even though that fort was little more than ruins after having been first abandoned by the British, then burned by the Americans. But instead of rebuilding on St. Joseph Island, a new site was chosen—Drummond Island at the Detour Passage, a more strategic site. And a new fort, Fort Collier, had been started there.

When the news had come about the war's end, Rebecca had begun to ponder her future. She could not stay on Mackinac Island after the Americans returned. Though the war was over, there might be those who would try to punish her for aiding the British in taking the island. On the other hand, she did not know how many passenger ships were traveling as yet between England and America. It might be difficult for several more months to secure passage on a schooner bound for London.

So, she supposed she might as well go on

to Fort Collier with the garrison. At least she would be among friends until the opportunity arose to travel to some eastern seaport and book passage home.

Pausing in her packing, Rebecca sat down and looked around the nearly empty cottage that had been her home for three years. She'd miss it, even though she'd spent some of the worst nights and days of her life here. She'd also passed some of the best nights here.

She thought back to those first days when she'd come to this island to spy. Beau had courted her sweetly, gently. What, she wondered, might have happened had she not been exposed as a British spy? If she had merely been a widow alone, it was not impossible that she and Beau might have been married. And there would have been a child, perhaps two.

The memory of the child she'd lost brought a glimmering tear to her eye. Beau's child. What wouldn't she give right now to be taking away a little golden-haired replica of him with her to Fort Collier?

As Sumner and Dr. Mitchell had planned, the American prisoners had been gone by the time they'd allowed her to leave Sumner's quarters. She'd been furious when she'd discovered they'd conspired together to keep her immured where Beau could not get to her. At least they had not underestimated Beau's daring. A pair of guards had flanked her door day and night lest Beau proved bold enough to try and come to her in the officers' barracks.

After returning to her home, she'd refused to speak to Sumner. When she did finally admit him, they'd fought over his "protection" of her. He did not understand how she could have any feelings save hatred for Beau. She smiled to herself. He simply could not comprehend that underlying their differences, the arguments, the quarrels, was a passion that could not be denied however much she might like to.

The winter that had followed had been long, cold, and lonely. She'd relented and Sumner had become a frequent visitor to her cottage. But she did not allow him to be her lover. She might be lonely, she might long to feel arms about her, hands caressing her skin, a man's strong body against her own, but it was Beau's arms, Beau's hands, and Beau's body she wanted and no other's.

Sumner had left more than a month before. He'd been sent to Drummond Island by Lieutenant Colonel McDouall to begin work on the new fort. The date chosen for the returning of the island to the Americans was July eighteenth and it was essential that the garrison have someplace to go when they left.

Sighing, she returned to her packing. The future stretched ahead of her, a long, empty, lonely parade of years. She knew that, despite what had happened between Beau and herself, Sumner was still in love with her and would marry her if she would agree. But she knew it was impossible. She had married William for love and when he'd died she'd thought never to love again. But then Beau had come into her life. Miraculously, she had found a deeper love, a more fiery passion, than she'd known even with William. It had been a tumultuous love, fraught with tension and tears, but after knowing what love could be, she could never settle for a comfortable, safe, boring existence with a man she did not love.

She looked up from her half-filled trunk, hearing footsteps approaching on the path outside. Not waiting for the knock, she opened the door.

Sumner stood there and Rebecca stepped back to let him enter.

"I was just thinking of you," she said, stooping to lay a folded blanket into the chest.

Sumner smiled, pleased. "Were you? I just got back from Drummond Island."

"What is it like there?" she asked.

"Much like Mackinac Island or St. Joseph Island," he answered. "Heavily wooded with different kinds of pines and hardwoods. There is a good harbor. That's where we've begun the fort."

"How is it coming?" Rebecca continued with her packing. She didn't really care about the new fort but she knew Sumner would want to tell her about it.

"We've built quarters for Commander McDouall and barracks for the men. A common mess. We've begun lookouts and placed the cannons we took with us. It's a good beginning."

"That's good, Sumner," she commented

obligingly. "I'm sure your commander will be pleased."

"I've found a place for you," he offered, frustrated as always by her lack of response to him.

"I'm glad. I knew I couldn't stay here."

Sumner was secretly relieved. He'd been afraid she might want to remain behind in the hopes that Beau McAllister might be posted back to the fort where he'd been at the start of the war.

"There are several small islands in the harbor at Drummond Island. On the one nearest the main island there is a small trapper's cabin. It's not as large as this, of course, but it's in good repair. I set the men to fixing the chimney and repairing the chinks between the logs."

"It's very kind of you, Sumner," she told him sincerely. "I do appreciate it. Truly, I do."

Feeling guilty, Rebecca turned away. She knew Sumner found hope in the fact that she was accompanying the garrison to Drummond. She knew she should tell him that she meant to stay there only long enough for shipping to be restored between England and America. She knew he meant to see the garrison safely housed and then he would begin offering to build a house—a house for her to live in with the hopes that eventually she would allow him to share it with her.

But somehow she could not find the words to tell him now. She went on packing, listening with half an ear to his extolling the virtues of the island to the east. She cursed herself for a coward for not telling him the truth, for not nipping these vain hopes of his in the bud. But she said nothing. He would be disabused of these notions soon enough and she was afraid that their final parting, when it came, would be a bitter one.

The Americans began arriving on the fifteenth of July, and made camp where the ground leveled off near the lakeshore below the fort. Their presence was like a constant stabbing to the British commander, who prowled the terrace of the officers' quarters, cursing again and again the negotiators who had made this day possible.

Against his will, he met with the American commander, Colonel Anthony Butler, and came to an agreement as to the day when the fort would pass from British hands to the Americans. But when the day arrived, he blustered and cursed and could hardly force himself to carry out his duties.

The garrison boarded the ships that would take them the forty miles to their new home. As they raised their white sails and watched them snap taut in the warm summer wind, the men crowded the rails for a last glimpse of what had been their home for three years and a day.

Rebecca was one of a handful of women going with the garrison. They were, all of them, facing difficulties, the chiefest being a lack of housing and necessities, but the women agreed they would rather face the deprivation of the new fort rather than remain behind while their men left. Most, like Rebecca, were uncertain of how they might fare if they remained behind on Mackinac Island. Like her, they did not know what treatment they might expect from the Americans. Unlike them, however, Rebecca had been a spy, had been instrumental in the loss of the fort to begin with. And so she knew it might not merely be uncomfortable for her to remain behind. It might well be dangerous.

She stood at the railing of one of the ships, watching the island diminish in size, watching the buildings blur and grow indistinct until she could no longer pick out her own cottage among the others on the street.

The fort seemed to glow starkly white in the summer sunshine. Above it on the heights stood Fort George—now to be renamed Fort Holmes in honor of a young American officer, Major Andrew Hunter Holmes, who had fallen during the abortive attack on the fort during the war.

"Here comes some more of the bastards!" a young private muttered as a ship approached going in the direction of the fort.

All heads turned toward the schooner flying the stars and stripes that was bearing down on them. The two ships passed close together and the British and American soldiers jeered at one another.

Rebecca, her black curls tickling her cheeks as they blew in the wind, scanned the men on deck. Her heart seemed to stop in her chest as she found herself gazing into the icy sapphire eyes she'd seen too often in her dreams.

"Beau," she whispered, involuntarily lifting a hand toward him. "Beau . . ."

He stared at her across the strip of water separating the two ships. But no glimmer of tenderness showed in his face, no sign of affection, no hint of love or passion.

As the ships passed, Rebecca pressed her fingers to her lips. If only he'd arrived sooner. If only they'd had a moment of privacy, perhaps she would have stayed. Now that the war was over, they might have worked out their differences. She would have stayed on the island had she known he would be there. Surely he could have protected her against any hostility against her.

But would he? He had stared at her with not so much as a trace of a smile. Why? Why?

Heartsore, she did not realize that Sumner stood behind her. She had not seen the look of triumph on his face when he'd exchanged stares with Beau McAllister. She had not realized how they'd looked standing there together with Sumner's arm nearly around her waist as he leaned on the railing. All she knew was that Beau had seen her, and rejected her.

Chapter Twenty-Five

Rebecca settled into her little cabin on her own speck of an island in Collier's Harbor. Across a narrow strip of water the new British outpost, Fort Collier, was growing on the shore of Drummond Island.

The cabin, as Sumner had told her, was much smaller than her home on St. Joseph Island and her cottage on Mackinac Island. It was really just one large room. One end was nearly taken up with a gaping stone fireplace. The windows had shutters which were all that stood between her and the outdoors. Rebecca knew that once winter set in no fire would banish the icy drafts blowing through those rough-hewn shutters. The floor was of hard-packed earth that she imagined would be torture once the ground froze.

Still, she comforted herself with the fact that she had a place to herself. The other women who had accompanied the garrison complained continually of the lack of privacy, of the primitive conditions and cramped quarters that existed at the new fort.

And, she told herself repeatedly, she would not be here so very long. Before the winter came, bringing hardships and illness and deprivation, she expected to be on her way east, perhaps even aboard a ship bound for England.

She had still not told Sumner of her plan. The weeks since they'd arrived had been busy ones and though he visited her frequently—and often, to her annoyance, late at night after she'd gone to bed—the moment had never seemed right to tell him she planned to leave.

But she would, she vowed, as she tidied her small cabin before retiring. The next time she saw him she would tell him of her plan. Better that than simply running away on the first schooner that passed by.

Blowing out her candle, she climbed into the creaky rope bed tucked into the corner at the opposite end from the fireplace. The wind whispered in the trees. The water rolled rhythmically against the rocky shore. Occasionally, she heard animals but Sumner had assured her that, apart from the occasional coyote, there were not many dangerous animals to worry about. Whether that was true or simply meant to assuage her fears of being alone here so far from everyone else, Rebecca did not know. But it didn't matter. With her doors and shutters closed, she felt safe from anything that might be crawling, flying, or slinking through the forest outside.

Lying in her bed, Rebecca thought of Beau. He was back on Mackinac Island, no doubt settling easily into the routine he had known before the war. Did he think of her? Did he miss her? How she longed to be with him. She could go back there, of course. The war was over, and though hostilities between the two countries remained, there was nothing really to prevent her returning to Mackinac.

It was possible, of course, that there would be those who would remember her part in the British capture of the fort and who might resent her and try to make trouble. But when she weighed that possibility against the thought of being with Beau again, the risk seemed very small.

But would Beau welcome her back? She could not help seeing his face again as she'd seen it when the two ships had passed one another on the day the British had returned the fort to the Americans. There had been no hint of tenderness, no sign of affection much less love. The thought of risking her freedom by returning to the now-American outpost only to find that Beau wanted nothing to do with her was a daunting one. Though she felt cowardly, she could not bring herself to risk the disillusionment, the humiliation of returning only to face rejection.

Rebecca yawned but the yawn was stifled. She'd heard a rustling outside, the snapping of a twig. An animal, she told herself, perhaps a deer or a fox. But then. . . .

Sitting up, she listened in the darkness. Were those footsteps? She was sure they were. Sighing, she rolled her eyes. Sumner. Why did he think he could come to her door at any hour of the day or night? Didn't he understand that she didn't like being awoken, dragged out of bed to listen to him go on and on with the plans for building the fort? She was really going to have to put a stop to it.

As she'd expected, she heard the muffled rapping at the door. Angry, determined to give Sumner a piece of her mind, Rebecca pushed back the blanket and climbed out of bed. Without bothering to light her candle, she went to the door and pulled it open.

"Sumner," she said sternly, "you simply must stop—"

She froze, a shudder of purest horror running through her. Standing there, bathed in the moonlight that filtered down through the trees, was not Sumner but Anthony Hawkins. A black patch covered his lost eye. He was dressed not in his uniform but in the rough cloth shirt and corduroy trousers of the *voyageur*.

Whirling away, Rebecca slammed the door and tried to lower the bar. But Anthony slammed his shoulder into it and the door flew open, knocking Rebecca sprawling to the earthen floor.

By Love Betrayed

Striding into the cabin, he closed and barred the door. He smirked as Rebecca pushed herself to her feet and rushed to one of the windows. She pushed open the shutters, intending to climb out the window, but a young, dark-haired man stood there.

"The cabin is surrounded," Anthony told her. "Close the shutter, Rebecca, you're not escaping me so easily."

Doing as she was told, Rebecca backed away from Anthony who had lit a candle and placed it on the table in the center of the room.

"Did you think I would let you go so easily?" he asked, taking pleasure in the naked terror he saw in her eyes.

"What do you want?" she managed, her voice hushed, caught in her throat.

"What do you imagine?" he asked. "I've come to take you back, of course."

"The war is over, Anthony," she reasoned. "Peace has been declared."

"Treason is treason," he told her. "You escaped justice but not forever. I'm going to take you back and see you pay for what you did."

"And if I refuse to go?"

Anthony laughed. "I hardly expected you to do otherwise. But I am prepared to see you bound and gagged and carried to the yawls we've beached on the far side of this poor excuse for an island."

Wrapping her arms around her, Rebecca shook her head. "You mean to see me die,

Anthony," she said wearily. "Why not just kill me and be done with it?"

"It's tempting," he admitted. "Very tempting. But, no, I mean you to have a trial, madam. I mean for justice to be done—and to see that it is. I mean for your death to serve as a warning to others like yourself."

"And you truly imagine your superiors will allow you to put a woman to death? Do you imagine Beau will allow—"

"Beau," Anthony mocked. "What your precious Beau will or will not 'allow' has nothing to do with it. He will, of course, be called upon to testify. He'll tell a pretty tale, I doubt not, and be a laughingstock when everyone hears how you duped him into giving you the information you needed. But in the end, you will be found guilty. And condemned."

"You believe your commander will order my death?" she asked.

"We are to have a new commander. Colonel Butler has gone. His replacement, Major Morgan, is said to be a man who brooks no treachery in his soldiers or civilians. He has been known to deal harshly with those who betray trust placed in them. I do not think your being a woman will weigh heavily with him. Not when placed against the evidence of your spying."

"And the officer left in charge until this Major Morgan arrives agreed to your coming to capture me?"

Anthony smirked. "I am the officer left in

charge. Your dear McAllister has gone with a squad of soldiers to escort Major Morgan to Mackinac. Until they return, the fort is all mine."

His eye glinted in the candlelight. "Now get dressed if you don't want to be taken back in your nightdress."

Rebecca laid a hand over the open neck of her nightdress. "Will you go outside while I change?" she asked. His sneering expression was her answer. "Will you at least turn around?"

Anthony sank into a chair, facing her, and casually crossed his legs. "Get dressed, Rebecca. I'm impatient to be away from this place."

Her face burning with embarrassment and humiliation, Rebecca struggled into her clothes, trying to dress as quickly as possible without revealing her body.

"Are you ready?" he asked as she laced her half-boots.

She retrieved a cloak from a chest against one wall, for she knew the night wind aboard ship would be cold. The miniature of Beau lay in a tiny compartment of the trunk and she slipped it into her pocket surreptitiously before turning to Anthony.

"I'm ready," she acquiesced, moving past him to the door.

Anthony drew a long hunting knife from a sheath at his hip. He laid the cold steel against Rebecca's throat.

"One sound from you," he said, his voice low and heavy with malice, "and I'll slit your throat. You may well be able to draw the attention of the sentries at the fort, but you'll be dead and we'll be gone long before they can get here."

Rebecca knew it was true. By the time the sentries reported hearing screams from this direction and by the time anyone was sent to investigate, she would be dead and Anthony and his men would be rowing out to their schooner, safe from their enemies.

"I won't scream," she said softly.

"Wise," he purred. "I mean for it to seem as if you are dead," he went on. "I don't want anyone investigating your disappearance."

"How do you plan to do that?" she asked as they left the cabin and started through the forest away from the fort on Drummond Island.

"You'll see," he promised.

With her arm clasped in his steely grip, Rebecca found herself half pulled, half dragged through the black forest with only the dappled moonlight to light their way. Several times she stumbled and was jerked to her feet and pushed onward. Branches slapped her face, bushes and brambles caught at her cloak and skirts, rocks and tree roots bruised her feet through the soles of her boots. But still they went on.

They emerged at last on the shore at the opposite side of the tiny island. A pair of small boats had been drawn up on the beach and Anthony shoved Rebecca into one, then helped as the boats were pushed out into the water.

The soldiers manned the oars and they were soon gliding over the inky water toward the schooner anchored well out from shore.

"Rebecca?" Anthony said, poking her through the folds of her cloak.

She turned toward him and he nodded toward the island.

"There is your answer. You will perish in a fire that will doubtless ravage that whole little speck of an island and, if we're lucky and the wind is right, might well burn down that pathetic excuse for a fort as well."

In the distance Rebecca could just make out her tiny cabin. Light glowed in the gaps of the shutters, far more light than her one candle could have accounted for. They had set it alight after Anthony had taken her out. It would burn and the surrounding forest with it. By the time the fire was out, there would be nothing left of her cabin and it would doubtless be assumed that she had perished in the fire and her remains lost in the charred wreckage of the cabin.

Tears glimmered in her eyes as she was pulled aboard the schooner. Sumner would assume she was dead. No investigation would be made into her disappearance. No one would know she'd been taken away against her will. The British would not protest her abduction. She could expect no help from her countrymen.

The best she could hope for, she realized as the schooner set sail for Mackinac, was that someone on Mackinac Island would come to her aid.

Beau, her heart whispered, *please, Beau, hurry back and save me from this monster!*

Chapter Twenty-Six

Her hands bound behind her back, Rebecca was led up the long ramp to the fort. She passed through the arched sally port, preceded and followed by guards, and was taken to the guardhouse just inside the gate.

The single cell in the guardhouse was about eight feet square. A door led into the second of the guardhouse's two rooms—the room where the guards remained. There was no window in Rebecca's cell. The only way in or out was through the guardroom. The cell door had a small window with iron bars, and the only light was what little that shone through.

A rough-hewn table and chair and a straw tick on the floor were the only furnishings. A bucket in the corner passed for a latrine.

It was clear from the moment she was pushed

Sandra DuBay

into the cell that Anthony had chosen Rebecca's guards from among those cronies loyal to him rather than to any commander likely to be sent to the fort from the south. They gave her no peace, jeering at her through the bars of her cell door, calling her names, accusing her of every crime known to man. They offered her their services if she were lonely, then abused her when she ignored them. They constantly watched her, making it impossible for her to find a moment's privacy for even her most intimate needs.

Nightly, as she lay on her straw tick, trying to sleep despite the grumbling and snoring of the guards outside her door, Rebecca prayed for Beau to hurry back to the fort. He had gone, so Anthony told her, to escort the new commander to the fort. What then was taking so long? Surely it wouldn't be much longer before he arrived. And when that day came, she was sure he could persuade the new commander to release her.

But he still had not appeared when she was brought out of her cell to be taken to Anthony's quarters for her "trial."

It was September, a cold, overcast day, but even so the daylight made her squint after so long in the comparative darkness of her cell.

She was taken to Anthony's quarters where he and four of his cronies sat behind a long table, prepared to decide her fate. Rebecca stood before them, her guards on either side of her as if they expected her to bolt from the

270

room and try to escape from the fortress.

"You are Mrs. Rebecca Carlyle," Anthony began, "a loyal subject of King George, the English tyrant?"

"A loyal subject of King George," Rebecca corrected, "a wise and benevolent king." She had, like everyone else, heard rumors that the king was mad and for that reason his son, the Prince of Wales, was to be Regent, but she would not swerve in her loyalties in front of her accusers.

Anthony's lip curled in a sneer. "Call him what you will, madam. You are accused of coming to this island with the purpose of gathering information that would help the enemy of the United States to invade and conquer this fort. Further, you are accused of subverting an officer of the First Artillery from his duty. Your actions resulted in the deaths of many American soldiers during their attempt to regain this island. You—"

"For God's sake, Anthony," Rebecca muttered, impatient with the farce he insisted on carrying out. "Be done with it!"

Anthony laid aside a paper presumably bearing the "charges" he'd leveled against her. "How do you plead to these charges, madam?"

"Would it matter how I pled?" she asked. "You've already decided my fate."

"You will enter a plea, madam," Anthony insisted, "or you will not leave this room."

"What a pity," she mocked. "You mean you would deny me a return to that elegant chamber you've allotted me? You mean you would deny these gentlemen"—she indicated the guards who flanked her—"the pleasure of spying on me while I sleep or eat or relieve myself?"

The other men who sat at the table with Anthony chuckled and he realized they were amused by her mocking of him. That she should make him look a fool even now, knowing she was facing almost certain death, infuriated him.

"How do you plea!" he roared, half rising from his chair.

Sighing, Rebecca shrugged. "Guilty, I suppose. It is true I came here to gather information to enable the British to capture this fort. There, is that what you wished to hear?"

Smiling, Anthony leaned back in his chair. "It will serve, madam, it will serve." He glanced at the men who sat to the right and left of him. "Gentlemen, you have heard the charges against this woman and you have heard her admit her guilt. She is a traitor to our country, she is responsible for the deaths of many of our friends and comrades. What is your sentence?"

One by one the men looked at Rebecca and in low, stern tones pronounced, "Death."

Pleased, Anthony smiled, the black patch that covered his lost eye making him seem more menacing.

"You have heard the will of this tribunal, madam. You will be put to death for your crimes at my pleasure."

"And doubtless it will be your pleasure," Rebecca snarled. "But tell me, Lieutenant, would you have been so eager to punish me for my 'treason' had I not rejected you for Beau McAllister?"

"That's enough!" Anthony growled. "Take her away!" he ordered.

Seized by her guards, Rebecca was taken back to the guardhouse and shoved into her cell. She stumbled, falling, skinning her palms on the rough boards of the floor.

In the darkness of her cell, she sat, her back to the wall, beside the door where her guards could not see her when they peered through the window. Her legs drawn up, she rested her forehead on her knees.

Death. She had been tried and sentenced to die. She half expected her guards to come in and drag her out to be shot, or hanged, or however Anthony decided to kill her. Surely he would want to put her to death quickly, before his new commander had time to arrive and perhaps overturn the sentence.

But a day passed, then two, and she heard nothing. No one entered her cell, no one gave a hint of what fate might be planned for her. Neither, however, did anyone come with food or even water for her.

By the evening of the second day, Rebecca's stomach growled. Her throat was dry, her lips cracked and parched. When she asked her guards for a drink of water or even of the grog they seemed to enjoy with such relish, they only

Sandra DuBay

laughed at her and went back to their endless gambling.

Slumped against the wall, Rebecca ran her tongue over her lips. Was it possible Anthony intended to starve her to death, or to leave her to die of thirst? Surely that would take too long.

She closed her eyes and listened to the rain thrumming on the roof of the guardhouse. If only she had a window to the outside, she could shove her arm between the bars and catch a few drops of the precious water to wet her lips, cool her face. As it was, she had to listen to the rain and imagine all that sweet cool water soaking into the ground, wasted.

She looked up as she heard the sudden scrambling of feet. Anthony's voice sounded unnaturally loud in the guardroom.

"You're all dismissed," he told them. "I'll call you back."

The guards filed out into the rainy night, and Rebecca rose as the lock on her cell door rattled. The door creaked and Anthony stepped inside. In one hand, he held a glass of clear, cold water.

Rebecca could not tear her eyes away from it. At that moment, it seemed the most tempting, the most appetizing thing she'd ever seen.

Anthony chuckled as he set it on the table in the opposite corner from where Rebecca stood. An evil grin split his dark-tanned face as he said, "I know you're hungry, Rebecca, and thirsty." He looked around the small, dank cell. "It's cold in here as well."

"All the comforts of home," Rebecca snapped. Her eyes strayed once more to the glass of water. "You surprise me, Anthony. I had thought perhaps, having sentenced me to die, you meant to leave me to starve or die of thirst."

"Not at all," he insisted. "But you must realize, madam, that your life is truly in my hands."

"I realize you mean to be my executioner, Anthony," she admitted. "You've made that clear. But why are you here?"

"I've come," he replied, his voice dropping to a low, intimate murmur, "to offer you mercy."

"Mercy?" Rebecca was taken aback. "What does that mean? You'll have me shot rather than starved? A quick death rather than a slow one?"

"Perhaps," he agreed. "Or perhaps I'll let you live."

Rebecca backed away but the wall of her cell was hard and unyielding behind her back. She felt she was being stalked by some cruel, pitiless animal who would give no quarter now that he was so near the kill. This was some ploy, some trick on Anthony's part, she was certain.

She cringed as his hand reached out and caressed her cheek. "I remember when you first came to this island, Rebecca," he said softly. "I had never seen a more beautiful woman. How jealous I was when you chose Beau over me."

"What did you expect?" she challenged. "You tried to rape me as I recall!"

"And Beau *did* rape you, didn't he? And after you nursed him so carefully. So what is the difference between us?"

"What happened with Beau was because of anger and betrayal. What you tried to do was because of animal lust."

"So, you can even excuse him that, can you? Well, I'm not so petty as to resent the past. I'm willing to let you make up for what's happened." His fingers toyed with her tangled curls and trailed down to her shoulder, her breast.

Shocked, Rebecca recoiled. "You're mad!" she cried. "You tried to kill me before. Now you've kidnapped me, brought me back here, dragged me before that farce of a trial, condemned me to death, denied me food and water, but now you offer me mercy if I'll lie with you?

"Let me tell you something, Anthony Hawkins. You disgust me, and I'd sooner die than lie with you!"

Dredging up the last bit of moisture in her mouth, she spat in his face.

Anthony's face flushed crimson, the jagged scar that ran from his forehead to chin turned scarlet. "You'll regret this," he snarled. "I promise you you'll regret this. You'll die, damn you, and you'll suffer until death is a welcome release!"

Backing away, he reached out and snatched up the glass of water from the table. Staring at her, he slowly, deliberately, poured the water out onto the floor and watched it soak into the boards.

"Guards!" he shouted, pushing open the door. "Guards! Come in here!"

The guards hurried back into the guardhouse and snapped to attention.

"Put her down below!" Anthony bellowed. And when they hesitated, he shouted, "Now, damn your eyes!"

Rebecca found herself dragged from her cell. Before her horrified eyes, a wooden trap door was pulled up in one corner of the guard room. Stone steps led downward and she found herself half dragged, half carried through a passage scarcely large enough to accommodate the soldier who held her arm.

A tiny chamber had been hewn out of the solid rock that formed the foundation for the fort. The walls were cold and damp, and an iron ring held a chain and manacle.

"Please," Rebecca whispered, already feeling the walls closing in on her. The ceiling was only a foot or so above her head as she sat on the floor. "Please, no!"

The soldier clamped the manacle about her ankle. He looked into her eyes for the briefest moment and she saw a surprising compassion there. But he could not help her and retreated to the room above.

"Lieutenant," one of the guards began, "is this necessary?"

"Are you questioning my authority?" Anthony demanded, his tone threatening.

"No, sir, but . . ."

"Close it!" he barked.

Unable to do other than obey, the soldiers lowered the trap door into the hole. There was no need to lock it; the chain of Rebecca's manacle would not allow her to reach it.

As Anthony turned and left the guardhouse, the guards exchanged a look. There wasn't a one of them who would not rather be shot than be confined in that limestone tomb.

Chapter Twenty-Seven

Upon reflection, Anthony had to question whether locking Rebecca in the tiny, tortuous cell had been a wise decision. True, he felt she deserved it and more. If he had had his way, he would have devised some even more diabolical way to put her to death, for in his mind she was responsible for more than merely the loss of the fort to the enemy. She was responsible for the deaths of the men who had died trying to regain possession of the island and also for the disfigurement he would carry with him the rest of his life.

Still, though the new commander, Major Morgan, was known to be a staunch patriot, a man who bore no love for the English and had no patience with those who would attempt to harm the country he loved, he might well think

Sandra DuBay

twice about inflicting such a harsh punishment on a woman, spy or not. He might disapprove and that would not bode well for Anthony's future prospects.

Anthony pondered his dilemma as he paced the ramparts. He had no eye for the beauty of nature laid before him. The blaze of red and gold and orange contrasted with the amazing blue of the water could not move him. He was too immersed in his own problems to notice the changing seasons or the magnificent autumn afternoon.

His eyes strayed to the guardhouse. She'd been down there for three days. Three days of thirst, of hunger, of damp and cold. Add to that the time she'd spent without food or water in the cell above and there seemed a good possibility that she was dead already.

Anthony's scarred face brightened. Perhaps that was the answer he sought. If she died before Major Morgan arrived, he could have her buried and only say in his report that a British spy lodged in the guardhouse had died. He smiled, oblivious to the sentries that saluted as they passed him. How much easier it was than his previous plan to have her executed. If he had her shot, as he'd planned to do, then Major Morgan might well want to know why he had not kept the spy in custody until his arrival. But if she died on her own. . . .

A new spring in his step, Anthony went to the guardhouse. The two guards snapped to attention as he entered.

280

"Have you heard anything from down there?" he asked, nodding toward the trap door.

The two privates exchanged a glance. "No, sir," the smaller one replied.

Anthony rocked back on his heels. "Well, then, as you were." Turning on his heel, he left the guardhouse, humming a gay ditty.

Perhaps, he told himself as he went to his quarters, he would check in the next day or two to be certain she was dead. And then, when he was sure she was, he would have her brought out and put into the cell above. There was no need for Major Morgan to know she'd ever been in the tiny lower cell, was there?

In the guardhouse, the two sentries looked at one another after their acting commander had left.

"I told you," the smaller man insisted, "he means for her to die down there."

"I don't like it," the larger of the two told his companion. "She might be a spy an' all, but she nursed me when I was wounded. She nursed everyone just the same, no matter what color his uniform. If she's to be executed for spying, then that's too bad, but I don't like seeing her starved like an animal."

"When Major Morgan gets here—" the smaller guard began.

"She'll be dead before then," the other guard interrupted. "She might be dead already."

The two guard looked at one another. There was a moment's hesitation. Neither had ever expressly disobeyed a command from a superior officer but both were of the opinion that Anthony Hawkins was a less than satisfactory commander and, moreover, that something had changed in him after he'd been savaged by the Indians on Round Island. He'd always been arrogant, conceited, sure his looks could gain him anything. Now, with his looks gone, his conceit had turned to cruelty. And his hatred of Rebecca Carlyle, the woman he blamed for all his troubles, was nothing less than maniacal.

"Let's go," the taller guard decided.

Dreading what they might find in the loathsome cell, they pulled up the trap door slowly, almost reluctantly.

"Is she dead?" the smaller one asked, trying to peer over his companion's shoulder.

"I can't tell. Go down and take a look."

Fearfully, the shorter guard stepped down the stone steps to the cell. Crouching, he peered in, unable to see much since his own body was blocking the light coming through the trap door hole.

A shapeless bundle lay on the stone floor. As the guard moved closer, it stirred. A fragile hand moved.

Rebecca turned her head slowly, painfully. Even the dim light filtering past the guard made her squint her eyes. Her tongue darted out but there was no moisture to wet her cracked and burning lips.

"Please," she whispered, "please, help me."

"She's alive," the guard whispered, more to himself than to the other man. He looked up into the anxious face above him. "She's alive!"

The larger guard got a dipper of water from the pail in the corner. His hand trembling, he passed it down to the guard crouched below.

On his hands and knees, the smaller guard moved over to Rebecca. Gently, he pushed the lank black hair out of her face. Her eyes, huge and darkly shadowed in her pale, gaunt face, gazed up at him as he held the dipper to her mouth.

"Try to drink a little," he told her.

Rebecca gulped at the water, feeling its cool wetness against her cracked lips, her dry tongue, her parched throat. She choked, coughing, but drained the dipper.

"Do you want more?" he asked.

She nodded her head and he passed the dipper up through the hole to be refilled. This time the other guard brought back the water and a piece of bread.

"Can you eat this?" the guard with Rebecca asked.

Eagerly, she chewed a bite of the bread but when she tried to swallow, she choked. The guard gave her the water and she managed to swallow it.

"Listen to me," he told her, suddenly afraid Anthony might come in and find them there. "Lieutenant Hawkins can't know about this. He's given orders that we, well, were supposed to . . ."

"To let me die," Rebecca finished for him.

"Yes," the guard confirmed. "So if he opens

the trap door and looks in here, don't move.
Don't make a sound."

"All right," she agreed. "When your new commander comes . . . Beau . . ."

"Lieutenant McAllister?" the guard asked.

Rebecca nodded. "Tell him I'm here. Please,
tell him."

"I will," the guard promised. "Now, we've
got to close the door again in case someone
comes. We'll bring you more water and more
bread when we can."

He moved away but Rebecca's hand on his
sleeve stopped him. Her amethyst eyes glittered
in the dark cell.

"Thank you," she whispered. "Thank you."

Nodding, the guard left the cell and climbed
the stone steps. Together the two men dropped
the trap door into place, leaving Rebecca in
darkness once more.

Another day passed, then two. With each sun-
rise Anthony was more confident, more certain,
that Rebecca could not have survived.

Happy, satisfied, he left the fort and went to
the village to the home of a very pretty young
woman who, if she did not love him, was
frightened enough of his cruelty and temper
not to refuse him when he came knocking on
her door.

Three hours later Anthony climbed the ramp
to the fort. He felt invigorated, inordinately
pleased with himself and the world around

him. So pleased, in fact, that he did not notice that a new ship was anchored in the harbor, that several new faces were to be seen inside the fort.

He cast a sidelong glance toward the guardhouse as he passed through the sally port. Under that floor, in her tomb of limestone, Rebecca Carlyle had paid with her life for her treachery. She had paid for the loss of this fine fort by the Americans and she had paid for the ruination of his life. He touched the jagged scar that creased his cheek and cursed Rebecca's soul to hell. If there was anything he regretted, it was that she hadn't suffered more.

Going to the officers' quarters, he was about to enter his rooms when a private approached him.

"What is it, soldier?" Anthony demanded.

"Major Morgan, sir. He wants to see you."

Anthony's face paled. "He's here?"

"He is, sir. Got here an hour ago."

Anthony's mind raced. He could send this soldier with orders to have Rebecca taken from the hole. That way, if Major Morgan asked. . . .

"Sir?" the soldier prompted. "I'm to bring you to him immediately."

Anthony knew he didn't dare refuse. Following the soldier to his new commander's rooms, Anthony could only hope Major Morgan took as dim a view of espionage as he did.

Chapter Twenty-Eight

Major Willoughby Morgan sat at his desk in the commander's quarters, reading a report he had found upon his arrival. It was a report, written the day before, by the officer left in charge of the fort until his arrival—one Lieutenant Anthony Hawkins.

According to the report, a spy was under guard, a British spy who had attacked Lieutenant Hawkins.

"Come," the major replied to the knock at the door.

"Lieutenant Hawkins, sir," the soldier announced, stepping back for Anthony to enter.

"Come in, Lieutenant, come in. I was just reading your report."

Anthony entered the room and heard the door being closed behind him. He took the chair the major indicated with a wave of his hand.

"I hope you found the fort in satisfactory order, sir," Anthony told him. "I've left the reports on provisioning, duty rosters, the arsenal, on your desk. If you have any questions . . ."

"They look fine, Lieutenant," the major replied. "If I have any questions when I've looked them over more carefully, you may rest assured I shall ask. It's this report that intrigues me. A spy, you say?"

"A spy, sir," Anthony confirmed. "Before the war, when the British were still at Fort St. Joseph, they sent an agent here to Mackinac to gather information. This agent gained the confidence of certain officers, pretended friendship with them, and duped them into providing the information the British needed. It was directly due to this agent's actions that the British were able to take the fort so easily. In addition, I believe this agent played a part in the failure of the American action against the British later in the war. I hold this person directly accountable for the deaths of those men."

"He sounds a dangerous man," Major Morgan said, automatically assuming the spy was male. "And he is still in custody?"

Anthony knew that this was the moment to tell the major exactly where the spy was and why. "I have ordered the spy put into the hole, Major."

"The hole? What might that be?"

"It is a cell, sir, cut into the limestone, beneath the guardhouse. It's where we put prisoners considered dangerous."

"Dangerous, Lieutenant?"

Anthony gestured toward the report. "As you can see there, sir, the person in question became violent. I was questioning the spy in the guardhouse and I was attacked. I had no choice."

Major Morgan leaned back in his chair. "Tell me, from the beginning, how you managed to get this person here. Surely he did not return to the island of his own volition."

"No, sir," Anthony admitted. "When the British left the island, the spy went with them. They settled, as you know, on Drummond Island. I led a raid there to return the spy to Mackinac."

"How long has he been in the hole, Lieutenant?" the major asked.

"Five days, sir," Anthony replied.

"Well, then, if he's still alive, he should be brought out and his case presented. If all that you say is true, he richly deserves to be punished for his crimes."

"Should I—" Anthony began.

A knock at the door interrupted him.

"Come," Major Morgan called. The door opened and Beau appeared. "Ah, McAllister, come in. You know Lieutenant Hawkins, of course."

"Of course," Beau agreed. "Anthony."

"What do you know, McAllister, about this spy who's been causing so much trouble here?"

289

Sandra DuBay

"Spy, Major?" Beau asked, his heart beating a little faster. "What spy?"

"Lieutenant Hawkins says there was a British spy here before the war. According to his report, this spy was directly responsible for the American loss of this outpost."

Beau knew it was useless to try to conceal the truth. The major would have to know eventually and it would look bad if he had been less than honest.

"It's true," he admitted. "She was sent here by the commander of Fort St. Joseph. She gathered the information the British needed by . . . by ingratiating herself with the soldiers at the fort. I . . ." he hesitated, unsure how to phrase his words. "I was close to her myself."

" 'She,' Lieutenant. 'Her?' " The major looked at Anthony, then back at Beau.

"Yes, sir," Beau confirmed. "Her name is Rebecca Carlyle. She is a widow. Her husband was William Carlyle, a British captain."

Major Morgan's ruddy face was the picture of puzzlement. He turned to Anthony. "Do you mean to tell me, Hawkins, that you've got a woman down there?"

Beau gaped at his new commander. "She's here?" he asked. "Rebecca's here?"

"Lieutenant Hawkins led a raid on Drummond Island," the commanding officer told him. "He brought this woman back here. Apparently she's been confined in the hole."

"The hole . . ." Beau's tanned face turned pasty-white. He turned toward Anthony. "You

290

put her down there? You bastard!"

Oblivious to his commander's presence, Beau launched himself at Anthony. Their bodies fell to the floor with a thunderous impact and Beau, nearly blind with fury, pummeled Anthony, his face mottled with murderous rage.

"McAllister!" Major Morgan shouted, shocked by the sight of two of his officers grappling on the floor. "McAllister, stop it! You're killing him!"

"I intend to," Beau growled, his hands at Anthony's throat.

"Guards!" the major shouted. "Guards!" The room was filled with soldiers a moment later. "Get him off!"

Beau struggled as a dozen hands pulled him off Anthony, who lay on the floor, gasping, his fingers tearing at the throat of his uniform, trying desperately to get air into his lungs. Wheezing, panting, he half sat up and pointed a shaking finger in Beau's direction.

"He was her lover!" he accused. "He was the one who gave her the information! He was in league with that British bitch!"

"Enough!" Major Morgan shouted. "I won't have my officers brawling on the floor like hooligans! Hawkins, go to the infirmary and let the doctor look you over. McAllister, go to the guardhouse and see if this woman, Carlyle, is still alive."

"She can't be alive," Anthony crowed as Beau strode out the door. "She's been down there five days without food or water!"

Sandra DuBay

Beau lunged at Anthony, but the soldiers kept the two men apart. "If she's dead," Beau told him under his breath, "you won't live to see the morning."

"Go to the guardhouse, McAllister," Major Morgan said. "And don't let me hear any more of these threats. If the woman is dead, Lieutenant Hawkins will have quite a few questions to answer."

Beau hurried away, ignoring Anthony who headed toward the infirmary in the opposite direction. As he went, Beau hoped against hope that Rebecca was still alive. But if what Anthony had said was true that Rebecca had been down in that hellhole without food or water for five days, then there seemed little chance that he would find her alive.

The sentries snapped to attention as Beau entered. Ignoring them, he went to the trap door and flung it open.

"Lieutenant?" one of the sentries began.

"The key," Beau said sharply, knowing there was a manacle in the hole and not doubting for a moment that Anthony would have used it. "Give me the key, damn you!"

The guard fumbled in his pocket and pulled out the heavy iron key. He handed it to Beau, then exchanged a look with his fellow guard as Beau took it and disappeared down the stone steps.

The tiny cell was dark, damp, and filthy. Beau was sickened by what he could see of Rebecca. Her cotton gown hung like a rag over her emaciated body. Her hair was lank, stringy, lying in lifeless tangles over her face and over the stone floor of the cell.

Beau groped under her skirt and found her leg. Following it down, he found the cold iron manacle clamped about her ankle, its sharp edges cutting into the soft flesh.

His hand trembling, Beau unlocked the manacle and pulled it off her ankle. It clanked against the limestone wall as he threw it away and gathered Rebecca into his arms.

Struggling, he pulled her out of the cell and up the shallow steps. The two sentries hovered close, trying to see her.

"We gave her water, sir," the shorter of the two men offered. "And bread, even though Lieutenant Hawkins said not to."

"When was the last time?" Beau asked, holding Rebecca's limp body in his arms.

"Yesterday," the larger sentry replied. "Yesterday afternoon. She's not . . ." he hesitated, not able to bring himself to ask the question.

But it didn't matter by then because Beau was already out the door, carrying Rebecca in the direction of the infirmary.

"Good God!" Dr. Day cried as he saw Beau appear in the doorway, Rebecca slung limply across his arms. "What's happened?"

"Hawkins brought her back from Drummond," Beau told him. "He's had her locked in the hole for five days."

"My God! Bring her over here."

293

Beau lay Rebecca on one of the narrow beds and he and the doctor stripped off her gown and underclothes. Her body was thin, her skin ghastly pale and cold to the touch. Her ankle, where the manacle had bitten into her flesh, was raw, infected, swollen.

Dr. Day laid his head on her chest, then held her delicate wrist between thumb and forefinger. He looked at Beau and nodded.

"She's alive," he confirmed. "But just barely."

Pouring a basin of water, he handed Beau a cloth and took one himself. Between them, the two men bathed her, taking care with her injured ankle.

"Will she live?" Beau asked, holding his breath, fearing the doctor's reply.

Dr. Day's face was grave, his tone guarded. "I don't know, Beau. I'll do everything I can, but right now, I don't know."

Beau sat with Rebecca while the doctor treated her ankle. She seemed so fragile, so lifeless, it was hard to believe that a heartbeat and blood pulsed in that starved, translucent body.

He held her hand, limp and too cold, between his two as if he could warm her, make up for the torture she'd suffered in that tiny, dank hold.

With every fiber of his being, he willed her to live, and with every bit of his heart, his soul, he vowed that Anthony Hawkins would pay for this atrocity.

Chapter Twenty-Nine

Night was falling over the island. The infirmary, empty of patients but for Rebecca who lay unconscious in one of the narrow beds, was lit by a single candle burning on a table near her bed. She was alone; Beau and Dr. Day, having bathed her, bandaged her ankle, and dressed her in a clean cotton shirt Beau provided, had gone to the officers' mess to eat.

The soft creak of the door hinges broke the eerie silence of the infirmary as the door swung open. A figure in silhouette appeared, hesitated, and then entered. His footfalls thudded on the wood floor as he passed between the double row of empty beds. He had come, unable to resist, to gloat. He had seen Beau carry Rebecca's limp form from the guardhouse, had known that Dr. Day was working over her, then had seen both

Dr. Day and Beau leave, and had assumed they had lost their battle to save Rebecca's life.

He moved around the screen that shielded Rebecca's bed. The candlelight wavered, casting undulating shadows across her pale face. Her face was serene, still, her hands were folded peacefully just below her breasts.

Anthony gazed down at her. He felt triumphant, jubilant. His only regret was that she had not had to suffer the indignity of a trial and a public execution.

"Damn you!" he growled. "I hope you're burning in hell this moment! I hope you . . ."

His voice dwindled away, the color faded from his face, as Rebecca's fingers moved slightly, almost imperceptibly.

"It can't be," he whispered. "It's not possible! You were down there five days without food or water! You can't be alive!"

Rebecca's sooty lashes fluttered, her lips parted and a single word issued from them, borne on a sigh, "Beau?"

"No!" Anthony cried. "It can't be!"

Rebecca's eyelids lifted, her great amethyst eyes fixed on the pallid face above her. For a moment time seemed to stand still. Neither could quite believe what they were seeing. Rebecca's eyes darted around, searching frantically for someone, anyone, to protect her from this madman who had sworn to kill her.

There was no one; they were alone. Trembling, Rebecca pushed herself backward, trying to scramble away from Anthony. She scarcely felt the pain of her ankle as she tried to kick away the blankets that hampered her movements.

Anthony's surprise turned to astonishment, then rage. He reached toward her and Rebecca's terror found vent in one long, agonized scream.

Anthony tried to grab her, unsure of what he should do but determined to silence her. But it was too late. The door of the infirmary burst open and Beau appeared followed by Dr. Day.

"What the hell are you doing in here?" Beau demanded. "Haven't you done enough harm already?"

Anthony's face was grim and filled with loathing. "Apparently not," he snarled, "she's still alive!"

Beau lunged at him but Dr. Day stepped between them. "Leave it, Beau." His face was the picture of distaste as he turned to Anthony. "I think you'd be wise to leave, Lieutenant. Whatever this lady's politics or past, you've shocked your new commander enough by having her locked in the hole. Don't make me add another page to my report."

Anthony cast a disgusted glance toward Rebecca who cowered, trembling, in Beau's arms as he sat on the edge of the bed.

"Coddle her if you want to, Doctor," Anthony spat, "wear yourself out healing her. It won't matter. In the end she'll pay for her crimes with her life. It may be that mine was the more merciful way."

"Get out, Hawkins," Beau snarled. "And don't

let me find you in here again or you'll be the one needing a doctor!"

Anthony opened his mouth to speak but then, thinking the better of it, turned on his heel and strode out of the infirmary, letting the door slam behind him.

"He's going to come back," Beau told Dr. Day as they helped Rebecca settle into the bed. "He's not going to leave her alone."

Dr. Day frowned as he rewrapped the bandages on Rebecca's ankle where her squirming had disarranged them. "I'm afraid you're right. The moment he thinks she's alone, he's all too likely to return. The best thing would be to get her out of the fort."

"How could we do that?" Beau asked.

Dr. Day arranged the blankets around Rebecca. "Let me go talk to Major Morgan," he replied. "I'll see if there isn't something we can do to prevent scenes like this."

Beau stroked Rebecca's hair as the doctor left to go to the commander's quarters. She leaned away, evading his touch.

"What's wrong, sweetheart?" he asked softly, touching the pale, cool flesh of her cheek with his fingertips. "Is it Hawkins? I'll keep that bastard away from you if it's the last thing I do."

"No," Rebecca whispered, struggling in vain to stay awake. She turned her head to stop the caress of his hand against her face. He was here with her now. He seemed so caring, so concerned, but she remembered the long, cool stare that had passed between them when their ships had passed and the lonely days and nights that had followed with no word from him. What wouldn't she have given then for some sign of this care, this concern? Now that she was back it seemed he gave a damn, but when she was away? Out of sight, out of mind. That seemed to be Beau McAllister's motto.

"Rebecca," he prompted, not understanding her reaction to his touches or the troubled look in her eyes. "What is it? Can't you tell me?"

Sighing, Rebecca shook her head. She felt weak, helpless, she had no choice but to trust Beau to protect her from Anthony. But he needn't think that all was forgiven. He would give her an explanation for the silence that had followed her leaving; she would demand some reason. But not now. Closing her eyes, she fell into a deep sleep and did not even notice that Beau had taken her small, cold hand between his own two and lifted it to his lips.

Beau looked up as Dr. Day returned. "Well?" he prompted as the doctor came to Rebecca's bedside. "What did he say?"

Dr. Day nodded. "He gave his permission for her to be taken to my home. We can take her there tonight. His only stipulation is that a pair of guards be posted at the front and back doors day and night."

"He thinks that's necessary?" It seemed to Beau a bad sign.

"Apparently so," the doctor confirmed. "I'm

afraid that, despite his disapproval of the way Hawkins handled the matter, he's inclined to take this business of Rebecca's spying seriously. He's in no mood to take chances. He doesn't want her to disappear from the island."

"Well, at least he's agreed to our taking her away from the fort and Anthony Hawkins," Beau mused. "I suppose that's the best we can hope for for the present."

While Dr. Day packed the medicines and supplies he would need to treat Rebecca at home, Beau went about rounding up guards for duty at the doctor's home and a cart in which she could be lain for the short trip down the hill to the village. It was not going to be easy, he knew, to roll a cart down that long, steep incline, but it was far less dangerous than trying to walk down, carrying Rebecca in his arms.

When both men were organized, Rebecca was carried out and lain atop the straw tick in the cart. Between Beau, the doctor, and the four guards, they managed to descend carefully, slowly, to the village and to reach Dr. Day's house not far from the water.

"Take her upstairs," Dr. Day told Beau. "She will be comfortable in the attic room and I'm certain it will be more acceptable to Major Morgan if I tell him she's upstairs where she can be locked in."

With Rebecca in his arms, Beau climbed the narrow stairway to the long attic room that ran the length of the rectangular house. A wide bed, made of logs with a straw tick laid over the ropes, stood opposite a small fireplace that shared a chimney with the fireplace in the downstairs sitting room. The roof slanted toward the front and back of the house, leaving only a narrow walkway down the middle where Beau could stand upright.

"How is she?" the doctor asked as he came up the stairs.

"She's all right," Beau said, gently smoothing a shining black curl from Rebecca's forehead. "I don't think the trip hurt her."

Dr. Day frowned as he turned back the coverlet and saw the crimson stains on the bandages covering her ankle. "This is what worries me most," he said. "It was left unattended so long while she was down there. There's almost certain to be an infection."

"If there is, you'll pull her through, I know you will," Beau replied fervently.

Dr. Day smiled. "I wish I had your confidence. Infections and fevers take more people than wars and Indians put together."

Rebecca stirred on the pillow. Her hand quivered, then lifted to touch her lips. Her tongue darted out to moisten them.

"What do you want?" Beau asked. "Water?"

Rebecca nodded. "Please," she whispered.

Dr. Day went downstairs and returned with a pitcher of water freshly drawn from the well and a mug. Pouring a mugful, he handed it to Beau. Rebecca held out her hand but Beau moved toward her, intending to prop her up in his arms as she drank.

Rebecca shrank away from him, her out-stretched hand trembling. "I can manage it alone!" she said, her voice strong if still hoarse.

Casting a perplexed glance at the doctor, Beau handed the mug to Rebecca, then watched as she struggled to balance herself on one still-weak arm and sip at the sweet, cold water.

When she'd finished, she held out the mug to Dr. Day, not Beau.

"Would you like more?" the doctor asked, prepared to refill the mug.

Rebecca shook her head. Lying back against her pillows, she closed her eyes, nearly exhausted by the effort.

"Is there anything else you need, Rebecca?" Dr. Day asked. "Are you hungry? In pain?"

"No," Rebecca assured him, her voice weak, "nothing, thank you, Doctor."

"Well, then, I think we should leave you alone to rest. I'll leave the candle burning for you to go to sleep with, shall I?"

With a soft half-smile, Rebecca nodded as she nestled into the warmth of her pillows and bedclothes. She watched as the doctor started toward the stairs.

Beau lagged behind. "Rebecca," he began, "I'm on duty tonight at the fort but I could stay a little while. I could sit with you until you sleep."

"No, thank you," she replied, her tone as icy as the November winds that would soon bear down on the island from the arctic regions far to the north. With a great effort, she pushed herself onto her side so her back was toward him.

Beau stared at her, at a loss to understand the change that had taken place in her since she'd left Mackinac Island with the British. He longed to say something, ask for a reason, but the resolute little form beneath the blankets seemed carved out of solid ice.

He turned and followed Dr. Day downstairs.

Huddled beneath the blankets, Rebecca listened to the men's footfalls as they descended the narrow, steep stairs. The door at the bottom closed behind them and she was left alone.

Turning onto her back, she gazed around the long, shadowy room. She didn't like being alone but it was a comfort that the room was not small and dark like that hellish cell in the guardhouse. And she took comfort from the fact that she knew Anthony could not come to her here, could not appear out of the darkness and harm her.

Below, Beau and Dr. Day stood together in the sitting room where a low fire burned to dispel the autumn chill.

"She'll be all right," the doctor assured Beau. "Don't worry about her."

"She might have nightmares," Beau suggested. "If she cried out in the night . . ."

"I'd hear her." The doctor patted Beau's arm. "I told you, don't worry. Now go along. You'll be late for duty."

With a wan smile and a nod, Beau left and

went along the darkened street toward the fort. He felt better knowing that Rebecca was at Dr. Day's house and under guard. Anthony Hawkins could not get to her there. She would be safe.

But would she be his? He did not begin to understand the way she was acting toward him. Her coldness toward him mystified him. What had he done to deserve it? Had he not rescued her from her hellish prison? Had he not protected her from Anthony Hawkins? Was he not prepared to do anything to make her more comfortable during her illness?

Perhaps it was merely that she hated all Americans. After all, the war was over, she was no longer a spy. There was no need for her to adopt a friendly demeanor toward the men who had so recently been her enemy. Perhaps, the unwelcome voice whispered inside his head, he was only now seeing her true feelings. If so, she was a consummate actress.

But, no, he told himself, that could not be. She was friendly enough to Dr. Day. It seemed all her anger, all her resentment and disdain was directed toward him and him alone. What could it mean? And how could he break through that icy shell she'd frozen about herself to find out the answer?

He glanced up at the fort, a ghostly white mass in the moonlight. A self-mocking smile curved his chiseled lips. Perhaps none of it mattered. Not the precautions to keep Rebecca safe, or the assiduous care Dr. Day was providing.

Not even the maddening, perplexing questions that haunted Beau.

They could keep Rebecca safe from Anthony Hawkins, they could nurse her carefully, diligently, to heal the wounds she'd suffered during her imprisonment. Beau could march into Rebecca's sickroom and demand a reason for her behavior toward him. But in the end, what would any of it signify if Major Morgan ordered her executed her as a spy?

Chapter Thirty

As Dr. Day had feared, Rebecca's ankle was soon swollen, angry, infected. She grew feverish despite the careful care lavished on her by both the doctor and Beau who spent his every spare moment by her bedside.

Together the two men cared for her, bathing her hot, moist body, keeping her linen, her nightclothes clean, replacing the blankets when she kicked them away, adding fuel to the fire kept burning day and night in the small fireplace that warmed her room. But in spite of it all, her fever grew worse, her ankle more swollen, and Dr. Day more concerned and watchful for the telltale signs of blood poisoning or, worse still, gangrene.

Sighing, the doctor leaned his head against the back of a chair in his sitting room. "I don't want to have to take it off," he said softly.

"Take what off?" Beau asked, kicking a smoldering log back into the fireplace with the toe of his boot.

"The leg," Dr. Day answered.

Beau stared at him, horrified. "Rebecca's leg?" he breathed. "My God! Do you think . . ."

"No, no, not yet. But this infection doesn't seem to be improving. If it spreads, turns poisonous, or gangrenous, it may be necessary to save her life."

Beau's stomach writhed at the thought of the doctor plying his saw on Rebecca's flesh. "There must be something more we can do to help her. Anything to keep from having to cut—"

"Easy, easy, Beau," Dr. Day soothed. "I didn't mean to frighten you so. I shouldn't have said anything. We're doing all we can do. It's out of our hands. Her fever has to break, first of all."

Restless, worried, Beau excused himself and climbed the stairs to the attic room above. It was sweltering in the long, narrow room. The fire blazed, banishing the slightest draft that might slip between the logs or around the windows and chill Rebecca's sweaty body.

Sinking into the chair beside the bed, Beau looked down at her. Was she more flushed than before, was her breathing more shallow, was her pallor more pronounced? After what the doctor had said, Beau searched frantically for some sign that she was better—or worse.

By Love Betrayed

It was near midnight when Beau was jolted out of his dozings. At first he was unsure of what had awakened him but then he realized that Rebecca, restlessly tossing, had struck his knee with her hand. He leaned over her, she was drenched in sweat. She had kicked the blankets off and her head moved restlessly on the pillow.

"Rebecca?" he said softly, reaching out to cover her. His hand touched her arm. It was cool and moist, completely unlike its hot, stickiness of the past days.

Going to the pitcher on the table, Beau dampened a cloth in the now-warm water. Wringing it out, he bathed Rebecca's face, her throat, her hands, and arms. She had calmed and lay quietly on her pillow, her ebony curls, reflecting the firelight, tumbled over the side of the bed.

Beau touched her cheek, she did not stir. He smoothed her hair, she gave no sign that she felt his touch. Frightened, Beau left the attic room and went down to awaken the doctor.

Sleepy, his nightshirt flapping against bare legs, Dr. Day climbed the stairs behind Beau. He went to the bed and crouched over Rebecca. As Beau watched anxiously, he felt Rebecca's brow, held her wrist to count her heartbeats.

"Well?" Beau asked. "Is she . . ."

Dr. Day smiled at him. "Her fever's broken, my boy. If we can heal the infection, she'll live."

Weak with relief, Beau sank into his chair. At least and at last there was hope. Rebecca would recover, she would! And she would be

309

whole and well and beautiful again. He knew it!

Within days, the infection in Rebecca's ankle began to heal, the swelling lessened, the angry red faded to a deep pink, growing lighter every day. There would be scars, two deep grooves encircling her slender leg, but after Dr. Day's fear that she might lose the leg entirely, they seemed a small price to pay.

It was a week after her fever broke that she took her first, tentative steps. A week after that she descended the attic stairs for the first time. She spent long evenings in front of the sitting-room fire with Beau and Dr. Day. She began caring for the doctor's house, cooking for him, feeling alive and useful once more.

There was an air of celebration when Rebecca, Beau, and Dr. Day sat down to a dinner of roast venison, potatoes, and vegetables from the doctor's garden. A bottle of wine was produced and they drank a toast to Rebecca's recovery.

"There were days when I wasn't sure we'd ever see you like this," the doctor said, "smiling, well, lovely as ever."

Rebecca flushed. "You're a born flatterer, Doctor," she teased. "Your charm is wasted out here in the wilderness."

They laughed but their laughter was interrupted by the knocking of one of the guards at the door.

"Probably smelled the roast," Dr. Day joked, rising from the table.

But at the door was a messenger from the fort. A private had been handling his musket when it had accidentally discharged. The doctor must come immediately even though it was thought the man could not survive.

With Dr. Day gone, the atmosphere in the room changed. It seemed to Beau that the temperature dropped and a chill, like the first breath of winter, invaded the room.

Rebecca rose and began clearing the table.

"Rebecca," Beau said softly. "Come back. Sit down and talk to me."

"What do you want to talk about?" she asked, not pausing in her labors.

"What do you think I want to talk about?" he demanded impatiently. "Rebecca!" He seized her wrist as she reached for the half-empty bottle of wine.

She jerked her wrist out of his grasp. "How should I know!" she countered.

"I want to know why you're acting this way? Your behavior, ever since we got you out of that godforsaken hole—"

"My behavior!" she snarled. "What about your behavior!"

"What have I done? Ever since you regained consciousness, I've tried to help you, to care for you, and what have you done? You've been as cold as ice toward me."

"And what did you expect? Should I have fallen into your arms? Should I have forgotten all those nights on Drummond Island simply because you've been kind to me now?"

"Drummond Island?" he asked, thoroughly confused. "What in hell has this to do with Drummond Island?"

"I spent weeks there—months!—before Anthony Hawkins came to force me back here. Long, long weeks, Beau, and day after day I longed for some word from you, some message, anything. But there was nothing." She closed her eyes, feeling again the loneliness, the longing and pain of those cold, lonely nights when she'd lain in her bed missing him, yearning for him, remembering the cold, disdainful look on his face when their ships had passed.

Beau pushed back his chair and stood. His expression was incredulous. "A message? You left Mackinac Island with Sumner Meade! You went with him, Rebecca, you did not stay behind to wait for me!"

"I went with my countrymen!" she disagreed. "I did not know what might happen to me if I stayed behind."

"The war was over before you left."

"The war was also over when Anthony Hawkins came after me and brought me back here to die," she reminded him.

"I would have protected you if you had stayed here," he insisted, his tone one of gentle admonition.

"How could I know that?" she demanded. "I remember the day we left for Drummond Island. Our ships passed; ours outward bound, yours inward. I called out to you . . ." She sighed at the memory. "The look you gave me across the water chilled my blood."

"It wasn't you," he told her. "Meade was standing beside you. His arm was about your waist, his hand resting on the railing. I thought—"

"You thought I was going away to be with him," she finished for him.

Beau nodded. "I did. I spent some lonely nights, too, Rebecca. I spent hours lying awake in my quarters, thinking of you with Meade, of his arms about you, of your marrying him."

"My God." She sighed, sinking into a chair. "I never intended to marry Sumner. Do you know what I had planned to do? I was going to board the first ship bound for the east and go home to England. There was nothing for me here in America any longer." Her voice dropped to a whisper. "Not without you."

"If I had known that," Beau said, reaching out but not quite daring to touch her, "I would have come for you. I would have brought you back."

"I wish you had," she breathed, reaching out to take the hand stretched toward her. "If you only knew how I longed for you to come for me. If you had any idea how it hurt to think that you hated me for what I had done to you and your friends."

"I was angry; I felt betrayed," he admitted. "But I did not hate you."

Their fingers intertwined as Beau pulled her out of her chair and into his arms. They had wasted too many days and nights when they could have been together.

He pulled her into his arms and turned his head to kiss her temple. Nestled against him, Rebecca smiled, feeling his fingers teasing her hair, her cheeks, burying themselves in the shining black silk of her hair.

"Well," she said, her tone light, airy, "now we've got all that out of the way. Dr. Day is gone; we're alone. What do you want to do with the rest of the evening?"

Glancing askance at Beau, she laughed at the look on his face. He took her glass from her hand and set it with his own on the table. Then, her hand clasped in his, he led her up the stairs to the attic room, where they'd spent so many hours in the past weeks.

Rebecca leaned weakly against him as he caressed her through the light wool of the gown one of the village women had given Dr. Day for her. She trembled in the circle of his embrace, sighed at the touch of his lips. When she felt his fingers working at the laces running up the gown's back, she, in turn, began unfastening the buttons of his white cotton shirt.

At last they stood in the firelight, their clothing a puddle of cotton and wool around their feet. Beau pulled Rebecca against him. She gasped, the hard, heady heat of his desire seemed to sear her flesh as their bodies pressed together. Her body quivered as he caressed her, savoring the satiny warmth of her skin.

Beau trailed hot, sweet kisses on her flesh as he fell slowly to his knees before her. He kissed her, loved her, tasted the sweetness of her. Rebecca buried her fingers in his hair, her head falling back, her lips parted as her breaths came in short, sharp gasps. Her heart galloped in her breast, her knees nearly buckled but she was lost, lost in a heaven of pure sensation.

"Beau," she whispered, "Beau, please."

He rose, his lips caressing her as they went, teasing her navel, taunting the aching, rosebud crests of her breasts. Lifting her, he lay her back on the patchwork coverlet of the bed. He drew her legs over his shoulders, pressed a kiss on either knee, and then Rebecca cried out, shuddering as his flesh parted hers. She reached up to caress him, stroke him, as he moved against her, within her. He took her to a place more beautiful than the virgin forests, ablaze with brilliant color, that surrounded them, as he gave her a pleasure more pure than the glittering white snow that would soon blanket the island, as he ignited in her an answering fire hotter than any that blazed in the hearth across the room, as he brought her, at last, utter peace and contentment.

It was late October when Dr. Day was summoned to Major Morgan's quarters. The officer waved him into a chair, then, without preamble, asked, "How is your patient coming along, Doctor?"

"Mrs. Carlyle?" The major nodded. "She's well. Her ankle is nearly completely healed. There will be scars, of course, but—"

"Does she need constant care any longer?" Major Morgan interrupted.

"No, Major," the doctor answered honestly.

"Then I think it's time she came back to the fort. You will see to it, Doctor."

Unable to refuse, Dr. Day rose from his chair and, giving the major his assurances that he would see to it without delay, left.

Outside, on the parade ground, he saw Beau speaking to a pair of soldiers. Beckoning him, he leaned close and spoke in low, urgent tones.

"The major wants Rebecca brought back to the fort immediately," he said.

Beau scowled. "Do you think he means to try her after all?"

Dr. Day shrugged. "He didn't say, but why else would he want her brought back here? If he weren't intending to try her, he'd simply ignore her or at most order her off the island."

Beau gazed off toward the officers' quarters. "I'm going to go talk to him," he decided. "Perhaps I can persuade him to let Rebecca leave the island in peace."

Arriving at his commander's quarters, Beau tapped on the door. Ordered inside, he stepped into the office and saluted.

"Well, McAllister?" the major prompted. "What can I do for you?"

"I came to speak to you, sir, about Mrs. Carlyle."

"You spoke to the doctor, I take it." Major Morgan leaned back in his chair.

"Yes, sir," Beau replied. "I wonder, sir, if it might not serve simply to send her back to Drummond Island, to the British garrison. She was settled there before Anthony Hawkins forced her to return."

"Sit down, McAllister." The major leaned forward on his desk, his hands clasped. "I am aware, Lieutenant, of your past relationship with this lady. Having looked into the matter, I know you and she were, shall we say, involved? That is, perhaps, understandable. I am told she is a very beautiful woman and this is a remote and lonely place. But it surprises me that you would want to free her after she betrayed whatever relationship existed between you by passing on information received from you to the enemy."

"It is true," Beau admitted, "that for a long time I felt angry, betrayed, by her. But the war is over, sir, how long should we harbor these old grievances?"

Major Morgan smiled grimly. "How long indeed? Are you aware that the British on Drummond Island have been interfering with trade? That Lieutenant Colonel McDouall has been telling the Indians who have traditionally been our allies that if they come here we will kill them? There are rumors, unsubstantiated, I grant you, that he is scheming with the notion of invading us once more."

He held up his hand to silence Beau who was about to speak. "Now, I do not approve of Hawkins's actions in chaining the lady like

317

an animal down in that hellish cell, but the fact remains that she was a spy and her actions resulted in the loss of this fort for three years—which might have been permanent had it not been for the Treaty of Ghent—and the loss of many fine soldiers. She must be called to account for her actions, Lieutenant. Not only because of the past, but as a warning to the British not to try such a ploy again. Go and get her, McAllister, and bring her to the guard-house. That's an order."

Rising, Beau saluted and left the major's quarters. His heart was heavy as he went to the village. Rebecca had been through so much, had nearly died in that tiny, tortuous cell, had been so ill and barely escaped death. And for what? To be put on trial as a spy and perhaps put to death as a warning to her countrymen? All the pain, all the worry, all the suffering she had endured, and for what? So Anthony Hawkins could ultimately triumph in his desire for revenge against a woman whose worst crime, in his mind, was in rejecting him.

Chapter Thirty-One

It seemed to Beau that he had to force his feet to take each step toward the village and Dr. Day's house. He hesitated at the path leading to the house, the two sentries guarding the front door stood at attention. Soon, Beau knew, they, along with the two at the back door, would form a guard to escort their prisoner back to the fort, back to the guardhouse that had been the scene of her most dreadful days and nights.

Taking a deep breath, he went to the door and entered the house. At first he did not see Rebecca. He thought, perhaps, she was upstairs resting. The thought of waking her with the news that she must return to the guardhouse dismayed him.

"Beau!" She sat in the sitting room, a book open on her lap. Her face was wreathed in smiles at his sudden, unexpected appearance. She knew he was on duty all day and hadn't expected to see him until evening.

Beau paused in the doorway of the sitting room. The deep crimson of her gown lent color to her alabaster cheeks; the sunshine flooding through the window glinted blue-black in the depths of her shining hair. Her beauty took his breath away and he felt at that moment that should Major Morgan order her killed a part of him would die with her.

Rebecca's smile faded. The look on his face warned her that something was wrong, something dreadful had happened.

"What is it, Beau?" she asked, laying her book aside. "What's wrong?"

Coming to her, Beau knelt on the floor before her. He took her hands in his and gazed deeply into her black-lashed amethyst eyes.

"You're frightening me," she said, her voice tremulous.

"I've come from Major Morgan," he told her. "I'm to take you to the fort."

"The fort," she whispered.

"To the guardhouse."

Rebecca recoiled, her body quaking. "No," she breathed, starting from the chair. "No!"

She tried to push past Beau but he caught her. Rising, he held her fast. His heart melted as he felt her trembling against him.

"Rebecca," he murmured, stroking her hair, soothing her as he would a child. "Rebecca, hush."

"He means to kill me, doesn't he?" she asked, her eyes shimmering with unshed tears. "He means for me to die! Doesn't he?"

Beau wanted to reassure her, to comfort her, to tell her it would be all right. But he could not. It was cruel to tell her the truth but even crueler to lie.

"You don't answer," Rebecca breathed, gazing up into his face. "My God!"

She sagged against him and he held her close. He could feel the beating of her heart, like the fluttering of a frightened bird, in her breast. She shivered like a child in his arms and he knew she desperately needed the comfort he could not offer her.

Leaving his arms, Rebecca turned her back to him. Her arms wrapped around her, she fought to steady herself. Her first impulse was to run, to flee from this house, but she knew it would do no good. Where could she go? How long could she hide even in the forest? This island, this God-cursed island, offered her no sanctuary, no hope, no escape.

"When do I have to go?" she asked.

"Now," Beau's voice answered from behind her.

"Now!" She turned toward him. Panic showed in her wide, haunted eyes but she fought it back. Lifting her chin, she gave a cool, solemn nod. "Let me get my cloak from upstairs."

Leaving Beau in the sitting room, she climbed the stairs to the attic. The room stretched before her, warm and bright with late-afternoon sunshine. Crossing the room, she took up her plain black cloak but it slipped through her fingers and fell in a whisper to the floor.

Reaching out a hand, Rebecca grasped one of the bed's posts. She sank onto the bed, the ropes creaking in protest. Memories flowed over her like a deluge, memories of this room, of Beau, of nights spent in a lover's embrace, of kisses, caresses, passion. She would never know those feelings again, never. Soon she would be cold and dead, beyond all pleasure, all pain.

Bowing her head, Rebecca willed away the despair that seized her. There was nothing she could do. If she ran, she would be captured. There was nowhere to go, no one to turn to, even Beau could not help her.

Resigned, she picked up her cloak and pulled it around her shoulders. Leaving the attic room for the last time, she descended the stairs and went to the door, waiting for Beau to come to her.

Beau gazed at her standing there, straight, strong, and yet the fear was there, hiding in her eyes, in the almost imperceptible trembling of her lips. His heart ached for her as he went to the back door and ordered the sentries to accompany them to the fort.

Surrounded by guards, Beau's steadying hand at her elbow, Rebecca made her way back up the long, steep ramp to the fort. With every step that took her closer to the sally port, closer to the guardhouse within it, her terror grew. Her legs shook beneath her, threatening to betray her, but her stubbornness drove her on. She refused to let the guards surrounding them or the sentries atop the ramparts watching their approach see how mortally afraid she was.

They entered the fort and she caught sight of Anthony Hawkins standing just outside the north blockhouse off to the right of the sally port. He leaned against the doorjamb watching her, his face filled with malicious pleasure. Rebecca stared at him, filled with unspeakable loathing. It was his vindictiveness that had placed her here; it was his unwavering hatred, his unyielding determination to see her dead that had brought her to this.

Turning her back on her enemy, Rebecca preceded Beau into the guardhouse. Her stomach roiled at the sight of the trap door that covered the steps leading to the hold. All the memories—the cold, the damp, the hunger and thirst, the pain and despair—came flooding back.

She stumbled and felt Beau's strong hand steadying her. She walked into the cell she'd first occupied and found it furnished now with a narrow bed—one of those from the infirmary, she supposed—and a pitcher and basin. A candle in a brass holder stood on the scarred table.

"It's not quite so bare as it was before," she mused aloud. "At least my last days will be comfortable."

She saw the look on Beau's face and regretted her sarcasm. Raising a hand to his face, she stroked his cheek. "I know you would help me if you could," she said softly.

"I will help you," he vowed, his voice a deep, urgent rumble. "Somehow . . ."

"Hush," she said quickly, well aware of the guards just outside the open door. She did not want them reporting any of Beau's rash promises to Major Morgan, promises that could be construed as aiding the enemy, conspiracy, treason. "Don't say anything."

Bowing to the wisdom of her warning, Beau stepped out of the cell and swung the door shut. His hand trembled as he turned the key in the lock. His eyes met hers through the bars in the cell door window and they gazed at one another for a long, lonely moment before Beau turned and left the guardhouse.

It was midmorning of the following day when Rebecca was led under guard to Major Morgan's chambers where her hearing would take place. Beau was there, and Anthony Hawkins, Dr. Day, and a pair of soldiers she had nursed in the infirmary who had volunteered to testify on her behalf.

Testimony was given. Rebecca's life on the island from the moment she'd arrived was recounted in embarrassing detail. Anthony, of course, denied his assault on her not long after her arrival, but Major Morgan seemed to believe him capable of such an action. Her love affair with Beau could not be concealed and Rebecca loathed hearing such intimate affairs being put forward in cold clinical detail for all and sundry to hear. Under oath, she testified that she had sent information to the British on St. Joseph Island, that she had known that the two countries were at war and had said nothing, that she had known invasion was imminent and had revealed nothing, even to her American lover. She named her contact as Pierre LaRoux but did not betray Michael Dousman who still lived on the island and who, like her, was open to a charge of espionage and treason.

When all the evidence had been presented, all the testimony had been heard, Rebecca was brought to stand before Major Morgan, her sole judge. His dark eyes swept over her as she stood before him; she returned his gaze with a calm that was pure bravado.

"Mrs. Carlyle," he said, leaning forward in his chair and toying with the papers on the desk before him, "I find you guilty of espionage and treason against the United States."

Rebecca wavered, feeling her heart thudding, her stomach roiling. She scarcely heard the major's words as he went on, "Will you admit, madam, that what you did was wrong?"

Rebecca looked at him levelly. "Tell me, Major, did you kill any British soldiers during the war?"

"Of course," Major Morgan replied. "We were at war."

"Do you believe that was wrong?"

"I do not," he answered. "I was defending my country."

"So was I. Simply because my country was the enemy does not make my actions more wrong than yours."

"Would you do it again?" he asked.

Rebecca hesitated. She knew Beau was mentally urging her to say no, to apologize for her actions and throw herself on the major's mercy. But she could not do that; she could not live a lie.

"If I believed it was the right thing to do," she replied at last.

She heard Beau's muffled groan behind her and Major Morgan's sigh. Her eyes never wavered as her judge sagged back in his chair.

"You leave me no choice, madam, but to make an example of you. It is the judgment of this court that you will be taken outside this fort at sunset tonight and will be summarily executed by firing squad."

Anthony Hawkins's bark of triumphant laughter was smothered by Beau's shout of outrage. Both men leapt to their feet as Dr. Day covered his face with his hands.

"I will have silence in this room!" Major Morgan shouted. "Guards, take the prisoner back to the guardhouse. The sentence will be carried out tonight. This hearing is adjourned!"

As her guards led her out of the room, Rebecca reached out toward Beau. He stretched a hand toward her but their fingers scarcely brushed before she was led away, back to the cell that would be her home until her death scarcely half a day from then.

Rebecca fought back her tears on the walk back to the guardhouse. She would not let them see her fear, her despair. If it took the last ounce of strength in her body, she would deny Anthony Hawkins the pleasure of seeing just now mortally afraid she was.

Chapter Thirty-Two

Looking through the window in her cell's door, Rebecca could see the shadows moving across the floor of the guards' room. Noon passed, the sun moved toward the west. Like sand running unstoppably through an hourglass, the sun lowered toward the horizon, heralding the last hours of Rebecca's life.

Seated at her table, she rested her arms upon its scarred top and laid her forehead on them. She was going to die. It seemed like a bad dream from which she couldn't awaken. Perhaps if she could get a message to Michael Dousman he could send word to the British garrison on Drummond Island. But what would they do? Send a protest? How long would that take? They, no doubt, believed she had died in the fire Anthony had started to destroy her cabin. How surprised they would be if they learned she lived. But by the time they had recovered from their surprise and acted on her message she would be long dead, moldering in some unmarked grave.

Dead. Every fiber in Rebecca's being rebelled against the thought. She was too young to die. She was filled with life and health and the desire to live. Was it all to end now? Was she never again to feel the sunshine on her face, see the fresh beauty of new fallen snow, trackless and pure, lying in shimmering drifts on the boughs of a towering pine? Was she never again to see the first green buds of spring venturing out into the still-chilled air of April? It was impossible to comprehend.

And Beau . . . What of Beau? She would never know his touch again, his love, never feel his arms around her, his body against hers. Tears shimmered in her eyes but she blinked them away. She would not go to her death whimpering and whining. If she had to die, she would do it with a dignity that would rob Anthony Hawkins of some of his pleasure, his triumph.

She heard voices outside her cell. Footsteps approached her door. "No," she whispered, "not yet. Please, please, not yet!"

For one irrational moment she wondered why, if this had to happen, it could not have happened in the summer when it stayed light well into the evening instead of late October when the darkness fell so early?

The key turned in the lock of her cell door and Rebecca rose and backed away. Though she willed herself not to tremble, her hands shook and she concealed them in the crimson skirts of her gown as the door opened.

A soldier appeared bearing a tray. On it was a bowl of some kind of stew, a piece of freshly baked bread, a bottle of wine, and a cup.

"Your supper, ma'am," the young man said, not quite meeting her eyes.

"Thank you," Rebecca told him as he laid it on the table. He started out but she stopped him. "What time is it?"

"Five o'clock," he told her. "About an hour before sunset."

"An hour," Rebecca murmured, averting her eyes as the soldier left her cell and relocked the door.

Going to the table, she sat down. An hour. Sixty minutes. She looked down at the steaming stew and still-warm bread but had no appetite. She poured a cupful of the sweet, red wine, but when she lifted it to her lips and sipped it, she could not force it past her tightly closed throat.

Resigned, she left the table and went to the cell door. Through the window in the door she could see the window in the guards' room. Outside the shadows were lengthening; the western sky was afire with shades of purple and mauve.

Its reflection tinged the very walls of the white-washed fort a pale pink. How beautiful it was—her last sunset.

Rebecca turned away from the door and went to sit on the edge of her bed. She could almost feel the minutes ticking by, dwindling away, the last grains in the hourglass tumbling to the bottom.

Her face buried in her hands, Rebecca did not hear the footsteps approaching her cell door. It was not until the door opened that she looked up, her eyes wide and filled with the fear she could not hope to conceal.

Beau stood there. The brass buttons and lacings of his uniform winked in the dim light spilling through the doorway. He gazed down at her, his eyes alight with compassion. He wanted to take her in his arms and hold her but what comfort could he offer her? He held out his hand.

"Beau!" Leaping to her feet, Rebecca ran to him. She embraced him, pressed her body to his, and waited for a response that did not come.

Stepping back, she looked up into his face. "What is it?" she asked, stung by his distance.

"It is time," he said simply. "Come with me."

"No." Shaking her head, she backed away from him. "Dear God, not you. Not you!"

He nodded. "Yes. I am to lead the squad. Major Morgan put me in charge of choosing the men and . . ." He shook his head. "It is my

punishment, Rebecca, for my part in all this."
He held out his hand. "Come now, it is time."

He picked up her cloak from the back of
the chair beside the table. Holding it open, he
waited for her to step into it, then wrapped it
around her.

Rebecca followed him out of the cell and out
of the guardhouse. Four soldiers stood there,
muskets in hand. Rebecca knew them all. Two
were the soldiers who had guarded her when
she'd been chained in the hole—the soldiers
who had taken pity on her and given her the
bread and water that had kept her alive. The
other two she had nursed after the Americans'
unsuccessful attempt to recapture the fort. How
ironic, she thought, that they had been chosen
to be her executioners.

Dr. Day stepped up to her, a wan attempt at
a smile flitting across his lips. "Courage, my
dear," he said softly.

Rebecca nodded. He need have no fear, she
thought, she did not intend to embarrass herself with hysterics.

With two guards in front of her and two
guards behind, Rebecca fell into step as Beau
ordered them on their way.

As they marched across the parade ground
to the north sally port which led toward the
forest behind the fort, Rebecca caught sight of
Anthony Hawkins standing on the ramparts,
watching them. She averted her eyes, staring
straight ahead. She would not let him have the
pleasure of showing her his triumphant sneer.

The little group passed out of the sally port just as the sun disappeared beneath the western horizon. The twilight was deepening, the purple and mauve turning to shades of gray and blue.

They entered the forest where the shadows were long and the darkness deeper than it had been in the open near the fort. Rebecca wondered where they were going. She was about to ask Beau when they reached a tiny clearing. In the center was a mound of dirt. Rebecca wondered at its purpose until she saw the hole beside it.

"Good God!" she breathed, recoiling. She was staring at her own grave. "No!"

She felt Dr. Day's hand on her elbow. "Steady," he said quietly, as though sensing that her impulse was to run away from this dreadful scene.

Rebecca felt her knees weakening beneath her. She was to be buried, like an animal in the forest, not even accorded the dignity of a real grave in a real cemetery. Soon the grass and weeds and wildflowers would grow over the raw earth and it would be forgotten that anyone lay there.

The squad stopped and Beau took Rebecca's wrist and drew her to the edge of the yawning hole. He positioned her with her back to it; his hands held her shoulders fast as he gazed down into her face.

"Do you want a blindfold?" he asked, about to offer her his handkerchief.

She shook her head, not trusting herself to speak. As he moved away, she caught at his sleeve. He looked back at her, his sapphire eyes filled with sadness and regret, but his hand closed over hers and loosed her fingers from the soft blue cloth of his sleeve.

She looked at Dr. Day who stood off to one side. Suddenly she realized what had not occurred to her before. He was not here to offer her the comfort of a friendly and familiar face. He was here to certify that she was dead! Shock ran through her, nearly driving the breath from her body.

She closed her eyes as Beau gave the order for her executioners to position themselves opposite her across a small expanse of ground. She held her breath, her fingers clenched, as she heard Beau's voice ring out in the evening stillness, "Ready!"

Rebecca's heart seemed to stand still in her breast. The air was charged with anticipation; her fear was an almost palpable thing.

"Aim!"

She ground her teeth not knowing what to expect. Would there be pain? Would she feel the musket balls, each a half-inch-diameter sphere of lead, tearing through her flesh, piercing her body? She felt giddy, light-headed with fear and dread. What would happen? Would there be anything more for her or only eternal darkness, buried in the cool, black earth?

"Fire!"

The bark of the four muskets was deafening, echoing through the forest and over the fort. All activity stopped for a moment; the soldiers exchanged glances. Major Morgan in his quarters looked up from his papers, his expression inscrutable even to the others in the room. Anthony Hawkins, still on the ramparts listening for the sound, was suffused with an ecstasy of malicious triumph that was almost rapture.

Rebecca heard the retort of the muskets—her ears rang with it—but, strangely, she felt no pain. There was only darkness, darkness, and then she was falling.

The four soldiers lowered their muskets as Rebecca fell backward, tumbling into the yawning hole. Dr. Day rushed forward, unceremoniously scrambling down into the grave where Rebecca lay, sprawled like a rag doll discarded by a bored child.

"Squad dismissed!" Beau shouted. "Go back to the fort. Dr. Day and I will fill it in."

The four soldiers exchanged glances. They had not wanted to be a part of this exercise. Each and every one had protested against being a party to the death of a woman—and a woman who had played some part in their lives. But they'd been ordered to obey and had had no choice in the matter.

Now, they were only too happy to obey. None of the four had any desire to go to the edge of the grave and peer down at their victim. None of the four had any desire to see the bloody havoc their musket balls must have wreaked on that beautiful, slender body.

And yet, they all knew what had happened in the past between Rebecca and Beau. They all knew that he, more than they, must be tormented by the part he was playing in her death. They wanted nothing more than to be away from this place, this scene, and yet they felt compelled to offer to take the burden of burying their lieutenant's lover off his shoulders.

"Are you certain, sir," one of them said, "that you wouldn't rather we took care of—"

"You have your orders, Private!" Beau snarled from where he knelt by the edge of the grave.

"But, sir," another protested, "we only thought it would be easier on you if—"

"Get back to the bloody fort, damn you!" Beau bellowed, and the soldiers, not venturing to offer any more assistance, left Beau and Dr. Day to deal with the burial of the executed spy.

Chapter Thirty-Three

Rebecca awoke slowly, regaining consciousness in stages as though her own unconscious
mind could not accept the fact that she was still
breathing, that her heart was still beating. Her
lips parted, she drew long, deep breaths as she
lay in some unknown bed in some unknown
place.

"Rebecca?" a familiar voice called her name.
A warm, rough hand felt her forehead, touched
her cheek. "Rebecca, can you hear me?"

Her lashes, like shining black fans on the
pale alabaster skin of her cheeks, fluttered, then
lifted. Her eyes adjusted slowly to the golden
candlelight illuminating the room. A face hovered far above her, shadowed by the darkness
in the dimly lit room.

Rebecca squinted up at the face, at first

unable to put a name to it. But then, suddenly, she remembered.

"Michael!"

Michael Dousman stood beside the bed. He smiled down at her as she pushed herself up against the pillows.

"Welcome back to the living," he said.

Rebecca pressed a hand to her forehead. "I don't understand," she said. "I heard the guns, I fell . . ."

"You fainted," he told her. "And you fell into the hole they had dug. It looked quite convincing, I'm told, but it's a wonder you didn't break your neck!"

"But they all fired! Are you telling me they all missed?"

Michael shook his head. He handed her a cup of water he'd dipped from the bucket in the kitchen when she'd begun to show signs of awakening.

"They didn't miss," he told her. "But they couldn't have killed you. Beau McAllister and Dr. Day apparently loaded the rifles. The charges were made of tow."

"Tow! But . . . then it was all a charade?" She felt a flash of anger that she had been put through all that nerve-wracking torment for nothing.

"It had to be done, Rebecca. Only Dr. Day and McAllister know the truth. They had to make it look real to convince Major Morgan and, more important, Anthony Hawkins that you were dead."

"Even the firing squad doesn't know the truth?"

Michael shrugged. "Apparently, McAllister chose men who had a certain regard for you for one reason or another. They weren't too anxious to examine their 'victim' too closely. When they fired and saw you fall, they were willing to take Dr. Day's word that you were dead. McAllister ordered them back to the fort, telling them he and the doctor would fill in the grave."

Rebecca shuddered, rubbing her arms. "Have you ever looked into your own grave?" she asked. "My God, what a horror!"

"It's over now," he soothed, lightly slipping an arm about her shoulders and hugging her. "Try not to think about it."

Rebecca nodded, grateful for his kindness but wishing it was Beau who offered her a comforting arm, a warm, strong shoulder to lean on.

"Where is Beau?" she asked. The house was quiet; it was apparent they were alone.

"He and Dr. Day had to go back to the fort right away. If either had stayed here, someone at the fort might have been suspicious."

"I suppose so," she admitted. "What will happen now? Am I to remain here, on your farm?"

Michael shook his head. "There's a schooner in the harbor. She sails at dawn. She will pass Drummond Island and you—"

"No!" Rebecca leapt to her feet. "I don't want to go back to Drummond Island! I want to be with Beau and—"

"It was Beau's idea, Rebecca," Michael told her.

"Beau's idea?" She frowned. "Beau wants to send me away?"

"What else can he do? Come now, Rebecca, he's right. You're far better off on Drummond, among your own people."

Biting her lip, Rebecca turned away from him to hide her emotion.

"Rebecca," Michael said soothingly, "come, lie back down and rest. You've been through a terrifying experience, you're overwrought. Now lie down and try to sleep. I'll wake you when it's time to go."

Obedient as a child, she lay down in the bed. Michael extinguished the candle in the bedroom and left her to rest.

But Rebecca did not sleep. Her mind was racing. Between the two of them, Dr. Day and Beau had saved her life. But now she was being sent away at Beau's insistence. And even though she knew it would be impossible for her to stay here, she felt rejected, hurt, by his insistence that she go to be with her "own people."

The thought of returning to Drummond Island, to Sumner, after being here with Beau, made her want to weep.

Though she'd thought she would not sleep, Rebecca was roused in the wee hours of the morning by Michael's hand on her shoulder.

"Rebecca," he said softly, "Rebecca, wake up, we have to go in a moment."

"All right," she agreed, wiping the sleep from her eyes with the backs of her hands. "I'm awake."

Rising, she washed her face and hands and combed her tousled hair. Then, pulling on her cloak, she followed Michael out into the frosty night air to the horse that waited to take them to the shore.

She rode behind him to the shore, where a canoe waited to ferry her out to the schooner, *Aurelia,* riding at anchor in the harbor.

"*Au revoir, madame,*" the *voyageur* who had paddled the canoe said as she started to board the *Aurelia.* "*Bonne chance.*"

"Thank you," she replied. "Good-bye."

Aboard the schooner Rebecca was shown to a small cabin on the side of the ship facing the island. After undressing, she lay down in her narrow bunk and gazed out the window at the shore.

The fort gleamed blue in the moonlight. A single light burned in one of the windows of the officers' quarters but Rebecca did not know if it was Beau's window.

"Beau," she whispered softly, loving the sound of the word in her ear, the roll of it on her tongue. "Beau, why does it seem the world is conspiring to part us?"

But at that moment, it seemed that not only was the world scheming to keep them apart, it seemed that Beau himself was parting them, sending her away, out of his life.

Rolling over in her bunk, Rebecca could no longer fight back the tears that burned behind her eyes. Muffling her sobs in her pillow, she gave vent to the horror of what had happened earlier in the evening: the fear that she was going to die; the terror of being taken into the forest and stood in front of that yawning grave; the moment when the musket fire had rung in her ears and she had felt herself falling as darkness closed around her.

But most of all she wept for the ache in her heart, the emptiness that only Beau could fill. She loved him, she needed him and wanted him and he was sending her away with no word of farewell, no promises, no hope that they had any future together. For all she knew, she would never see him again. For all she knew, he had no desire to see her again.

It stood to reason that he could not love her. If he had, wouldn't he have left some parting message for her with Michael Dousman? Even if he could not have stayed with her until she left, couldn't he have spared a moment to put pen to paper and let her at least have some small part of him to take away with her? Some words of love to cling to? Some small hint of whether he saw her as a part of his future?

But there was nothing. They had come to a parting of the ways and Beau seemed only too willing to see them part.

Sniffling, she tried to push her anguish out of her mind. Despite her few hours of sleep at

Michael Dousman's she was exhausted, physically and mentally. Sleep was a refuge that welcomed her, drawing her down into a nothingness where she could forget, if only for a few brief, precious hours, the pain that seemed to pierce her to her very soul.

Dawn had scarcely broken over the island when the schooner *Aurelia* weighed anchor and set sail out of the harbor and away from Mackinac Island, Anthony Hawkins, and Beau.

Rebecca stood at the rail as the sails caught the wind and drove the ship away from the shore. She pulled the hood of her black cloak up, shielding her face from the biting wind that whipped her skirts against her legs and snapped the sails and rigging above her head.

Tears stung her eyes as she gazed at the fort. She knew, in her heart, she would never return. And she feared, at the same time, she would never again set eyes on the man she loved— the man who was sending her from him.

At the same moment, Beau stood on the ramparts of the fort, hidden from Rebecca's view by the bulk of the guardhouse. His woolen overcoat was rippled by the wind. His sapphire eyes were filled with regret as he watched the schooner growing smaller in the distance.

He wished, for a moment, that he had left a letter for her with Michael Dousman. But what could he have said? She could not stay. It was essential that Anthony Hawkins believe she was dead or else he would pursue her to the end of the earth. Beau was an officer in the Army of the United States, she a condemned traitor—what future was there for them? And he remembered what she'd once said about returning to England. It might be right for her, but America was and would always be his home.

No, it was better that they part, better that they make a clean break of it. The pain would be wild and fierce for a while, but in the end it would become clear that it had been the right thing to do.

"Well?" a voice said from behind him. "Is she aboard?"

Beau looked around. Major Morgan stood behind him, hunched against the chilling wind.

Beau saluted. "I don't know what you mean, sir," he said uneasily.

Major Morgan laughed. "Come now, Mc-Allister, don't ask me to believe that you really had her shot. I'm not so great a fool as all that."

"But, sir," Beau protested. "My orders were—"

"I know what your orders were," the major interrupted. "I also know that you were in love with the lady. Not that I blame you. I'd heard she was beautiful and I must say she is." He eyed Beau curiously. "You didn't have her shot, did you?"

Beau hesitated and the major went on, "Good heavens, my boy, why in hell do you think I put you in charge of the firing squad? I assumed you'd come up with a way to make it seem she'd been killed and then smuggle her off the island. If I'd really meant for her to die, I'd have given her to Anthony Hawkins."

He nodded toward the water where the schooner was little more than a spot on the far horizon. "Now tell me the truth. She is aboard that ship, isn't she?"

Smiling, Beau nodded. "She is, sir."

"And on her way back to British territory?"

Beau nodded again. "The schooner will put in at Drummond Island. That's where she was living before Anthony brought her here."

"So long as she's not on American soil she's not my problem," the major declared. "You did well, Lieutenant."

"After Dr. Day and I filled in the grave, we took her to—"

"Never mind," Major Morgan said, holding up a hand to silence Beau. "I don't want to know the details. I'm not going to be here much longer. A new commander is being sent. I think I can report only the bare facts of this case without compromising my honor as an officer or your future in the military."

"Thank you, sir," Beau said softly, his gaze straying out to the water where the schooner carrying Rebecca away was now scarcely visible.

"You know, don't you, McAllister, that you could be court-martialed for this little escapade? I don't only mean the so-called firing

347

squad incident, but the whole situation."

"Yes, sir," Beau acknowledged.

"Don't let it happen again, will you?" Clapping Beau on the shoulder, the major turned to walk away. "Carry on, Lieutenant," he said quietly as he left.

Beau nodded but, before he went about his duties, he cast a last glance in the direction of the ship that was carrying Rebecca out of his life—forever.

Chapter Thirty-Four

1819 Philadelphia

"Rebecca, say you'll marry me."

Standing in the drawing room of her Philadelphia townhouse, Rebecca paused in drawing on the long white gloves that completed her ensemble. She gazed across the room at the gentleman, elegant in evening dress, who watched her with dark eyes alight with admiration.

"Jonathan, you promised we'd have no more of that," she chided gently.

Abashed, Jonathan Gibbons toyed like a disappointed child with his tall hat and kid gloves. He'd been in love with this beautiful, maddening creature ever since she'd walked into his bank and asked him to make arrangements for her English inheritances to be paid from her London account to his bank in Philadelphia.

He remembered that day as if it were yesterday instead of nearly three years ago.

He remembered looking up from his desk to find her there, gazing at him with those bewitching amethyst eyes. Her shining, blue-black hair was a mass of curls, caught up with a mother-of-pearl comb. She had arrived, she told him, from the west a few days before. She had intended to return to England but had decided instead to remain in America. A gentleman aboard the schooner she'd traveled on had recommended Philadelphia as a city of culture and beauty; so here she was.

She told him she was a widow and that she had an inheritance both from her family and her late husband in London banks. She'd asked him to arrange to have the monies transferred and he'd done as she wished. Their business had not required that he spend a great deal of time in her company but he'd managed, just the same, to find excuses to see her. He'd helped her find this modest, but charming, townhouse. He'd helped her through trying times. He'd fallen in love with her and asked her, many times, to be his wife. For reasons she could not, or would not, explain, she'd always refused. But he would not abandon hope.

Tonight he was taking her to the theater which meant hours closeted with her in the intimate semiprivacy of his box. Sitting close beside her, he would find reasons to reach out and touch her hand, her arm, to speak softly, leaning close, to smell the sweet jasmine perfume that seemed to emanate from her very skin.

"We're going to be late," Rebecca prompted. The pale yellow silk coat that matched her low-necked, short-sleeved gown lay over her shoulders.

"Of course, forgive me," Jonathan said quickly, stepping forward to take her coat from her and hold it so she could slip into it.

"What are we seeing?" she asked as they went to the door and outside where Jonathan's carriage waited in the street.

"The play is called *The Heart's Souvenirs*. It's by Charles Duprey. Do you remember? We saw another of his plays."

"Yes, I remember," Rebecca answered as he handed her up into the carriage and climbed in beside her.

The carriage started off and Rebecca folded her gloved hands in her lap. She felt a twinge of guilt at the way she had thwarted Jonathan's proposal. He loved her, she knew. He was a good man, a kind man. Certainly he could provide her with a comfortable, carefree life. She'd been to the beautiful home he owned outside the city. Why couldn't she let go of the past and build a future with this man?

Sighing, she looked out the window at the houses and shops they passed. Beau. It all came back to Beau. Not a night had passed in the three years since that morning she'd sailed away from Mackinac Island that she hadn't lain awake in her bed thinking of him. Sometimes she wept for him, sometimes she cursed him, but she never forgot him.

She remembered arriving back at Drummond Island. Sumner and all of them had been astonished. They'd believed her dead in the fire that had destroyed her cabin just as Anthony Hawkins had hoped they would.

They'd welcomed her back with open arms, but she'd soon realized she could not stay. She'd remained for the winter, but had left on the first eastbound schooner in the spring. By then she had decided to remain in America and had heard from a fellow passenger of the city of Philadelphia.

And she'd met Jonathan within days of her arrival. She cast a sidelong glance at him. He was a good-looking man. He did not have the breathtaking, almost brutally handsome gold-and-bronze masculine beauty Beau had had, of course, but in the state of mind she'd been in when she'd met him that had been to his advantage. He was several inches taller than she, with dark brown wavy hair and soft, soulful brown eyes that gazed at her with unspoken admiration and longing. In the nearly three years she'd been seeing him, she'd never allowed him more than a kiss, an embrace, but still he courted her. He was a gentle, patient man, a kind man, a sensitive man. But she did not love him.

"Rebecca?" Jonathan prompted as the carriage stopped before the theater. "Rebecca, we're here."

As they walked through the lobby, Jonathan stopped to speak to business and social acquaintances. Rebecca smiled and exchanged greetings with those she knew—people to whose homes she had been invited as Jonathan's guest. She felt a certain hostility in the air and knew much of it came from the women, young and not so young, who had set their caps for Jonathan but had lost their chances once the beautiful, mysterious Mrs. Carlyle had come to town. Most, she knew, would give their eyeteeth to be Mrs. Jonathan Gibbons. If they knew how many times he had proposed that she become just that and that she had refused, they'd think her mad. Sometimes she thought herself mad.

Jonathan stepped back and let her enter his box first. He took her coat as she slipped out of it, and she sat down in one of the red velvet-seated, gilded chairs. She knew quite a few of the people seated below and smiled and waved at some of them. She smiled up at Jonathan as he sat beside her.

Rebecca leaned forward as the curtain was about to rise. She glanced to her left toward the next box and it seemed at that moment that the world stopped turning.

Two couples sat there, one older, one younger. The older gentleman, a distinguished-looking man with steel-gray hair and impressive side whiskers. His lady, beside him, dressed in lilac velvet and purple silk, was stately, not beautiful, perhaps, but grand like an imperious duchess from Rebecca's native England.

The younger couple sat slightly behind them. The lady gave every indication that she would one day be as grand and as elegant as the older woman. For now, she was lovely, not precisely pretty perhaps, but pale and pretty with ash-blonde hair threaded with ribbons and plumes. Her gown was of a pale pink that complimented her alabaster complexion.

But it was her companion who held Rebecca's gaze. She tried to tell herself it wasn't true. She tried to believe her eyes were deceiving her, turning a chance resemblance into something more. But in the end, she had to accept the truth.

There, in the next box, leaning close to hear something his pretty companion was saying, was Beau McAllister. He wore a dark blue frock coat not unlike the shade of the uniform he'd worn on Mackinac Island. His shirt was of the same white as his trousers and the brass buttons of his waistcoat caught the light like the gilded strands of his golden hair.

Trembling, pale, Rebecca leaned back in her chair so the crimson-draped pillar separating the boxes hid Beau and his companion from her sight. She forced herself to breathe slowly and deeply. She clasped her shaking hands in her lap, nearly cracking the ebony sticks of her fan.

The curtain rose and the play began, but the

voices of the players, their lines and gestures, meant nothing to Rebecca. She saw nothing, heard nothing, was aware of nothing, but the nearness of the man she'd longed for, dreamed of, loved, and hated for three long, lonely years.

Jonathan reached out and took her hand in his. Rebecca looked up, startled. Apparently, from the look on his face, she had missed some particularly touching and romantic scene in the play. She had no idea what was happening on stage but she forced a fond smile and allowed Jonathan to raise her gloved hand to his lips. But when he released it, she quickly returned it to her own lap, clasping it with her other hand to still its trembling.

Surreptitiously, she leaned forward and peered into the neighboring box. Beau's companion sat close beside him, her gloved hand on his arm. She spoke to him, apparently softly, for he leaned toward her, and when she'd finished, he grinned, his smile brilliant, those deep, sapphire-blue eyes shimmering in the candlelight.

His smile was like a stiletto through her heart. She bit her lip to stop its quivering. She blinked to quell the tears that threatened to spill down her cheeks. Damn him. Damn him! Why, of all the cities in this benighted country did he have to come to Philadelphia. She wanted to scream, to cry, to charge into the next box and claw that smiling face to ribbons!

Jonathan's voice reached her ears. "Rebecca?" he said, his hand on her wrist. "What's

wrong? You're so pale. And you're trembling!
You look as if you've seen a ghost."

"I . . ." She tried to steady her voice. "I've
seen someone I knew a long time ago," she
managed.

"Who is that?" he asked.

She bit her lip. "In the next box," she whispered, though the noise from the stage would
have kept anyone from overhearing. "Beau
McAllister."

Jonathan leaned a little forward and glanced
discreetly into the neighboring box. "Ah, Captain McAllister."

"Captain?" Rebecca asked. "He was a lieutenant when I knew him. He's not wearing a
uniform."

"I don't think he has to when he's not on
duty," Jonathan told her.

"Who are the people with him?" Rebecca
forced herself to sound casual, but her heart
was pounding as she waited for him to answer.

Jonathan looked again. "The older gentleman
is Colonel Nicholson, McAllister's commanding
officer. The older lady is his wife. The young
woman is their daughter, Caroline."

"Caroline Nicholson," Rebecca whispered to
herself. She asked Jonathan. "What is Beau . . .
Captain McAllister's connection to the Nicholsons?"

"He is Colonel Nicholson's aide," Jonathan
replied. "But he often escorts Caroline Nicholson to social affairs. Rumor has it an announce-

ment will soon be made of their engagement."

Rebecca felt her stomach turn over. Engagement! Beau was going to marry that spun-sugar blonde? Oh, God, why here? Why now?

Rebecca said no more. She felt numb, mute, she could not think much less talk. She wanted only for the interminable play to end so that she could go home and try to make some sense of this evening.

At last the curtain fell and Rebecca quickly snatched up her coat and slipped it on.

They left their box, and Jonathan took her elbow to slow her down as she would have barreled through the crowd to reach the lobby and the safety of his carriage.

"Rebecca," Jonathan said, "don't you want to say hello to Captain McAllister?"

"No!" Rebecca cried. She blushed, aware of several curious looks aimed in her direction. "Please, Jonathan, I'd just like to go home."

"As you wish," he acquiesced, leading her out to the street and into his coach.

As they started out, he eyed her curiously. "Where do you know Beau McAllister from?"

Rebecca gazed out the window. "When I was in the west," she answered evasively. "He was posted to a fort there. It was a long time ago, Jonathan. I was just surprised at seeing him, that's all. I can't understand why I haven't run into him somewhere before tonight."

"From what I understand," Jonathan explained, "Colonel Nicholson was in Washington until recently. He came here to Philadelphia and

brought his aide, Captain McAllister, with him."
Jonathan laughed. "No doubt he didn't want to
let a prospective son-in-law slip through his
fingers."

Rebecca said no more as they rode through
the night-shrouded city. How cozy, she thought
bitterly, that Beau had been posted to the capi-
tal as an aide to the colonel. He'd become his
superior officer's daughter's favorite escort and
when the colonel had been transferred he'd
brought Beau with him. Had it been the colonel's idea? Or his daughter's? Or Beau's? Whatever it was, judging from what she'd seen at
the theater, he didn't seem to find escorting his
colonel's daughter a particularly onerous duty.

The carriage drew up before Rebecca's townhouse and Jonathan stepped out and held up a
hand to help her down. Together they walked
to the door and she took out her key.

"May I come in?" Jonathan asked.

Apologetically, Rebecca shook her head. "It's
very late," she said. "And I'm awfully tired." She
glanced up at the lighted windows on the second floor of the three-story house. "Mrs. Bailey
will be waiting up for me."

Jonathan sighed. Mrs. Bailey was Rebecca's
housekeeper and he knew she would not say
a word if Rebecca were to invite him into the
house. It was only an excuse but he felt he had
no choice but to accept it gracefully.

"Well, then, good night," he said. "Will I see
you tomorrow?"

"If you like," she said gently, knowing she

had hurt his feelings. "Why don't you come for supper?"

Smiling, he nodded. He leaned close and she allowed him to kiss her softly on the lips.

Rebecca fitted her key in the lock and opened her front door. With a last smile for Jonathan, she closed the door behind her.

All pretense gratefully abandoned, she pulled off her coat and tossed it over a chair. Her fan landed on top of it and she sank onto a damask-covered settee and buried her face in her hands.

"What is it, dearie?" Mrs. Bailey asked. The stout, motherly woman in nightdress, wrapper, and nightcap came to hover over her. "I heard you come in and Mr. Jonathan's carriage drive away. Did he upset you?"

"No," Rebecca whispered, lifting her head. "It was not Jonathan. It was someone at the theater tonight."

"Who?" the housekeeper asked.

"A ghost," Rebecca replied, reaching up to take the housekeeper's hand. "A ghost from the past."

Chapter Thirty-Five

"A ghost, you say?" Mrs. Bailey set her candlestick on a table and sat down beside Rebecca. "Whatever can you mean?"

Wiping her cheeks with her fingertips, Rebecca shook her head. "It's nothing. A man I once knew, that's all." She forced a smile. "How is Monty?"

"I haven't heard a peep out of him since I put him down," the housekeeper answered. "He's a little angel."

Rebecca laughed. "You're prejudiced, Mrs. Bailey. I love him with all my heart, but I'd never accuse him of being an angel."

Rising, she reached out and squeezed the older woman's hand. "I think I'll look in on him before I go to bed. Good night."

"Sleep well, my dear," the housekeeper said,

taking up her candle once more.

Rebecca nodded as she started for the stairs but she doubted it would be possible after what she had heard and seen at the theater tonight.

Upstairs she went to a door across from her own bedroom. Quietly, she opened it and peered inside. The room was dimly lit, a single candle burned in a brass holder, its etched-glass cover protecting the flame from drafts. Across from the light stood a small bed with ornately carved guards running halfway to the foot.

Rebecca went to the little bed and bent over it. Lying there, his cheeks flushed, his lashes lying over pink-and-white cheeks, was her two-and-a-half-year-old son.

He was the reason she had decided to leave Drummond Island. Once she had learned she carried Beau's child, she had known she could not remain. And he was the reason she had decided to live in America, partly because she knew Beau would want his child raised an American and partly because she could not imagine returning to England and telling her parents she was alone, unmarried, and bearing another man's child so soon after William's death. The second was a cowardly reason, she admitted, but there it was.

She'd been heavily pregnant by the time she'd reached Philadelphia. When she'd gone to Jonathan's bank, she'd told him she was a widow. He'd assumed the child she was carrying was her late husband's and she'd done nothing to disabuse him of the notion. He'd helped her arrange for her finances, helped her find this house, and Mrs. Bailey, the housekeeper-nanny, without whose support and common sense she didn't know what she'd do.

And it was a good thing that Jonathan assumed her child belonged to her dead husband. For if he had stopped to think about her reaction tonight to Beau and remembered her young son, he might all too easily realize the truth.

Smiling softly, she touched her son's downy cheek with tender fingers. Here, then, was the Beau-in-miniature she'd thought she'd lost with her miscarriage on Mackinac Island. His hair was the same burnished gold, his face gave every promise of one day having the same chiseled male beauty Beau possessed. And his eyes, when he was awake, were a clear, dark, sapphire-blue.

She'd wanted to name him after Beau when he'd been born, even though he would carry her last name. It was only then she had realized she'd never asked what the name Beau might be short for. And so she'd named him Beaumont and from then on he'd been Monty to one and all.

Gently, she tucked the quilts around him and smoothed his golden curls. She smiled as his lashes fluttered and his eyes opened.

"Mama?" he said, stretching a hand out toward her.

"Yes, darling, I'm here," she said, taking his hand and kissing it before tucking his arm under the blanket. "Go back to sleep now."

The deep blue eyes, so like another pair she'd never thought to see again, closed and he went back to sleep quickly with all the carefree trust of a little boy.

Rising, Rebecca quietly left the room. But instead of going to her own room, she went back downstairs to the drawing room and poured herself a glass of claret.

"It's little Monty's father, isn't it?" a voice from behind her asked.

Rebecca started, nearly dropping her glass. Turning, she saw Mrs. Bailey standing there, her long gray braid hanging over her shoulder, her ruffled nightcap framing her round, concerned face.

Sighing, Rebecca nodded. "Beau McAllister," she admitted. "He is an aide to Colonel Nicholson. From what Jonathan said, this colonel has recently been transferred from Washington and brought Beau with him."

She sank into a chair and took a long sip of her wine. "I never thought I would see him again, Elinor." She shook her head. "After I left Mackinac Island, I thought he was out of my life forever."

Elinor Bailey, who alone of anyone in Philadelphia knew what had happened to Rebecca in the years before she came to Philadelphia, sat down beside her.

"Was it so difficult, then, seeing him again? I was under the impression that you loved him."

"I did," Rebecca admitted, adding softly, "I do. But he sent me away. He wanted nothing more to do with me. But then, tonight, there he was. I could have reached out and touched him, Elinor!"

"Then why didn't you?"

"He was with someone," she said softly, draining her glass and setting it aside.

"A woman?"

Rebecca nodded. "Jonathan said she is the colonel's daughter. He says the gossip is that Beau and she will marry."

"Oh, my dear!" Elinor cooed, reaching out to take Rebecca's hand. "I'm so sorry." She frowned, leaning toward Rebecca. "But does he know about little Monty?"

"No, of course not, how could he?"

"Why don't you tell him?" She went on before Rebecca could object. "But surely if he knew he had a son—"

"No." Rebecca shook her head. "If he wants to marry this girl, I'll not use my son to prevent it. Monty is better off without a father than with a father who wants to be with someone else."

"A little boy needs a father," Elinor pointed out. "If you really don't want to tell this Beau McAllister that Monty is his, then why don't you consider marrying Mr. Jonathan? He loves you so, and I know he's proposed to you more than once."

Rebecca laughed in spite of herself. "You are an incorrigible matchmaker, Elinor," she chided. "Why are you so interested in seeing me married?"

"Because Monty needs a father and you need someone to love you, to care for you. Oh, I know"—she held up a hand to silence Rebecca's protests—"you can take care of yourself. I'm not talking about financial affairs. I'm talking about a beautiful, lonely young woman who doesn't have to be lonely. Mr. Jonathan loves you."

"But I don't love him," Rebecca pointed out.

"Do you love Monty's father?"

Reluctantly, Rebecca nodded. "Yes, I love Beau. It seems I always have." She dropped her eyes. "But he doesn't love me."

Elinor sighed. "What's to be done then?" she asked, reaching out to squeeze Rebecca's hand.

Rebecca smiled wanly and returned the squeeze. "For tonight," she said, "nothing. I'm going to go to bed and try to forget the whole thing if only for a little while."

Getting up, she impulsively bent down and kissed Mrs. Bailey's cheek. "Good night," she said fondly, smiling at the woman who had become more than a housekeeper, and more like a mother to Rebecca and a doting grandmother to Monty.

"Good night, my dear," Elinor Bailey said, watching with a wistful expression as the woman she'd come to love like a daughter mounted the stairs and disappeared into her bedroom.

Dressed in her nightdress, Rebecca sat before her looking glass, brushing out her hair after having taken out the mother-of-pearl comb. The woman who gazed back at her from the depths of the silvered glass looked older than she had three years before, world-weary, wiser.

Perhaps Mrs. Bailey was right, she mused. Perhaps she should have said something to Beau at the theater. If he knew she was here, in Philadelphia . . . If he knew they had a child. . . .

Unbidden, the image of Beau seated beside the pretty blonde appeared in Rebecca's mind. Was he in love with her? Caroline, that was her name. Was he somewhere, even then, making love to her? Were they whispering together, intimate endearments, planning their future?

Rebecca gasped at the pain that thought caused her. She pressed her fingertips to her lips.

"Beau," she whispered, "I don't understand."

She remembered the nights on Mackinac Island when she was recovering in the attic room at Dr. Day's house. Whenever they could, she and Beau had been together in that creaking bed with its sagging ropes and straw-tick mattress. The love they made was like nothing she'd ever known or could ever hope to know again. But he had sent her away, apparently without a backward glance.

She had waited and waited, throughout that long, lonely winter at Fort Collier on Drummond Island. She had hoped against hope every time a mailbag arrived that there might be some small message from Beau. But there was nothing. Beau's child was growing within her, a testament to those nights of passion, but from Beau not a word of love. She might as well have disappeared from the face of the earth for all he'd seemed to care.

Now here he was, in Philadelphia, a lovely young girl at his side. She remembered how he'd smiled at the girl, how he'd leaned close to hear what she'd said to him, how the girl's fingers had settled on the blue cloth of his sleeve. She remembered Jonathan telling her that the gossips said that Captain McAllister would marry Caroline Nicholson.

"Caroline McAllister," Rebecca whispered, hating the sound of it.

Sighing, she tossed her brush aside. Why was she torturing herself? Beau had made his decision, he had made his choice, and she'd be damned if she'd use her sweet, precious son to try to lure back a man who did not want to be with her.

"Beau McAllister can go to hell for all I care!" she hissed, throwing off her wrapper and dragging back the coverlet on her bed.

She climbed into bed and jerked the covers up under her chin. So much for Captain Beau McAllister! She wouldn't cry for him anymore, she wouldn't regret what might have been! Let him have his pretty little featherpate! Much joy may she bring him! She would make a life for herself and her son without him.

"I'll marry Jonathan!" she vowed, her eyes

bright and shining fiercely. She frowned. "Well, maybe I won't marry Jonathan. But I'll think about it!"

Rolling over, she banished the image of Beau from her mind. She wouldn't even think about him. From now on, it would be as if he'd never been a part of her life.

But that was easier said than done. While she was awake, she could banish Beau from her thoughts by sheer force of will. But once she fell asleep, her dreams seemed to center on him, troubling, restless dreams of what might have been but never would be.

Chapter Thirty-Six

Rebecca stood patiently as *Madame* Celeste, her dressmaker, fitted a gown of emerald silk she had ordered weeks before.

"You have grown thinner since the gown was cut out," *Madame* Celeste said, taking in a seam. "You must eat. The gentlemen like their ladies to be plump and pretty."

Rebecca smiled wanly. *Madame* Celeste herself could be described by only the politest of people as merely "plump." But she was an excellent dressmaker with exquisite taste and Rebecca was willing to allow her her opinions.

"*Monsieur* Gibbons has not broken your heart, has he?" the dressmaker asked.

"Not at all, *madame*," Rebecca assured her. "It is only that I've had little appetite of late."

"Well, you must force yourself. Your beauty depends upon your health and your health depends upon your eating well and sleeping well. Do not forget it."

"I won't forget, *madame*," Rebecca promised absently.

"And where is that sweet little son of yours today?" *Madame* Celeste went on, for she liked to know all the details of her client's lives. "Is your faithful Mrs. Bailey attending him?"

"No," Rebecca replied. "Mrs. Bailey stayed at home. Monty is out playing in the park across the street with my maid-of-all-work, Letty."

"Such a beautiful child he is," the dressmaker mumbled around a mouthful of pins. "His father must have been a very handsome man."

"Yes," Rebecca murmured, Beau's face appearing in her imagination. "A very handsome man indeed."

The bell over the door in the shop chimed and *Madame* Celeste took the pins from her mouth and dropped them into a china dish.

"If you will excuse me a moment, *madame*, I will see who it is."

The dressmaker left the fitting room and went out into the shop, whose somber woodwork was a dark backdrop for the rainbow of silks and satins spread over the tables for her customers' perusal. Fashion dolls in the latest Paris styles stood on the countertops and sketches littered tables and chairs. In one corner a fireplace warmed the room and kept the water hot for the tea *Madame* Celeste invariably offered her customers.

"Ah! *Mademoiselle* Nicholson," the dress-maker cooed. "Your gown is finished. Would you like to try it on before you take it home?"

"I would, *madame,*" Caroline Nicholson replied. "Thought I'm certain it's perfect."

"How sweet you are. Mimi!" There was silence until *Madame* Celeste's assistant appeared from the sewing room at the back of the shop. "Take *Mademoiselle* Nicholson into that fitting room and help her with her gown. Some tea, perhaps, *mademoiselle?*"

"Thank you, no, *madame,*" Caroline answered as she followed the tiny, dark-haired assistant into the fitting room next to the one where Rebecca waited.

Rebecca stood, expecting the dressmaker to return to finish her fitting. Instead, she heard *Madame* Celeste say, "And you, *Monsieur* McAllister. May I offer you some tea?"

"Not today, *madame,*" Beau's voice replied. "I've just come from tea with the Nicholsons. Are you well, *madame?* You look as lovely as ever."

Cautiously, Rebecca peeked between the blue velvet draperies that divided the fitting rooms from the front of the shop. Beau stood there, resplendent in his uniform, so tall and handsome that Rebecca's heart seemed to stop in her breast. *Madame* Celeste, her face flushed with girlish pleasure at his company, bustled about seeing that he was comfortable while he waited for Caroline to finish her fitting.

Letting the curtains fall together, Rebecca turned away. Now he was accompanying Caroline Nicholson to the dressmakers! she thought bitterly. How very domestic of him! Tears stung her eyes. And he had been to tea at Caroline's home!

With her fingertips, Rebecca rubbed away the tears blurring her vision. What did she care, she told herself fiercely, if Beau could think of nothing better to do than follow that featherpate around on her errands! He had seemed so strong, so masterful, so brave and bold on Mackinac Island. Now what was he but some faithful lapdog for a girl scarcely out of the schoolroom.

She frowned, impatient for the dressmaker to come help her out of her pinned-together gown. She wanted nothing more than to leave, though she could not think how she could get out of the shop with Beau sitting there.

"Come back, *madame*," she whispered to herself. "Get me out of this dress!"

She heard the click of the woman's heels approaching the fitting room and thought help was at last on its way. But just as *Madame* Celeste would have entered the fitting room, the bell over the door rang again, signaling another arrival.

"Oh, damn!" she muttered, feeling suddenly like a prisoner in a green silk prison.

She heard *Madame* Celeste's lilting, accented voice cry out, "Be careful, little one, you're going to—"

There was a thud, then the loud, piercing cry of a child, more surprised than hurt, filled the shop.

Rebecca, recognizing Monty's cry, started for the curtains, more worried for her child's safety than whether Beau saw her. But by the time she reached the fitting-room door, Monty's cries had stopped.

Rebecca opened the curtains to peek out. Letty, the young maid stood watching, a dazzled look on her face, as Beau bounced the little boy in his arms.

Rebecca held her breath. Her son, usually standoffish with strangers, regarded Beau with calm interest, fascinated by the gold buttons and braid of Beau's uniform.

Seeing them, their golden heads so close together, so alike, the resemblance seemed, to Rebecca, unmistakable. Sapphire eyes gazed into sapphire eyes as Beau and the little boy looked at one another.

Rebecca pressed her fingers to her lips. Didn't Beau feel some kinship with the child? she wondered. Didn't some sixth sense tell him that the sturdy, handsome little boy he held in his arms was his own flesh and blood?

Beau smiled at Monty and Rebecca thought her heart would break. She felt a rush of guilt that she was keeping her secret. Beau had a right to know that he had a son; he had a right to get acquainted with his child. Even if fate had decreed that he and Rebecca take separate paths, Beau was Monty's father. It was wrong of her to deprive a father of his child and a child of his father. Was she being selfish to deprive them both? Even if there was no future for her with Beau, surely it would be good for Monty to have a father in his life and not be constantly surrounded by women.

Steeling herself, Rebecca started toward the door, determined to confront Beau and ask him to call on her her at his earliest convenience. She would not tell him now. It was far too private and sensitive a matter to be discussed in a dress shop in front of *Madame* Celeste, who would, no doubt, tell the news to every lady who walked through her door.

No, she would ask Beau to call, and in the privacy of her own home, she would tell him he was Monty's father and see if he wished to become a part of his son's life.

Taking a deep breath, she reached out to separate the velvet draperies. But before she could, she heard the high, giddy voice of Caroline Nicholson filling the air.

"Look at my gown, Beau!" she cried, sweeping out of the other fitting room. "Isn't it delicious! Oh, *madame*, you are a wonder!"

Peering between the curtains, Rebecca saw the ash-blonde Caroline Nicholson twirling to show off the canary-yellow satin gown with its tiers of delicate lace. She seemed so young, so heedless of anything but her own pleasure, so sure of herself and the world around her, that beside her Rebecca felt old and weary.

"Beau!" Caroline cried, noticing for the first time, the child he held in his arms. "What an adorable little boy! I declare, he looks just like you! Whose is he?"

Rebecca held her breath, wondering if *Madame* Celeste would reveal the truth. But the dressmaker, mercifully, had gone back to the sewing room for more pins.

"He is the child of another of *Madame's* customers," Beau answered.

"Aren't you darling?" Caroline cooed, leaning close to Monty as if to kiss his cheek.

But the little boy, attracted to the shimmer of Caroline's dangling earrings, reached out and gave one a sharp tug, making the wire dig into her ear lobe.

"Oh!" Caroline cried, clasping a hand to her ear, then checking her fingers for blood. "The little brat!"

She made a motion toward Monty with her hand and Rebecca, not caring if Beau saw her, started to open the curtains, determined that no one would hurt her child.

But Beau quickly handed Monty to the maid and followed Caroline back into the fitting room where she'd retreated to nurse her stinging ear.

"*Madame?*" Rebecca called as the dressmaker appeared from the sewing room. "*Madame,* please, help me out of this gown. I must leave at once!"

"Of course, *madame*. I am so sorry to have left you here so long. Where is *Mademoiselle*

Nicholson and *Monsieur* McAllister?"

"In the other fitting room, I believe," Rebecca replied, stepping out of the green gown and reaching for the gown of pale lilac silk she'd come in.

"Ah, doubtless they wished to be alone. These young lovers."

"Just so," Rebecca agreed, reaching for her bonnet and shawl as *Madame* Celeste fastened the back of her gown. "I must go, *madame*. The gown will be lovely, I'm certain. Good-bye."

Taking Monty from the maid as she passed, Rebecca went out to her carriage and climbed inside. As they rode toward home, Rebecca cuddled her little boy, stroking his golden hair, remembering Caroline Nicholson's face as she'd drawn back a hand to slap him for tugging at her earring.

"Never!" she whispered fiercely, her amethyst eyes sparkling, her tone too low for the maid, Letty, sitting opposite to hear. "I'll never let that woman touch my son! Beau can have her if he wants her. He can marry that she-cat! I wish him the joy of her! But she'll never be a stepmother to my son!"

Chapter Thirty-Seven

"Will you come with me?" Jonathan asked, handing Monty's stuffed toy back to the baby who toddled up to him, his hands outstretched.

"I don't know," Rebecca hedged, carefully not looking up from the embroidery hoop she held in her lap. "I've been leaving Monty home alone so much lately and—"

"Come now, Rebecca," Jonathan chided. "You know perfectly well that Monty will be almost ready for bed by the time we leave."

"I suppose so, but . . . Monty, no, no!" She laid aside her hoop and retrieved her basket of brilliantly colored silks from the baby, who was happily tangling them into a multihued ball of knots.

"Rebecca, what's the real reason you're hesitating? You've been to balls at Fairfield before.

I thought you liked Philip and Judith Lamont."

"I do like them," she insisted. "And Fairfield is a beautiful home. It's only . . ."

"Only?" Jonathan studied the golden charm dangling from his watch fob. "Tell me the truth, Rebecca. Is it the man we saw at the theater? Captain McAllister? Are you afraid he'll be there?"

"Jonathan, please." Rebecca sighed. "You're being ridiculous."

"Am I? You were never this reluctant to go anywhere with me before. Now, all of a sudden, you don't want to leave Monty."

"All right!" she agreed impatiently. "I'll go to Fairfield with you! Now can we end this ridiculous conversation, please?"

Mollified, Jonathan allowed her to change the subject but Rebecca realized the seeds of suspicion were firmly planted in his mind. She wondered if the ball at Fairfield would confirm or deny those suspicions.

On the night of the ball, Rebecca sat in her gown of emerald silk, its four deep flounces around the skirt echoed in ruffles banding the short puffed sleeves and the deep, rounded neckline. At her throat, an emerald pendant hung from a thin gold chain and emeralds dangled from her ears. They were gifts from Jonathan who'd insisted she take them despite her protests that they were far too costly.

"There you are, my dear," Mrs. Bailey said as she positioned the emerald silk ribbon that caught back Rebecca's curls and let them fall in a shining black cascade down over her shoulders. "You'll be the belle of the ball."

"I doubt it," Rebecca replied, standing and drawing on her long, buff-colored gloves.

"Do you think Captain McAllister will be there?"

Rebecca gave her a worried glance. "I'm afraid so." She forced a wan smile. "Of course, he'll probably be so enraptured by Caroline Nicholson he won't notice me."

"Come now, Rebecca," the housekeeper said cajolingly, "don't you think you should speak to him if he's there? For Monty's sake."

"It's for Monty's sake that I shouldn't speak to him," Rebecca insisted. "What if he felt obligated to be with me because of Monty? How happy could he be, being with me because he felt he had to and not because he wanted to?"

"Even so," Mrs. Bailey argued, "I think he has a right to know he has a son. No doubt he'd—"

But at that moment the downstairs bell rang and Mrs. Bailey had no choice but to go down and admit Jonathan. Rebecca followed, pulling on her green silk pelisse. She knew Elinor was dying to say more, but the housekeeper was silent as she handed Rebecca her straw bonnet with its green ribbons and plumes.

"Good night, Elinor," Rebecca said.

"Good night, dear," Elinor said, tight-lipped.

"Is she angry about something?" Jonathan asked as they went to the waiting carriage.

"We had a slight disagreement," Rebecca explained vaguely. "Nothing important."

Little was said on the ride to Fairfield. It was not a long ride but Rebecca felt tension in the silence that reigned in the carriage. She was relieved when they arrived, drawing up before the elegant, three-story brick mansion with its steep-hipped, dormer-pierced roof and twin curving wings.

"How lovely you look tonight," Philip Lamont told Rebecca as one of his servants relieved her of her hat and pelisse.

Rebecca smiled up at the distinguished-looking financier. "Flatterer," she teased.

"Not at all," he insisted. "You must promise me a dance."

Laughing, Rebecca promised, then went into the ballroom on Jonathan's arm.

Discreetly, over the rim of a glass, she scanned the room. There was no sign of Beau or Caroline, Colonel or Mrs. Nicholson. Was it possible, she wondered, that they had not been invited? They had not been in Philadelphia long, it was possible they did not know Philip Lamont.

"Come dance with me," Jonathan invited as the musicians began to play.

Rebecca stepped into his arms as they moved with the other couples around the long, elegant room with its beautiful woodwork and gleaming, polished floor. The dowagers sat gossiping in the rows of tapestry-cushioned chairs in the corner. In an adjoining room a table of refreshments had been laid out with a selection of wines, pastries, and cakes.

She looked up into Jonathan's dark eyes and found him gazing down at her. He was in love with her, and her heart ached with guilt and regret that she could not return his love.

She sighed as he lifted her hand to his lips and kissed her gloved fingers. If only Beau had not reappeared, she might have learned to love Jonathan. They might have built a comfortable life together.

The dance ended and they walked to the edge of the dance floor where several of Jonathan's business acquaintances stood talking. As they began discussing some complicated financial business, Rebecca excused herself and went into the refreshment room where the aroma of fresh-cut flowers arranged in vases vied with the delicate scent of the pastries and cakes on fine porcelain plates.

A pair of French doors opened onto the garden behind the house. A creek wound its way through the garden and the graveled path led through the beautiful beds and over an ornate stone bridge. Lanterns had been lit and cast dim golden circles of light along the path.

Rebecca stood gazing through the doors toward the garden and she did not at first hear the Lamonts greeting their newly arrived guests. It was only when she turned around that she caught sight of Colonel and Mrs. Nicholson standing in the foyer, which opened onto both the ballroom and the smaller room where Rebecca was.

She watched, curious, wondering if their daughter was with them. In a moment she saw Caroline Nicholson, pretty in canary-yellow satin with cascades of lace rippling as she walked. Her blonde curls framed her delicate, pink-and-white face, making her seem as delicate and delectable as one of the pretty pastries.

Holding her breath, Rebecca waited to see if Beau was with them. As she watched, Colonel Nicholson, his wife, and their daughter disappeared into the ballroom.

"He didn't come," she whispered to herself, secretly pleased.

But she'd relaxed too early. He was in the foyer, speaking to someone she could not see. He smiled and Rebecca felt her heart turn over. His evening dress, a deep wine-red frock coat, cream pantaloons, and a cream-and-burgundy waistcoat trimmed with gold buttons, was even more flattering than his uniform had been. He seemed so handsome, so elegant. It seemed incredible to Rebecca that she had once upon a time lain in those arms, kissed those lips, trembled under the caresses of those hands. She could scarcely believe that the beautiful little boy sleeping at home had been fathered by this elegant gentleman.

Rebecca's eyes narrowed as Caroline Nicholson once more appeared. Wrapping her hands around Beau's arm, she pulled him away from his conversation and out of Rebecca's line of vision.

Unable to stop herself, Rebecca went to the doorway and peered into the ballroom. As she'd imagined, Beau held Caroline in his arms and they twirled about the floor as the orchestra played a waltz. Beau smiled down at his pretty partner who scarcely reached his broad shoulder with the top of her curly head.

As she watched, Rebecca felt a twinge of jealousy. She had never danced with Beau. He had never held her in his arms as they circled an elegant room to the strains of a beautiful melody. Of course, she had to admit there weren't many balls on Mackinac Island. But, still, the sight of him holding Caroline, looking so handsome, and so happy. . . .

She looked around for Jonathan, intending to think of some excuse to talk him into taking her home. But he was still engrossed in his conversation and showed no sign of leaving it soon.

Sighing, she resigned herself to being stuck there for several hours to come. Retreating to the refreshment room, she let herself out into the garden, where the night air was warm, the darkness welcome, and the scent of the flowers a soft, beguiling perfume borne on the night breezes.

Sinking onto a bench beside the path, she felt overwhelmed with sadness. For three long years she had longed for Beau, pined for him, almost mourned him, and now here he was, so close she could almost feel him, holding another woman in his arms.

Longing to be out of earshot of the music that wafted over the garden, she left the bench and wandered onto the little stone bridge spanning the creek. The moon was a silvery sliver high above, casting little light.

The stone balustrade was rough against her palms as she rested them upon it. She gazed down into the black creek below, its calm surface showing her a dark reflection of her own melancholy face.

What would happen? she wondered. She could not put off the inevitable forever. She could not run and hide every time society threw her and Beau together. Sooner or later they would come face to face and then what? If she weren't such a coward, she would march back into that ballroom and face him. She would dance and laugh and flirt with Jonathan and show Beau McAllister that he was not the only man in the world; show him that she could get along without him as well as he could get along without her.

But for now, the thought of meeting him threw her into a panic. She knew she could not maintain her composure; she knew she would cry or shake or be hopelessly tongue-tied. And she couldn't bear the thought of embarrassing herself in front of Caroline Nicholson.

A noise on the path between the bridge and the house startled her. For a moment she hoped Jonathan had come searching for her. Then she could ask him to take her home—plead a headache or something—and they could leave discreetly with little fuss.

But the man who appeared around the bend in the path was Beau, his mouth agape, staring at her as she stood bathed in the weak moonlight.

"Rebecca!" he breathed, frozen to the spot. "Rebecca!"

He took a step toward her and she panicked. Turning away, she fled into the night on the far side of the bridge.

"Rebecca, wait!" Beau called, starting after her.

But she was gone. Skirts lifted away from her feet, she ran along the path, darting between the flower beds, intent only on escape. The thought of meeting him again in this intimate place, knowing his new love was just inside those beautiful walls, frightened her.

His footsteps were softer now, fading. She had been here many times before and knew the twists and turns of the serpentine garden paths.

From the sound of his footfalls, she knew where he was and she doubled back and recrossed the bridge while he was still searching the far corners of the sprawling park.

Her breasts heaving, she reentered the house and made for Jonathan, who had finally left his acquaintances and had come looking for her.

"Rebecca, here you are," he said. "Would you like a glass of wine? You're out of breath."

"Take me home, Jonathan," she asked. "Now, please. I want to go home."

"But why?" he asked.

"I mean it," she insisted. "If you won't come with me, I'll go alone and send the carriage back for you."

He put down his glass. "Of course I'll come with you. But won't you tell me—"

"In the carriage," she promised.

But they were nearly to her home and she still had said nothing when at last Jonathan prompted, "Was it McAllister?" She said nothing and he went on, a note of impatience in his voice, "Rebecca, I think I have a right to know."

"All right," she acquiesced. "It was Beau. I had gone into the garden and suddenly there he was. He came toward me. I ran away."

"But why?" Jonathan raised a hand, then let it fall into his lap. "Can't you tell me what all this is about?"

"Oh, Jonathan," she whispered. "I never thought to see him again. I thought it was all in the past."

"What was in the past?" he persisted. "What was between the two of you?"

Looking up at him, she said softly, "He is Monty's father."

Even in the near darkness of the carriage, she could see the shocked pallor of his face. "Jonathan, I didn't think I'd ever see him again. I didn't think the truth about Monty's parentage would ever be an issue."

"I thought Monty was your late husband's child," Jonathan said quietly.

"I know," Rebecca admitted.

"You never corrected my thinking."

"I didn't think . . ."

"You didn't think the truth would ever come to light," he supplied.

"Oh, Jonathan," she said, leaning toward him, "I thought Beau was a part of the past. The truth was so complicated, so . . ." She looked away as the carriage drew up before her door. "I didn't want anyone to know."

The carriage door opened and Jonathan stepped down, then reached up to help Rebecca out. He walked with her to the door and when she opened it, followed her inside, uninvited.

"I want to know the truth, Rebecca," he said as she pulled off her pelisse and bonnet. "And I intend to know it all before I leave here tonight."

"Once you know," she warned, "you may not want to see me anymore."

Reaching out, he touched the cascading curls that fell like black silk over her creamy shoulder. "I'm willing to take that risk."

"Well, then," she said, resigned, "come in and make yourself comfortable. It's a long, long story."

Chapter Thirty-Eight

Jonathan stood, his hands clasped behind his back, gazing up at the landscape hanging above the fireplace in Rebecca's drawing room. Silence hung heavy in the room as Rebecca finished her story.

"Say something, Jonathan," she said when the silence dragged on.

He turned toward her. "Why didn't you tell me any of this before? You knew I assumed Monty was the child of your husband."

Rebecca toyed with the gloves that lay across her lap. "I thought you would despise me—a condemned British spy pregnant with the child of a man who was not her husband?"

Sighing, Jonathan sank down into a chair near the fireplace. "I would have been taken aback," he admitted. "But, tell me, did you love Beau McAllister?"

Rebecca drew a deep, shuddering breath. "At first, I meant only to use him to gather the information I'd been sent there for. I was serving my country. He was the enemy. But then . . . yes, I fell in love with him."

"And now? Now that you've seen him again? Do you still love him?"

Rebecca sighed, laying her gloves aside on the sofa. "What difference does it make, Jonathan? He's with—"

"Do you!" Jonathan persisted, his voice rising.

Rebecca hesitated, then answered softly, "Yes."

The breath Jonathan had not realized he'd been holding left his body in a rush. "Then why did you run away from him at Fairfield?"

"I don't know," she replied. "I didn't know what to say. I didn't know what he would say."

"Rebecca, you love this man. You bore his child. How can you not know what to say to him?"

"He sent me away, Jonathan."

"He saved your life! You couldn't stay on Mackinac Island with him."

"I know. But he knew where I was going. Surely he could have written to me. If he loved me . . ."

Jonathan sighed. "Give him a chance to explain."

"Explain what? If he had cared for me, he would have written to me at Fort Collier. And, anyway, what does it matter now? He's found someone else." She turned away to hide her expression. "You, yourself, told me he is going to marry Caroline Nicholson."

"I told you?"

"At the theater, remember?"

Jonathan scowled, exasperated. "I told you that was what the gossips said. It may not be true."

He went to Rebecca and turned her toward him. "You have to see him, Rebecca," he told her gently. "You must, at least, tell him about Monty. A man has a right to know he has a son."

Rebecca nodded. "I'll think about it, Jonathan. I promise."

"Think seriously about it," he said sternly. "Don't leave it too long."

Touching her cheek, Jonathan leaned forward and kissed her forehead. Then, bidding her good night, he left, leaving Rebecca alone with her fears and misgivings.

Later, lying in bed, Rebecca thought of Beau, wondering what might have happened had she not run away from him in the garden at Fairfield.

A week passed, a week during which Rebecca neither saw nor heard from Jonathan. He wanted nothing more to do with her, she supposed. It reminded her of Sumner's reaction once he discovered she was carrying Beau's child. He had been bitter, disillusioned, angry. They had seen little of one another after he'd found out the truth.

She returned home on a sunny afternoon after a shopping expedition. The carriage drew up before her townhouse and she stepped down and reached inside for her packages.

She had not yet gotten to the door when it opened and Mrs. Bailey beckoned her in, her round face flushed with excitement.

"Let me take those," she said, plucking Rebecca's packages from her arms. She put them aside and came back to untie the ribbons of Rebecca's bonnet.

"What's happening?" Rebecca asked as she pulled off her pelisse and had it all but snatched out of her hand.

"There's a gentleman in the drawing room to see you," her housekeeper answered, fluttering around Rebecca, tidying her hair, smoothing a wrinkle from her gown.

"Beau?" Rebecca whispered, her eyes going to the closed drawing-room doors.

Mrs. Bailey nodded. "He's been here about a half hour. I told him you'd gone shopping and he said he'd wait."

Rebecca drew a deep breath and pressed a hand to her stomach which seemed aflutter with nerves. "Does he know about Monty?"

Mrs. Bailey shrugged. "He didn't say anything about him. So I suppose he doesn't. You're going to tell him, aren't you?"

"I don't know," Rebecca replied.

"Rebecca!" Mrs. Bailey argued. "You have to tell him—"

"Hush now," Rebecca interrupted. "I'll speak with him and then I'll decide."

"But he should know! Even Mr. Jonathan says—"

"I know what Mr. Jonathan says," Rebecca told her. "But the decision will be mine."

Taking a deep breath, Rebecca went to the drawing-room door and opened it.

Beau stood up as she entered the room. He wore white pantaloons, a deep blue coat that matched his eyes, and a waistcoat of blue brocade. As Rebecca paused in the doorway, she drew a shaky breath. The sight of him, so handsome, so close, was like a physical blow to her system.

"I see Mrs. Bailey has brought you tea," she said, noticing the tea set and biscuits on the table.

"Yes," Beau agreed. "She's been very kind to me."

"She's a wonderful person." Gesturing for him to sit down, Rebecca took a seat opposite him on the sofa.

"How did you find me?" she asked, adding, "No, don't tell me. Jonathan Gibbons."

Beau nodded. "At Fairfield I asked Philip Lamont who you'd come with. He told me and I went to Jonathan Gibbons and asked him how to find you." Beau hesitated then went on, "He said you'd seen me at the theater."

"Yes," Rebecca admitted. "I almost didn't recognize you. I'd never seen you out of uniform before."

Beau grinned. "Come now, Rebecca, you've seen me out of my uniform more than a few times."

Blushing, Rebecca had to laugh. "You know perfectly well what I mean," she chided.

"Why didn't you say something at the theater?" he asked, his grin fading.

Rebecca shook her head. "I don't know," she said softly. "I . . . I didn't know what to say."

"If I'd known you were here, in Philadelphia . . ." He stopped. "Why didn't you go back to England?"

"I decided to stay in America," she said vaguely. "I heard about Philadelphia and it sounded like a good place to . . ." she hesitated. She'd been about say "to raise my son" but she couldn't bring herself to say the words. "To live," she finished lamely.

Beau sensed there was more she wasn't saying but he didn't feel he could press her at this point.

"How long did you stay on Drummond Island?"

"For that first winter," she replied. "In the spring, in April, I boarded the first schooner that came along."

"All winter." His blue eyes narrowed. "Did you miss me at all, Rebecca?"

She stared at him, taken aback not only by his question but by the anger in his tone and his face. "Of course I missed you," she answered honestly.

"Then why didn't you answer my letter?"

Rebecca was speechless. She'd been so hurt, so wounded by his silence after she'd left Mackinac Island. "What letter?" she managed, her voice breathless, her thoughts jumbled.

"I wrote to you shortly before Christmas. A ship docked at Mackinac. I assumed it would be the last ship before the ice closed the waterways. I sent you a letter. The captain promised to deliver it to Fort Collier for me. He had some dispatches for the fort so he was planning on stopping."

"I never received it," she told him, dazed by the thought that she'd suffered all that pain for nothing. She remembered those long, lonely months before she'd left Drummond Island. She would have given her soul to know that he cared, that the man she loved, the father of the child growing within her, hadn't simply dismissed her from his heart as he had banished her from the island where he lived.

"I assumed you didn't . . ." she began, then faltered.

"Didn't what?" he prompted. But she only shook her head and dismissed the subject.

"What about Sumner Meade?" he asked. "He must have been delighted to have you back among the living."

Rebecca nodded. "He was—at first. But he was a bit disenchanted with me when he found out that I was going—"

"Yes?" Beau prompted when she said no more. He had the maddening feeling that there was so much she was not saying, but he feared that if he pressed her she would withdraw from him.

Rebecca clasped her trembling hands in her lap. This was the moment to speak. This was the moment to tell him about Monty. But she could not force the words. She opened her mouth but nothing would come out.

"Rebecca, what is it?" Beau urged. "Tell me, please."

Rising, Rebecca went to the windows that overlooked the street. *Tell him. Tell him!* a voice commanded inside her. She heard again both Mrs. Bailey and Jonathan telling her that he had a right to know that he had fathered a son. She did not dispute that, but could not rid herself of the image of him dancing with Caroline Nicholson.

If he were really engaged to the girl and they married, might he not want to take the boy for extended visits? She closed her eyes. The thought of her son—all she had of Beau—going to live with him and another woman broke her heart. What if Monty decided he wanted to live with Beau and Caroline? She would be left with nothing. Nothing!

Tears stung her eyes and she blinked furiously to hold them at bay. She couldn't do it. She couldn't! Monty was all she had. He was the most precious thing in her life. She couldn't risk losing him.

"Rebecca?" Beau came to stand behind her, so close his chest nearly touched her back.

She quivered. She could feel the heat of his body, feel his strength, smell the clean, masculine scent of him. She wanted to turn to him, feel his arms about her, lay her head on his shoulder, and weep for the time they had lost. But she could not.

"Rebecca," he said again more softly this time, as though he could sense the turmoil within her. He wanted to hold her, reassure her that there was surely nothing so terrible that she could not tell him. "Please," he said gently. "Please tell me what this is all about. Let me help you."

But before Rebecca could reply, the drawing-room door opened. A little face topped with golden curls peered around it. Two sapphire eyes lit with pleasure as they came to rest on Rebecca. A brilliant smile appeared on lips soft and tender that would one day become strong, chiseled replicas of another pair Rebecca remembered all too well.

"Mama!" Monty cried, toddling toward her on his small, sturdy legs. "What did you buy for me at the shops?"

Mrs. Bailey appeared in the doorway. "I'm sorry, dear," she said, no trace of regret on her face or in her voice. "I tried to keep him away, but when he discovered that his mama had returned from shopping, he had to see you."

Rebecca cast a pointed glance at the housekeeper who returned a tiny smile and then disappeared, closing the door behind her. She wondered if Mrs. Bailey had been listening and had decided, when it became clear that Rebecca could bring herself to say nothing, to take matters into her own hands.

"Come here, darling," she said softly, holding out her arms to her son.

The little boy came to her and she lifted him in her arms. Slowly, hesitantly, she raised her eyes to Beau's face. He was gaping at her, dumbfounded.

Chapter Thirty-Nine

Seeing the unspoken question in his eyes, Rebecca nodded. "Yes," she said softly. "He's your son."

Beau held out his hands toward the child and Monty trustingly went to him. Wordlessly, they gazed at one another, nose to nose, two faces, so alike, one but a smaller, softer version of the other.

"What's his name?" Beau asked, his eyes straying again and again to the child in his arms.

"We call him Monty," Rebecca told him. "I wanted to name him after you but I didn't know what Beau might be short for. I thought perhaps Beaumont?"

Monty squirmed in Beau's arms and Beau gently stood him on the floor. He watched as the child went to the table where the tea tray was and selected one of Mrs. Bailey's sweet tea biscuits.

"No," he said at last, smiling as he watched his son demolish the tea biscuit and reach for another. "Actually, it's short for Beauregard."

"Beauregard?" Rebecca asked, wrinkling her nose.

Beau laughed. "It's a family name. My mother's maiden name." He chuckled as Monty picked up his tall hat and set it on his head. It immediately fell to his chin and Beau plucked it off before the child could stagger blindly into the furniture. While Monty stood patiently, Beau balanced the hat on the back of the little boy's head. "He's beautiful, Rebecca," he said sincerely.

"I agree," Rebecca replied, her eyes soft and filled with love as she watched her son play with his father's hat.

"Is he the reason Sumner Meade was angry with you?"

Rebecca nodded. "I suppose he always hoped I would be with him. Once he discovered I was pregnant with your child, he knew there could never be more than friendship between us."

"I suppose that when the mail packet came to Fort Collier, he managed to get his hands on the letter I wrote you and destroy it."

"I suppose he did," Rebecca agreed. Considering the pain and loneliness that Beau's apparent silence had caused her, it seemed utterly malicious and cruel of Sumner.

"And Monty is the reason you decided to stay in America rather than go back to England," Beau went on.

"Yes," Rebecca admitted. "I thought you would prefer that your son be raised an American. When I left Fort Collier, a man aboard the schooner told me about Philadelphia. It sounded like a good place to live and to raise a child."

"And it would have been difficult to explain him to your family in England, wouldn't it?" he added.

Rebecca laughed. "All right, that was part of it as well. They knew when William died. Had I arrived in England about to bear a child with no husband in sight, I would have been hard pressed for a plausible explanation."

Beau's smile faded. "Rebecca," he said softly, coming to stand before her. "Why didn't you send word to me? Why didn't you let me know you were carrying my child?"

"I thought you didn't care for me. I heard nothing from you."

"I tried!" he insisted. "I wrote to you. Haven't I told you that?"

"I never got the letter!"

"That's not my fault!"

"I know!" she replied, nearly shouting.

"Mama!" Monty cried, coming to her side, frightened by the obvious distress in her voice.

"It's all right, sweetheart," she soothed, cuddling him and kissing his cheek. "Come, let's go see what Mrs. Bailey is doing, shall we?" She glanced at Beau. "I'll be back in a moment."

Beau watched as she left the room and waited impatiently until she returned without the child.

"The tea is cold," she said vaguely, touching the pot on the tray. "I could send for some more if you like."

"No, thank you." Beau knew she was stalling because the subject was a painful one for her but he was determined to get to the heart of it all.

"I tried to write to you," he said gently, reopening the subject between them.

"I know that—now," she replied. "But at the time I was hurt. Even though I knew I couldn't stay on Mackinac Island, I was hurt that you sent me away." She smiled wanly. "Don't ask me to explain it. I only know that when I didn't hear from you once I reached Fort Collier, I convinced myself you didn't care for me. I decided to build a life for me and my child here in America."

"If only my letter had reached you," he said, his voice filled with regret. "If only you had written to me, told me you were pregnant."

"What could you have done?" Rebecca countered. "Could I have come back to Fort Mackinac? Could you have come to Fort Collier?"

"No, of course not," Beau admitted. "But I could have made arrangements for you to go to my family in Baltimore. You wouldn't have had to be alone. You wouldn't have had to go through all this by yourself."

"Baltimore," Rebecca mused. "Is that where you send all the prisoners you get pregnant?"

"Rebecca," he said reproachfully.

"All right," she said, "I'm sorry. I didn't contact you because I thought you wanted no more to do with me. I thought our differences would always stand between us. Do you remember the argument we had on Mackinac Island? I wanted to see England again and you wanted to remain in America? We never resolved that. And, don't forget, I am a condemned traitor to the country you love."

Beau gazed at her. He reached out toward her but his hand fell to his side. "I love you, Rebecca," he said simply.

Rebecca felt as if her heart had turned over in her breast. How many nights had she lain awake yearning to hear those words from him? How often had she thought she would give anything on earth to know that he cared for her a hundredth as much as she cared for him?

But there were other issues that needed to be resolved. She hated to shatter the moment by bringing it up, but she forced herself to ask, "What about your fiancée?"

Beau stared at her, apparently bewildered. "What fiancée?" he asked.

"On the night I first saw you at the theater, Jonathan told me that rumor had it you were going to marry the young lady you were with."

"The young lady . . ." Beau's face cleared and he began to laugh. "Caroline Nicholson?" he asked, chuckling.

"What's so funny about it?" Rebecca demanded. "I saw you with her at the theater. I saw you dancing with her at Fairfield."

"I know, but that does not mean we're engaged. I swear to you, Rebecca, I'll never marry Caroline Nicholson."

"Why not?" For a moment, Rebecca felt angry. Was he merely flirting with the girl, leading her on to curry favor with his superior officer, her father? "She seems like a perfectly lovely young girl!"

Beau laughed. "A few moments ago you were irritated because you thought I was going to marry Caroline. Now you're annoyed because I'm not?"

"Well . . ." Rebecca scowled. "If you're going to break her heart—" She flushed, growing angrier as she saw the amusement on his face. "I think it's despicable, Beau. You can't go on allowing this poor girl to think—"

"Rebecca!" he interrupted. "Rebecca, calm down. I'm not leading Caroline on. She knows I've no intention of marrying her. She's my cousin."

"Your . . . But . . ." Rebecca stared at him. "Your cousin?"

"Yes." He laughed. "Her mother, Mrs. Nicholson, and my mother are sisters. I only escort her because she doesn't know anyone in Philadelphia yet."

Relief flooded through Rebecca. When she thought of all the needless pain she'd put herself through, the nights of agonizing, the jealousy, all for nothing!

"I wish I had known," she said.

"I wish you had come to speak to me at the theater," he said. "I would have introduced you to my uncle and aunt and my cousin, Caroline."

"Oh, Beau." She sighed. "I was so afraid you'd fallen in love with someone else."

"Impossible," he said softly

They gazed into one another's eyes for a long, silent moment that spoke more clearly than any words could. But Beau could not help breaking the silence. "What about you and Jonathan Gibbons? Philip Lamont told me he's surprised the two of you aren't married."

"He's proposed to me several times," Rebecca admitted.

"Why haven't you accepted?"

Rebecca looked away. "Do you want me to tell you I haven't married him because I couldn't forget you?"

"I want you to tell me the truth," Beau corrected.

She gazed up into those sapphire eyes that had haunted her dreams. "I haven't married him because I couldn't forget you."

"Rebecca . . ." Beau reached out and took her into his arms. Holding her close, he kissed her, softly, tenderly, with all the love he harbored for her.

Rebecca melted against him. She felt as if she'd finally come home after a long, lonely journey in a harsh and hostile land.

"Marry me, Rebecca," he said, his lips brushing her ear. "I want you to be my wife. I want us to be a family, you and me and Monty."

Troubled, Rebecca stepped out of his arms. "I keep remembering that argument we had on Mackinac Island. I know you love America. I've grown to love it as well. But my family is in England. I want them to know you, to know Monty. What if I wanted to go there someday to visit them?"

Beau shrugged. "It might be interesting. So long as we could come home again."

"Home," Rebecca repeated. "If I were with you, anywhere would be home."

"Does that mean you'll marry me, Mrs. Carlyle?" he asked, a teasing tone in his voice.

"Yes," Rebecca answered, going into his arms and reveling in the warm welcome she found there. "Oh, Beau, yes!"

Outside the drawing-room door, Mrs. Bailey, who had been eavesdropping, broke into a delighted and relieved smile, and went to the kitchen to begin planning the wedding dinner. She would have to pretend to be surprised when Rebecca came to tell her the news, but a little pretense was well worth it to see her dear girl happy at last.

Epilogue

Philadelphia
Three Months Later

The beautiful mansion that was the centerpiece of Hartwick, Jonathan Gibbons's country estate, was awash with light as his guests celebrated his marriage to Caroline Nicholson.

In the ballroom the groom and his pretty blonde bride danced and laughed, and accepted the good wishes of the cream of Philadelphia society. Everyone agreed that the sweet, demure Caroline was a perfect bride for the kindhearted banker. No one denied that the former Miss Nicholson had stolen a march on those young eligible Philadelphia girls who for some time had been trying to distract Jonathan from his former love, Rebecca Carlyle.

Of course, there were some who said that Jonathan had married his pretty wife on the rebound after Rebecca's astonishingly sudden marriage to Miss Nicholson's cousin, the handsome Captain McAllister.

But whatever the truth of the matter, both couples seemed completely contented, utterly delighted with the outcome.

In the garden behind Hartwick, Beau and Rebecca strolled hand in hand in the scented darkness. The light of a full moon bathed the garden with a silvery glow that shone through the trees, dappling the paths.

"You might have been mistress of this beautiful place," Beau reminded her, his tone teasing.

"I suppose so," Rebecca said. "But I wouldn't have been happy."

"Jonathan seems a very nice fellow."

"Oh, yes, he's very kind and gentle. But I didn't love him." Stopping in the shade of a gnarled oak tree, Rebecca looked up at her husband. "I wouldn't trade these last three months with you for a hundred such mansions, Beau," she said passionately. "I wouldn't trade our life together for all the world."

Cupping her face in his hands, Beau kissed her, moved by her sentiments. Politics and war, governments and misunderstandings had conspired to tear them apart, but love, fate had brought them together again and he was determined that they would never again be parted.

"Wouldn't it be nice for Monty to have a little

brother or sister?" he asked, his voice low and husky.

"It would," she agreed, nuzzling his shoulder through the soft, dark green cloth of his coat.

She laughed when she felt his hands at the laces fastening the back of her gown. "Beau!" she chided.

He looked down at her, his face the picture of innocence. "You said it would be nice."

"I didn't mean we should start on it now."

Bending toward her, he kissed her throat, her shoulders, the curve of her breast above the low neckline of her gown.

"Why not?" he asked, his voice hushed, breathless.

Rebecca gasped as his hands caressed her breasts through the thin silk of her gown. *Why not, indeed?* she reasoned to herself as, her fingers buried in the heavy silk of his golden hair, they sank together to the soft grass of the moonlit garden.

"Do you think Jonathan and Caroline will be as happy as we are?" she asked as Beau drew her gown from her shoulders.

"Impossible," he declared, then silenced the wife he loved with kisses.

SPECIAL SNEAK PREVIEW!

By Connie Mason

Storm Kennedy can't believe her bad luck! With six million fertile acres open to settlers in the Oklahoma Territory, she loses her claim to Grady Stryker, a Cheyenne half-breed she holds responsible for her young husband's death. And the only way Storm can ever win back the land is by marrying the virile Stryker and raising his motherless son. No spineless Sooner, Storm agrees to his terms, then denies him access to her last asset—the lush body he thinks is his for the taking. But the more Storm fights him, the harder Grady works to sow the seeds of a desire that promised a bountiful love.

Don't Miss *A Promise of Thunder!*
On Sale In June
At Booksellers And Newsstands Everywhere.

Storm had her makeshift shelter erected before the inky blackness of night descended over the prairie. She and Buddy had prepared well, having purchased stakes, canvas and supplies to last them several months, or until the land started producing. Buddy had used an inheritance from his grandmother to finance their trip and there were still sufficient funds left in the bank in Guthrie to build a snug cabin on her new land.

Using some of the extra stakes, Storm built a fire and started coffee boiling. She was famished, having eaten nothing since early that morning. Rummaging in the back of the wagon, she found a tin of beans, another of fruit and some hardtack. The next day, when she went to Guthrie to file her claim, she'd buy bacon, eggs, flour, sugar and the other supplies necessary for her survival.

In a very short time she was seated before the fire shoveling beans into her mouth and thinking how lonely it was without Buddy. He had been her constant companion for so long, the loss sent a sharp pang through her innards. She hadn't really cried or had a chance to mourn Buddy since his death, and when tears appeared suddenly she didn't try to stop them. She let them course down her cheeks, finding solace in the healing flood of tears. When it was over she knew she could continue, with or without Buddy. She would always mourn her husband, but she had never been one to dwell overlong on the injustices of life. Life simply went on.

When she and Buddy had struck out for Oklahoma, she had eagerly welcomed the challenge of pioneer life, and not even Buddy's death would make her give up the dream of owning one of the last tracts of free land in the country. Abruptly Storm's thoughts wandered in another direction. She wondered if the half-breed had managed a fire and meal. When she glanced over toward his claim, she saw nothing but dark stretches of land for as far as the eye could see. The moon and the stars provided the only light, except for that projected by her meager campfire.

Storm didn't want to worry about the half-breed, didn't even want to think about him, but somehow his image intruded upon her thoughts. It was difficult to hate a man who was wounded and helpless. Although helpless hardly described Grady Stryker, Storm realized that he couldn't have entered the race as fully prepared as she and Buddy had been, for to her knowledge his decision to homestead had been one made on the spur of the moment. He probably had no food or even a spare blanket to keep him warm during the coolness of the night.

Suddenly Storm came to a decision. She filled a tin plate with the remainder of the food she had prepared, picked up the coffee-pot and started walking the short distance to Grady's claim. Since it was full dark and she had to pick her way carefully, it took fifteen minutes to reach his roped-off claim. Stepping over the barrier, she saw that Grady had indeed erected a shelter. Upon closer inspection she saw that his tent consisted of a shotgun stuck into the ground as a tent pole and a blanket stretched over it and staked down on all four sides. There was absolutely no way he could stuff his tall lean frame into the small enclosure. Setting the plate and coffeepot on the ground before the tent, she called his name.

She heard his tethered horse snort softly in response, but Grady was nowhere in sight. She was ready to return to her own claim when the sound of rippling water caught her attention. Since she wanted to wash up before she retired, she headed in the direction of the river, wishing that she had been one of the lucky ones to claim land bordering the water. As things stood now, she'd be forced to negotiate with the half-breed for her water until a well could be dug.

The moon lit her way as Storm walked across the lush prairie, happily aware of the fact that she had claimed a piece of prime farmland. Though she didn't know a great deal about farming or raising animals, she was determined to learn. Surely she wasn't the only woman to claim a piece of Oklahoma for herself, nor was she the first woman pioneer whose man was killed before he could realize his dream.

Storm stumbled upon Grady quite suddenly. He was poised at the edge of the water, his back to her, nude except for a breechclout covering his loins. He looked like an ancient heathen god, standing as tall and straight as a towering spruce. His stance emphasized the strength of his thighs and the slimness of his hips. Moonlight danced along the ropy muscles of his biceps, highlighting his shoulders, a yard wide and molded bronze. In fact, he was gilded bronze all over, even the taut mounds of his buttocks. His midnight hair shone with glistening pearls of water, as if he had just emerged from the river. Storm's breath lodged in her throat as she stared at him, fascinated by the pagan splendor of his powerful body.

He was the closest thing to an unclothed man Storm had ever seen. She and Buddy had never undressed before one another. They had discreetly shed their clothes in private and when they made love, Buddy, in order to protect her sensibilities, had raised her voluminous nightdress without looking. Though Storm had never seen her husband without his clothes she knew he had looked nothing like Grady Stryker. Was there a man anywhere on earth the equal of him?

Grady tensed, sensing that he wasn't alone. In the past his keen senses had served him well, but this time he detected no menace, felt no danger from the intruder. He had bathed in the river to cool his feverish body. Then he silently communed with the moon and river, both of which the People worshiped as givers of life. He had heard the nearly silent footsteps and stood ready to spring, until the sweet scent of violets wafted to him on the breeze.

"Have you come to bathe, Mrs. Kennedy, or merely to watch me?"

A startled squeak escaped from Storm's lips. "How—how did you know I was here?"

"My reflexes have been honed to recognize danger no matter what guise it takes," Grady said, turning to face her. "Had I not recognized the scent that lingers on your skin and on your hair, I would have attacked you. Next time announce yourself."

"I—came upon you suddenly and—and—" Her tongue seemed glued to the roof of her mouth as she stumbled over the words. "I

419

wasn't spying," she finally spit out.

"What *are* you doing here?"

"I brought you something to eat and when I didn't find you, I decided to wash up before I returned to my claim."

"You brought me food?" Grady asked, incredulous.

She was grateful the darkness hid her flushed face. "If you want it," she said, shrugging. "You couldn't have carried many supplies on your horse."

"You're a strange woman, Mrs. Kennedy— Storm." He grew pensive, then asked, "Why do you have an Indian name?" He left the water's edge and her eyes fell unbidden to the bulging muscles of his thighs and the intriguing way they flexed with each step he took. He didn't stop until he stood close enough to feel her soft breath against his cheek.

Her lips went suddenly dry and she had to lick them before she could speak. "It's not an Indian name, not really. I was born during a violent storm and my parents thought it appropriate to name me Storm."

"It is the same with the People."

"Why do you have blue eyes?" Storm asked before she realized what she was saying.

Grady's features turned grim, as if recalling something painful from his past he didn't like. But to Storm's surprise, he answered readily enough. "They come from my mother. She is a white woman."

"You look like a savage."

Grady's eyes turned flinty. "Looks are often deceiving."

"Was your mother a captive?"

"Captive?" Grady's laughter vibrated the air around them. "Those who know my parents say my father is the one held captive by my mother."

"But how—"

"You ask too many questions, Storm Kennedy."

And look much too lovely in the moonlight, he thought but did not say.

"Thank you for the food but I think you should leave. Aren't you afraid of being here alone with me? I'm a renegade. If you aren't afraid, you should be."

"I'm not afraid of you," Storm retorted, "but I'll be all too happy to go. If you'd kindly leave me alone for a few moments I'll clean up and be on my way."

"If I recall, your land does not border on the river."

"That's why I'm asking permission to cross your property to reach the water." She hated being beholden to the half-breed but there was no help for it.

"I'll have to think about it."

"Are you always so disagreeable?" Storm asked, stomping her foot furiously.

"I am when dealing with White Eyes. For the most part they are untrustworthy, prejudiced, and dishonest."

"Your mother is white," Storm shot back.

"My mother lives far away on a ranch in Wyoming. Leave her out of this," Grady said tightly. "Most whites are evil."

"And most Indians are dirty savages. You don't even have a proper Indian name."

"I am called Thunder by the People."

"Thunder," Storm repeated softly. The name conjured up visions of violence, mayhem and destruction—it fit him perfectly.

"My parents named me Grady. When I left the People to live among the White Eyes I assumed that name."

"You left the—I don't understand."

"There is nothing for you to understand," Grady said tersely. "You may cross my land to the river whenever it pleases you." He turned to leave with an abruptness that startled Storm, as if he couldn't wait to be rid of her. The bandage she had tied around his chest shone stark against his bronzed flesh, yet she hadn't thought to ask him about his wound.

Let him suffer, she thought, it would serve him right for being so darn ornery. Had he learned no manners at his mother's knee?

Kneeling at the river's edge, Storm plunged her hands into the cool water and proceeded to wash her hands, face and neck, unaware that Grady had turned to watch her as she unfastened the top buttons of her blouse and dribbled water between her breasts. Moonlight beamed down benevolently upon her, turning her hair into a halo of pure gold as she bent forward. Grady couldn't recall when he had seen

422

a more entrancing sight or witnessed anything quite as sexually arousing as Storm, raising her face to the stars, splashing water on her face, neck and breasts. And what made it even more provocative was the fact that she wasn't even aware of what it was doing to him.

Grady smiled in spite of himself, envisioning what it would be like to quench his lust in the cradle of Storm's loins. He wondered if she would be as tempestuous, wild and untamed as her name implied. Those forbidden thoughts made his flesh rise and harden with a need he had thought subdued long ago. He had wanted no woman in his heart but Summer Sky; now suddenly he was overwhelmed with desire for a white woman named Storm who had whirled into his life with all the fury of a tornado.

Shaking his dark head in denial of what his flesh was demanding, Grady spun on his heel and stomped away. When Storm passed by his crude tent a short time later, Grady was just finishing the plate of beans and bacon she had left for him.

"If you're finished, I'll take the plate." Her voice was cool.

Grady handed her the plate and coffeepot. "Thank you, it was very good." He hadn't realized just how hungry he was until he had picked up the fork. Tomorrow he'd have to see about getting some supplies out there and building some sort of shanty to serve as a dwelling. Getting them out to his claim was going to be a problem unless. . . .

Storm took the plate and coffeepot from Grady's hands and started to trek back to her own claim. "Storm, wait."

Storm paused, uncomfortable with the idea of the half-breed using her first name. "Was there something you wanted to say to me?"

"I told you earlier that you could cross my land to use the river whenever you liked. Perhaps in return you could accommodate me?"

Storm stiffened, her face twisted into a mask of shock and dismay. "Accommodate you, Mr. Stryker? In what way?"

"We both need to go to Guthrie tomorrow to file our claims and we both need supplies. Perhaps you'd be good enough to carry some of my supplies back in your wagon since we are going to be neighbors."

Immediately Storm relaxed, realizing she had jumped to the wrong conclusion. But she'd be a fool to trust the half-breed renegade. Obviously he hated whites, and his hatred extended to women as well as men. He seemed to hold white women in as much contempt as he did white men. Curiously she wondered what had happened in his past to turn him against the white race. He was intelligent and well educated, and he spoke English as well as she did, better even. Yet something had turned him against all white men and their ways.

Grady Stryker was secretive concerning his past. All she knew about him was that he was born in Wyoming on a ranch, hated whites and could handle a gun like a pro.

And he was heart-stoppingly handsome in a rugged way that brought shivers to her flesh.

"It's a deal," Storm agreed. "Though it boggles my mind to think of a man like you settling down on a farm, we *are* going to be neighbors, and it would behoove us to help one another. But don't get the wrong idea, Mr. Stryker. I still hate you for what you are and the way my life has changed because of you. If Buddy was alive today we would have been here first to claim land on the river. Good night, Mr. Stryker, I'll be by for you in the morning."

Grady was waiting for Storm early the next morning when she drove the wagon past his claim. Dressed in skintight buckskins, and moccasins, he had his long ebony hair tied back with a leather thong. He must have been wearing his spare shirt, for there were no telltale holes where the bullet had entered or exited his flesh. In fact, he gave little sign that he had been wounded at all. Was the man not human? Did he not feel pain like other mortals? Though the wound hadn't been life threatening, it surely was serious enough to cause him distress. Yet there he was, looking as hale and hardy as he had the first time she saw him in Guthrie.

"I'll tie Lightning to the back of the wagon and ride beside you," Grady said as he led his saddled horse over to the wagon.

Lightning and Thunder, they made a good pair, Storm thought, fascinated by the blatant play of muscles beneath Grady's buckskins as he moved gracefully to the rear of the wagon. And where did Storm come into the scheme of things? Had their meeting been preordained? Thunder and Storm. She shook her head at such a silly notion. Their meeting had been purely coincidental, and unhappily for her, an unforeseen tragedy. When Grady leaped into the wagon beside her, the brief pressure of his leg pressing against hers sent a shudder through her body.

"Are you cold? Perhaps you should have worn a jacket."

She was dressed in a split skirt and blouse, and if it wasn't for the half-breed sitting beside her, she would have been perfectly comfortable. His presence confused her and made what she had felt for Buddy seem tame.

It made her angry.

"I'm fine," Storm snapped as she slapped the reins against the horses' rumps. "I just don't want you to think our being neighborly is anything but a mutual need for survival. Until I can get my well dug I'll need to use the river that flows through your land. And you'll need—"

"You may not be willing to provide what I need," Grady said with slow relish. His blue eyes, so incongruous in his dark face, blazed with an unholy light.

Storm gasped, stunned at the sexual innuendo inherent in his words. "You, Mr. Stryker, are an unprincipled rogue. How dare you speak to me in such a suggestive manner. If Buddy were alive you wouldn't dare—"

"I said nothing to offend you," Grady said, quickly defending himself. His innocent stare made her want to give him a thorough tongue-lashing. "Don't you think that we should be on a first-name basis after all we've shared?"

"What we shared is the tragic death of my husband, Mr. Stryker. If you don't stop badgering me, we can forget all about the cooperation between us. I'll bargain with another homesteader for water until my well is dug."

"Don't get your dander up, Storm," Grady said, trying not to smile, but failing miserably. Why was he feeling more lighthearted than he had in years? He couldn't recall when he'd smiled last or bantered with a woman as lovely and provocative as Storm Kennedy. It felt good, damn good. Perhaps abandoning his renegade life, settling on his own land and making a home for his son was the wisest decision he had ever made. If he could accomplish that much, there was hope of reconciling with his parents, he reasoned. And he had Storm Kennedy to thank for it. . . .

HISTORICAL ROMANCE AT ITS FINEST

BY LEISURE'S LEADING LADIES OF LOVE!

Ice & Rapture by Connie Mason. Cold and hot, reserved and brazen, Maggie and Chase are a study in opposites. But when they join forces during the Klondike gold rush, the fiery sparks of their searing desire burn brighter than the northern lights.

_3376-3 $4.99 US/$5.99 CAN

Child Of The Mist by Kathleen Morgan. Betrothed to the leader of the cursed clan Campbell, young Anne MacGregor has no desire to marry the dreaded warrior. But soon she eagerly succumbs to Niall's fiery kisses—only to discover a secret foe who has the power to crush their newfound love like a handful of heather.

_3379-8 $4.50 US/$5.50 CAN

Love's Golden Promise by Lynette Vinet. An act of piracy on the high seas leaves Wynter McChesney at the mercy of arrogant Cort Van Linden. And while she vows never to become his doxy, Wynter discovers in his wild embrace that she will give anything to know the achingly sweet fulfillment of love's golden promise.

_3381-X $4.50 US/$5.50 CAN

LEISURE BOOKS
ATTN: Order Department
276 5th Avenue, New York, NY 10001

Please add $1.50 for shipping and handling for the first book and $.35 for each book thereafter. PA., N.Y.S. and N.Y.C. residents, please add appropriate sales tax. No cash, stamps, or C.O.D.s. All orders shipped within 6 weeks via postal service book rate. Canadian orders require $2.00 extra postage and must be paid in U.S. dollars through a U.S. banking facility.

Name _____

Address _____

City _____ State _____ Zip _____

I have enclosed $_____in payment for the checked book(s). Payment <u>must</u> accompany all orders.☐ Please send a free catalog.

Winner of the *Romantic Times* Storyteller of the Year Award!

Storm Kennedy can't believe her bad luck! With six million acres of fertile territory open to settlers in the Oklahoma Territory, she loses her land claim to Grady Stryker, the virile Cheyenne half-breed she holds responsible for her young husband's death. And the only way to get it back is by agreeing to marry the arrogant Stryker and raise his motherless son. But while she accepts his proposal, Storm is determined to deny him access to her last asset—the lush body Grady thinks is his for the taking.

_3444-1 $4.99 US/$5.99 CAN